# ARMED AND FABULOUS

## LEXI GRAVES MYSTERIES

*Camilla Chafer*

Copyright: Camilla Chafer, 2012

All rights reserved. The right of Camilla Chafer to be identified as author of this Work has been asserted by her in accordance with sections 77 and 78 of the Copyright, Designs and Patents Act 1988.

First published in 2012.

No part of this publication may be reproduced, stored in retrieval system, copied in any form or by any means, electronic, mechanical, photocopying, recording or otherwise transmitted without written permission from the publisher. You must not circulate this book in any format.

This book is licensed for your personal enjoyment only.

ISBN: 1481113704
ISBN-13: 978-1481113700

Visit the author online at www.camillachafer.com

# ALSO BY CAMILLA CHAFER

*Lexi Graves Mysteries:*
Armed and Fabulous
Who Glares Wins
Command Indecision
Shock and Awesome
Weapons of Mass Distraction
Laugh or Death
Kissing in Action
Trigger Snappy
A Few Good Women
Ready, Aim, Under Fire
Rules of Engagement
Very Special Forces
In the Line of Ire
Mission: Possible
Pied Sniper
Charmed Forces

*Deadlines Mystery Trilogy:*
Deadlines
Dead to the World
Dead Ringers

*Calendar Murder Mysteries:*
Murder in the Library
Poison Rose Murder
Murder by the Book
Murder at Blackberry Inn
Curated Murder
Dressed for Murder

# CHAPTER ONE

Finding dead bodies wasn't in my job description.

Of course, sneaking out of work wasn't in my job description either, but that never stopped me from doing it. There are a lot of things wrong with being a temp, the doormat of the office totem pole, but fortunately, I've learned how to take advantage of just about any weak boss, and outsmart the smartest ones. For starters, I'm super bright, but everyone thinks I'm utterly dim, possibly on account of my super long and very gorgeous blonde hair, (if I don't say so myself, so long as we gloss over its expensive bi-monthly bleach and upkeep), along with a pair of upright and out there assets. No, not my boobs: they're courtesy of Wonderbra. I mean my inquisitive and determined nature. At least my school careers counselor told me they were assets; mostly, however, they seem to get me into trouble. Given my current position as office dogsbody at Green Hand Insurance, they certainly hadn't landed me a decent job.

I was startled and jumped as my annoying boss,

Adam Shepherd, loomed over my desk, appearing as if from nowhere. "Lexi, what is it that you're doing?" he asked, his eyebrows knitting together suspiciously.

Shepherd was annoying for two reasons. One: he never seemed to do anything in the way of work, and I had no idea how he actually got a job as my manager! After six months, I was still relegated to being a temp, without even a whiff of a permanent job upgrade at the firm. Two: he is so crazy good-looking, it's unfair to the rest of the male species. It's something between his dark, unruly, hair (that looks like it rarely sees a comb and has no clue which direction to grow), and his smoky blue eyes. It also could have a whole lot to do with his super sexy body, today hidden beneath dark pants, plain white shirt and striped tie. Not that I was even looking. Much.

"Um," I said, sneaking a finger sideways on my keyboard to change screens so he couldn't see the Victoria's Secret webpage I was browsing. I was supposed to be writing a report. Of course, the report was already written, but any good temp knows that you never admit to how fast you can complete a task; otherwise, you could end up unemployed, seeking a new assignment since you'd already accomplished your first. And I could only take so much of my temp manager at the agency before I started getting visions that involved her, me, a boxing ring and a wet kipper, with me winning, of course. So, naturally both my bi-monthly check and I didn't want to get hassled by her for another couple of months.

"Yes?" Shepherd raised his eyebrows, waiting.

"Just finished your report, Adam," I said brightly, moving the mouse so I could click "print." "I sent it to your printer just this minute." See? Super smart! I can online window shop secretly, pretend to just finish a report I actually finished hours ago, and send it to the boss' printer all at the same time! Could you?

"Right, thanks, Lexi," said Adam and I flashed another brilliant smile at him, which I wiped off my face as soon as he turned to walk away. The printer was no more than ten feet away, near his large corner desk. In my peripheral vision, I saw him pick up a piece of paper.

One *single* sheet of paper.

There should have been ten sheets.

Maybe someone forgot to fill the paper tray with frickin' paper again? But Adam wasn't looking at the paper tray, or hitting it; he was looking at me, then down at the single sheet of paper… and at me again… smiling like a smug puppy that had just eaten a slipper, but knew it was too cute to be punished.

I rolled my castered office chair slightly to the left until I was concealed behind the big, beige monitor that dominated my desk. Except… I couldn't help peeking again.

Adam's chest rose and fell in sharp rapid movements, his mouth a tight line as if he were trying very hard not to laugh. Then he looked up.

I ducked behind my monitor again as he crossed the floor—towards me.

God. What had I done this time? I checked the screen. My mouse pointer hovered over the "print" button. Only it wasn't the report screen. Somehow, I had managed to slightly minimize the screen with my report, and instead, my pointer hovered over the "print'" option on the screen below.

I nudged it, clicked on the screen and paled.

*Shit. Shit. Shit.*

My heart plummeted and my stomach did an Olympic-sized backflip as I realized what I had done. *Why wasn't there an "unprint" button? Why? Why? Why!* "Urrrgh," I squeaked as I hit keys at random, thinking someone should invent one and make all unwanted printouts combust before anyone else got their filthy hands on them.

"Lexi?" Adam was standing next to me, the piece of paper in his hand.

I plastered on my "I'm-so-happy-to-serve-you, you-patron-saint-of-temps!" bullshit smile that I was so proud of, (after a painful amateur drama workshop my best friend, Lily Shuler, forced me to attend), and went for the best defense I could think of. That's right. None.

"Sir?" I grinned like an empty-headed bimbo.

"What's this?" asked Shepherd. Then the bastard laughed.

"Sir?" I chirped again, flicking my mane of blonde hair. There's absolutely no point people thinking you're stupid if you don't act like it occasionally. Of course, it's purely so I can get away with loads of stuff, you see? Like "not understanding" how the photocopier works, or "Oh! These files are *so* heavy, I couldn't possibly carry them," or "What does that do?" and hitting something irreversible on a spreadsheet. But people think I'm sweet for trying and never bother me by asking for my help again. Yes, yes, I know, it's gaming the stupid system; to which I say, this is why I would have made a fabulous spy. I could game the best of them.

"This isn't the report I requested."

"It isn't?"

"No. Do you know what it is?"

"Someone else's report?" I asked, keeping my face blank, while twirling a lock.

He leaned in, his eyes narrowing. He was close enough to kiss. "Does that ever work?"

"All the time." I gulped, recoiling in horror as the words slipped out. *Damn. Busted.* Knocked senseless by his cologne and coffee scent, not to mention the way his eyes sparkled.

"I think this is yours." Adam held out the sheet, print side up. My body edged away, and my eyes took a good look. Yep, I'd printed out a page of Victoria's Secret lingerie. When I didn't take it, he thrust the page a bit closer to me, leaning in again, his eyes glazing over momentarily as he got a good view down my top. At least, he was distracted enough for me to smooth over my goof. I thanked the Wonderbra deity and got on with it.

"Not mine," I lied deftly.

Adam's forehead knitted into a frown. He flipped the page over, scanned the contents, then looked at me, or more precisely, at my boobs, and then back to the sheet.

"Looks like your size," he said softly and my mouth dropped open. Was he sizing up my lady lumps? In the office? *How rude.* He continued, in the same low voice, too low for any of my neighboring idiots, um, colleagues, to hear. "Personally, I like the lemon set better. Sexy, but not too revealing. Leaves a bit of mystery." Then he dumped the page on my desk and marched off, adding over his shoulder. "Send that report to the printer again, would you?"

I gaped at him. But this time, I was really, *really* careful what I sent to the printer. Five minutes later, I put the lemon silk bra with the lace edging into my virtual shopping basket, along with the matching thong, and purchased them. Well, if Adam said they were sexy, who was I to argue? He was built like a Greek god, but with worse hair. I suspected his middle name was "Yum." I also suspected he knew a lot about women's lingerie and not in a secret, blinds-drawn, don't tell, sort of way.

But... was he *flirting*?

Hmm.

Not sure what I thought about that. A nice office flirt did make the day go faster, but Adam was my boss, not to mention an annoying one, and I was nothing, if not professional.

Snort. Yeah. That made me laugh too.

The downside of Adam having my report in his hot manly hands was that he now knew I had finished it, which meant I'd have to begin a new report. Something which I could preferably complete in three hours flat, spend at least a couple of hours "researching" in the basement library (read: go to Starbucks, call Lily, and do my nails), but could spin into at least four days of "concentrated work."

It took Adam fifteen minutes to send me an email—despite being within talking, not hollering, distance—to request a report on the latest public survey regarding insurance claims. Why he didn't just get up and ask, I don't know. Of course, I'd emailed Bob, who sat merely four desks away, for two months without realizing who he was, so who was I to talk?

My job as an admin/researcher/dogsbody for Green Hand Insurance was full of various and wonderful things. *Not. Do people even say "not" anymore?* Largely, it meant I wrote reports whenever some kind of new legislation, survey, policy, or some other documentation came out that no one truly cared about. As long as it affected insurance, the powers that be at Green Hand could adjust their insurance lending, while feeding the sales department with their latest information. Along with my endless and dull reports, I also filed, typed and took notes. I have no doubt in my mind that somewhere far, far away, someone thought my job was an important and useful one. I can't say I shared that thought; but at least, it meant my mother could say the youngest of her brood did something respectable. I didn't follow my three older brothers into law enforcement, or my older sister into an actual career, after all. Besides, someone had to keep the wheels oiled, the sales agents' information stocked, as well as ensure that the real, live office workers didn't have to bust a gut doing the grunt work that temps like me were drafted for.

And heaven forbid Adam, here just a month, brought in from some other dull department, had to do any of the research himself. He caught my eye and raised his eyebrows while I ducked behind the monitor, called up my email and started to type.

*Adam,*

*This looks like a tough one. I'll need to go to the library and research some of the points. Is it okay if I go now while it's quiet?*

*Lexi*

I hit "send" and looked around. Of course, it was quiet. No one appeared to be doing anything. Well, Bob was doing a crossword, his eyes pinched and studious. I could see the corner of the newspaper peeking out from the large black binder he was pretending to peruse. Across from him, Anne's hands flew across the keyboard, but I would bet twenty bucks that she was emailing one of her cronies. A few desks over, Vincent, our accountant, was bobbing his head and I figured he had his headphones on. Still, kudos to them all for pretending.

An instant message window popped up on the bottom bar of my screen.

Adam: *Are you really going to the library?*

I sighed. So distrustful.

Me: *Yes.*

Lie. I was going to Starbucks to get an iced caramel macchiato and a muffin.

Adam: *How long will you be?*

Me: *A couple hours? I need to make sure I have up-to-date information on the survey.*

Hah. Can't complain about that, can you? I added the question mark to the time frame in case I couldn't be bothered to come back before my day officially ended. Then I could technically claim that I was guesstimating the time and had his approval.

Adam: *Fine. Put a copy of the report on Martin Dean's desk before you go. He'll need to read it before tomorrow's morning briefing.*

Me: *Okay.*

I rifled around in my drawer for a new notepad and a pen, then rummaged in my purse for my emergency coffee money. I found a filthy ten-dollar bill tucked into a pocket of my wallet, and I folded it and taped it into my notepad. If I took my purse, Adam would totally know I was sneaking out; and I was way smarter than that. The IM box showed that Adam was typing something else, so I waited, my fingers tapping the desk softly until his message popped up.

Adam: *When you go to Starbucks, get me a tall Americano.*

My mouth dropped open. Out-bloody-rageous. Not even the question of an "if"! What was he typing now?

Adam: *And one of those cake things you like. With the marshmallows.*

I think I made a cross little noise. When I peeked out from my monitor, Adam was focusing on his screen, face completely blank. He caught my eye and... I think he winked at me! It's entirely possible my heart skipped a beat.

Me: *I am NOT going to the library. I am going to Starbucks.* I typed crossly, then realized what I had typed and went to hit the "delete" button. Instead, I got "enter." Shit. Why did the gods of keyboards decide that putting the "enter" and "delete" keys so close together was such a good idea? Morons.

Me: *I meant that the other way round, obviously.*

Adam: *Obviously.*

Then...

Adam: *Regular is fine. I'll give you the money when you come back.*

That was it. I was going to sacrifice my yummy macchiato on principle today. I signed off the IM, locked my screen, picked up my notepad and pen, and swanned out of the office. Swiping my identity card through the scanner, I passed into the corridor to the bank of elevators and hit the "down" button.

The basement library was made up of a series of stacks that spanned the length of one wall, while a few computer stations and a cluster of reading cubicles occupied two other walls, leaving the last free for the elevator and the exit to the stairs. Without natural light, or a heating system that could sustain human life for longer than a couple of hours, it wasn't a very popular space. The whole room had a deathly air of quiet about it. Just for kicks, I loudly faux sneezed. Three people jumped.

Finding a free terminal, I dropped onto the plastic seat and typed in my search keywords, waiting for a list to come up that would show me every yawn-inducing pamphlet, journal, book or article that had been tagged with those words in the system. It was a blessedly short list, so I printed it out and went to round up my afternoon reading, along with the current year's survey file, before settling into one of the desks. Sometimes, it reminded me of being at college with the windowless room and fluorescent lights over a broad bank of desks where people quietly read and scribbled notes. The piles of books that surrounded us were the kind not a single person would choose to read unless said person was as dull as dishwater. But seeing as this was the insurance industry, they probably were, but that was beside the point.

Actually, as I got into reading and making notes, it wasn't quite as dull as I first estimated and the survey would definitely change the information and statistics the brokers who worked with Green Hand would give to clients, as well as alter their premiums.

Insurance depended on many factors and it was hard to keep the various policies straight in my mind, causing me to drift and play my favorite game of pretending to be a spy. I can attest, hand on heart, that I have seen every single James Bond film ever made and I have the theme song CD too. Once again,

I cursed the government that wouldn't let me be a glamorous operative, or even a senator, even though that might be pushing it a bit, given that I have neither the drive nor the patience to get that far. So I made a career of being a temp and actually doing the work of a glorified gofer instead. Life was so unfair.

When I had accumulated ten pages of notes on how the statistics had changed, along with various highlighted sections to paste into my report, I glanced at my watch. Crap. It was seven p.m. How had I spent three *hours* in here? I smiled. Adam hadn't gotten his coffee. That showed him dedication, alright.

I returned my reading to the stacks and headed back to the single elevator that served the basement. Just as my finger hovered over "Reception," I remembered my purse still tucked under my desk. That, and I hadn't given Green Hand Insurance's vice president the report, so I hit the sixth floor and trundled up. I felt slightly buoyed by the thought that I could claim almost two extra hours of overtime, which would more than pay for cocktails on Saturday night with Lily.

Someone had propped the door open with a wedge so I slipped through, assuming the custodians were doing their thing. The room was still and silent. Everyone else had gone home. I walked over to my desk, jabbed a button on the keyboard and my monitor whirred back to life. Logging in, I called up the report Adam had requested and sent it to the printer, dashing over to make sure I hadn't printed any lingerie pictures again. I hadn't. Thank goodness for that. It was bad enough Adam had seen my bra choices; he was healthy. Green Hand's vice president,

Martin Dean, hadn't seen a day of exercise inside of a decade and would probably have had a heart attack. Then I'd never get a decent reference out of him to get a proper job doing something cool. I know. I know. I'm selfish like that. Actually, come to think of it, *maybe* sending him thong shots would get me a reference faster.

Inside my head, I vomited at the thought.

Back at my desk, I raced through the motions of closing the computer screen, logging off and shutting down. Leaving a computer on in this building was akin to looking at porn. You might think about it occasionally, but you didn't want to get caught. So I'm told.

Picking up my purse and swinging it over my shoulder, I shoved my notepad into my drawer and locked it, then stapled the report together and headed across the room to Dean's office.

Martin Dean, being the resident big shot, had an office far away from the plebian workers and behind a set of double doors, outside of which his executive assistant, Dominic, sat. Dominic's monitor was off so he had gone home already, which meant I would have to take the report in and leave it on the desk myself.

I raised my hand to knock on Martin Dean's door and hesitated, hearing voices inside.

My heart sank.

Dean was still in and probably cross he would have to read my report this evening, instead of doing whatever he usually did in his downtime. Even worse, the voices sounded heated and angry.

At least, I hadn't barged in before remembering that he always liked an extra photocopy so Dominic could read it too. Dominic was in his early thirties and smart. I thought, privately, he was the one really running the show.

Turning on my heel, I sloped back the way I came, veering off into the corridor on the left that led to the nearest photocopy room, and shutting the door behind me. Inside, I wasted precious minutes as the machine crawled back to life. Finally, I photocopied the pages, in sequence, and rooted around on the overhanging shelf for another stapler so I could attach the pages together.

Gathering both sets of papers, I returned to Dean's office, pressing my ear to the door. All was quiet inside. I knocked on the door and waited. Nothing. I knocked again.

Maybe I'd struck lucky and Dean had gone home? I could ditch the papers and pretend I'd left them earlier. I pushed open the door and stepped inside, the door falling shut behind me with a light click.

The office was empty. I quickly checked the handle, in case I'd done something stupid, like locking myself in. Thankfully, I hadn't. I wouldn't have to phone the security guards twice in a week. Yay me!

With a bounce in my step, I strode up to the desk, leaning over to put the reports square and center on top... and that's when I saw him.

Sprawled on the floor, not moving.

"Sir?" I said hesitantly, in case Martin Dean was doing some really weird form of meditating. Face down.

No reply. I moved around the desk, and slipped on something, sending my legs in different directions. I landed heavily on my palms, cursing. One hand hit the carpet and stung as I steadied myself; my other hand hit something wet.

I raised my hand to my face and my stomach flipped. "Shit!" It wasn't just wet; it was blood and it was seeping from under Dean's body. "Double shit!" I squeaked.

I sat on my haunches for a moment, too freaked out to move; then I shuffled round and saw exactly what had caused Martin Dean to be lying in a pool of his own blood.

His head lay on the right side. He'd been shot between the eyes, a powder burn marring the ragged wound, and there was a second wound in his back. Point blank range. Well, I assumed it was point blank. I'd never seen anyone shot between the eyes before.

He'd been alive just a few minutes ago. I'd heard him through the door, his voice raised. God, someone had just shot him while I was in the photocopy room! They might still be in the building.

Despite my heart racing and the blood rushing in my ears, I heard footsteps.

I clutched the sheaf of photocopies in my hand until my knuckles went white while I panicked.

If I went out the door, whoever had just put a bullet between Martin Dean's eyes would see me. And I'd see them. Then they'd probably shoot me too and my mom would cry the hardest at my funeral because the only thing I would be remembered for was the moment of madness when I ran away to join the Army. Oh God, I did not want to die! I had nowhere near enough good stuff to put in my eulogy, which would probably be performed by my sniveling sister, after strong-arming the rest of my family out of the way. You could just bet she'd manage to work her Harvard degree into the speech too, insulting my lack of aptitude even in death.

What if no one turned up? It's not like I'd made a big effort to stay in touch with school friends or was making a ton of pals at work. My funeral would be social death. Literally.

The footsteps got closer.

I looked down at the puddle of blood underneath Martin Dean as it bloomed towards me. Shit! I'd left a handprint in it. I'd left fingerprints. Evidence! My TV husband, Horatio Caine, would be all over that and do his little side-on serious look thing as he peered over his sunglasses at me and told me my rights. It totally did not go that way in my dreams. Plus, all the hot women on *CSI: Miami* had their giraffe-like legs clad in white pants and wore ridiculous heels, considering they were always getting messed up by corpses on murder scenes. I didn't even have any white pants. I was wearing my favorite blue dress with its super-cute flared skirt. And now I'd gotten blood on it, because like an idiot, I put my bloody palm on my lap. My mug shots would look terrible! They'd think I had killed him.

I'd probably go to prison.

Even more pressing, there was at least one murderer on his? —her? —way back to the office and they would see my handprint. Reality hit me with a thump.

My heart pounding, I took his warm—*oh God, dead!* —hand between my thumb and forefinger and gingerly moved it on top of my handprint; then I pressed down and rubbed the palm and fingerprints out with his own, all the time trying not to squeal like the big scaredy cat I was. I moved his leg to cover my footprint and smooshed it in, trying hard not to squeak as I slipped off my heels.

I had officially tampered with my first crime scene. And last, I hoped. Not that it really mattered. It wasn't like I popped him anyway. Surely someone would believe me. A second set of footsteps sounded as the murderers made their way to the office.

Standing up, I looked around for somewhere to hide and finally, *finally,* clapped eyes on the big wall unit where Dean stored his spare suits and other things when he needed to change in a hurry after a long day. I knew it was mostly empty because Dominic had roped me into cleaning it out on Monday, when Dean was away at a conference in Boston, and I took the bags to the dry cleaners.

Trotting towards the closet, I used a tissue from my purse to pull one slim door open. I backed in, tugging the door shut. Sinking to the floor, I made myself as small as possible, hunkering down, my heart beating twice as fast as normal, just as I saw the handle to the office door turn down through the crack in the closet doors.

Which was almost the exact same second a hand clamped over my mouth and my eyes nearly popped out of my head in fear. So *not* a good look... even in a dark closet!

## CHAPTER TWO

"Stop wriggling," hissed a man's voice. His breath brushed my ear and my heartbeat ramped up to marathon speed. "If they find us, we're dead."

Okay. So here's the good news. I was probably not wedged inside Martin Dean's closet with his murderer. That, at least, had the potential for some reassurance. Powerful arms remained clamped around me, even though I stopped trying to wriggle my way free, and the hand stayed over my mouth, despite my attempts to stifle my whimper. For a brief moment, I contemplated licking the hand because that always made my brothers and sister let go when we were kids, but that was too gross to do to a stranger. In a closet. With a corpse a few feet away.

"If you scream, they'll shoot us in the head and you're far too pretty to die," came the man's urgent whisper. Well, I had to agree with that. I really was too pretty to die. Also compliments totally worked on me. "I'm going to uncover your mouth. Don't scream. Nod if you understand."

I nodded and the hand slid away, while the other stayed firmly clamped around my upper body as we looked through the slim crack in the doors. Two men came into the room and walked over to Dean's body. I remained huddled against the mystery man, shivering with fear as the men stared down at my boss' corpse. The blood had spread a bit and the carpet was screwed. I knew that because I once cut my hand in my parents' kitchen and ran into the dining room for help. I tripped and promptly stained their new wool carpet with my bloody handprint. In my opinion, there had been too much whining about the ruined carpet, too much giggling about what forensics would make of it, and not enough sympathy for my potentially early demise. Well, not that I would have *actually* died, but I was seven and a bit dramatic at the time. Blood did that to me as a kid. Even so, the stain leaking from Dean was decidedly larger than my splotchy handprint and they would never get it out.

More pressing was Dean's warm corpse on top of it.

"We'll have to get rid of it," said one of the men to the other. They were both tall and broad with shaven heads, flat faces and flatter noses. They wore black suits that hugged brawny shoulders. Their ties matched. Slightly less business-like were the rubber gloves they both wore. Despite their effort at business disguise, "thug" could have been printed on their foreheads. I was certain I'd never seen them before.

"Can't get it past security," said the second man, giving Dean's leg a poke with a shiny shoe. "There's a twenty-four hour desk."

"Can't leave it here." The second man shrugged.

They looked down at Dean's body. A bit too hopefully, I thought. It wasn't like he was going to oblige them by getting up and trotting away.

"Shoulda shot him outside," said the first man. "Coulda made it look like a mugging. I didn't think of that." He was slightly bigger than his friend and clearly the rougher of the two. He looked like he'd led a hard life. Despite his smart suit and polished shoes, just one wrong look, and you'd be in the river, wearing a not-so-stylish pair of concrete stilettos. I shivered. The arm tightened about me for a moment before relaxing.

"Let's see if there's anything we can move him with," said number two, making for the door. *Heh-heh. Number two.* I know. Immature. But I'd take a laugh anywhere I could get it right now.

Number one grunted and followed him out the room, closing the door behind him.

Just as soon as the door shut, the man holding me whispered, "What are you doing here, Lexi?"

I twisted my neck and blinked in the gloom. Now that I thought about it, that voice sounded awfully familiar. "Adam?" I whispered.

"Yeah."

I thought about all the things I should ask next. "What are you doing in Dean's closet?"

"I asked first."

"I was dropping off the report." I still had it clutched in my, literally, bloody hand.

"I thought you'd gone home."

"No. I was working in the library."

"Really?" Adam was incredulous.

Honestly, we were stuck in a closet, no more than ten feet away from a man who had just been murdered minutes before, his murderers now freely trotting about the floor and my boss was giving me grief about my work ethic. *Typical.*

"Yes, really," I replied with as much indignation as I could muster, given the circumstances.

"I thought you went to Starbucks, then home."

I gaped into the darkness. "I. Was. Working."

"Really?"

"Oh for God's sake." We were quiet for a moment, then, "Adam, what are *you* doing here?"

"Trying not to get shot."

"Oh. Well... well done."

"Hmm?"

"You've not been shot yet."

"Yet, being the important bit." That was quite a sobering thought.

"Why are you in the closet?" I persisted.

"I don't want to say."

"Why not? Did you have something to do with..." I flapped my hand and caught my knuckles on the door. We both froze.

"Okay, fine. I came to talk to Martin. He got a call and told me to get in here."

"How... odd." No one had ever told me to get into the closet when a friend came to visit. Well, except that time at college when I was about to get it on with some guy, and his girlfriend, (don't judge. I didn't know and he wasn't exactly forthcoming), knocked on his door. I resolved that by climbing out the first floor window, rather than hide and see God knows—his idea, ugh! *The perv*—and walking home. I try not to think about it.

"I'm glad he did." Adam exhaled softly.

"Yes, I suppose you are."

"We need to get out of here, Lexi."

"Any bright ideas?"

"I'm thinking. Shh! I hear something. They're coming back." We fell silent again while the two goons trundled a mail delivery cart into the room, with a large box balanced on top. Behind me, Adam shifted and then put both arms around me, and, *oh*, that was quite nice, actually. So long as I didn't think too much about our impending deaths anyway.

I relaxed slightly, partly because I was scared of getting a cramp and partly because being cuddled up to Adam had featured prominently in today's daydream of choice. Minus the corpse.

The goons set the box on the floor, then number one picked up Martin Dean's hands and number two got his feet. Together, they dragged him over to the box, a thick smear of blood trailing in their wake. His chest oozed more blood. Ick. I never knew a human body held so much.

They dropped him. Dean's head rolled to face us, his eyes open and glassy. I squeezed my eyes shut and Adam hugged me a bit tighter again. I turned to press my head into his big, hard, manly chest, while trying not to make a sound. *Wow*. Adam was quite muscular. That was a surprise. He smelled really nice too, sort of minty. He tightened his arms around me, one hand stroked my hair and... okay, I'm not ashamed to admit it. I *snuggled*. And I stayed there right through the quiet argument the goons had with each other, even while picking Dean up and folding him into the box before carrying it, and right up until the cart was wheeled out of the room. Adam leaned forward slightly to angle his head to peek through the sliver of space between the doors.

"They're gone. We need to get out of here before they come back."

"Why would they come back?"

"Because they want one of the files on the desk and they didn't take it."

"Which one? What's in it?" I might have been scared, but I couldn't help asking. It was the nosy gene. My whole family had it, which probably explains why most of them became cops.

"Some report."

"A report?"

"They were talking about a report and Martin wouldn't tell them where it was," Adam explained.

"We could take them?" I suggested.

"Then they would know we were here and they have guns."

I thought about the bullet wound in Dean's head. "Oh, right. Bad idea."

"Do you know what reports were on Dean's desk?"

"Not right now. Dominic guards this office."

"Remind me why you're here again?"

"Because I forgot to put this report on his desk and he wanted it today." I flapped the sheets of paper at Adam.

"Does Martin keep copies anywhere?"

"Sometimes Dominic has a copy on his desk. See? I have two here. One for Dean, one for Dominic."

"We'll have to check and see which reports are on the desk."

"Okay." Neither of us moved.

"Today," said Adam, giving me a little push.

"I'm not going out there! What if they see me?"

"Fine. Wait here." Adam edged around me and

slid out of the closet, skirting Dean's blood as he crossed to the desk. A small stack of reports sat squarely in the center and Adam rifled through them, quickly checking the cover sheet of each one before knocking them back into a precise pile again.

"Do you keep copies of your reports?" he asked, pulling the door open and beckoning me out. He pressed the door shut again.

"Yes. On the hard drive."

"Shit. They'll probably delete it."

I swallowed. "Um... Why?"

"Your reports are the only ones on the desk."

My breath caught in my throat. "They killed Dean over one of my reports?"

"I don't know. Maybe."

"I might have another copy," I mumbled, my thoughts whirring.

Adam glanced back at me as he moved towards the door. "What?"

"I might have another copy. On a memory stick." I wasn't quite sure how he was going to take that. I added, in a mumbled whisper, barely audible, "Of all my reports." It's not my fault, okay? I had to. I had a habit of accidentally deleting stuff, so now I was super organized and backed up everything. It was a practice that allowed me to save my own bacon a whole bunch of times.

"Lexi, you do know that's highly unethical? Didn't you sign loads of secrecy waivers and stuff?"

"Oh, tons." God, it had taken *ages*.

Adam sighed. "Where's the memory stick?"

"At my apartment."

"At your apartment! You've been sneaking files out of the building! Fucking hell, Lexi!" I could feel him fuming.

"So you don't want them?" Hah. Got him.

"Yeah, I do," he conceded, "but we need to get out now. Do you know another way out that doesn't involve using the elevator or getting spotted by security or cameras?"

"Um... yes, actually I do." See? This is another reason why I should have been a spy. Not only could I sneak documents in and out of the building for months without ever being noticed, but I also knew how to physically get out without being caught.

"How long will it take us to get there?"

I did a quick calculation. "Thirty seconds to the door. Five minutes to get downstairs." Adam darted to the door, opened it slightly and looked through the crack. After a moment, he signaled to me and I lurched forward, clutching my papers, purse and stained heels, taking the hand he extended towards me.

"Let's go," he said. "Let's get out of here."

Holding Adam's hand would have been a lot nicer if we weren't running from two murderers who were, at this moment, somewhere in the building with our boss' corpse. I tugged him along as I ran to the rear stairwell, slamming to a stop when I saw the pass card swipe slot. Shit, I'd forgotten about those. If anyone checked the logs, they would see me swiping out minutes after Martin Dean bit it, a sure sign that I had been on the floor.

Adam reached around me and ran his pass through the machine as he pushed me through the door, shutting it quickly after us.

"You'll show up in the system," I said, as we took the stairs down. "If anyone checks, they'll know you were here. You'll be a suspect."

"It's an unregistered all access pass," said Adam as he ran after me.

"How did you get one of those?"

"Uh, can't tell you."

I shot him a glance as we ran. "Did you 'borrow' it?" I asked, adding bunny ears with my forefingers.

"No!"

We descended six floors in, by my guess, less than five minutes. I signaled to Adam to use his magical swipe card again, which he did, and we entered the mailroom. I had been in here a couple of times when I had to sign for a package, so I knew the layout fairly well. Each time it had been busy with deliveries arriving and mail being sorted and loaded into carts. The day's work lay discarded on the long table and in the pigeon holes that flanked one side. The mailroom was completely dead.

Oh, I wish I hadn't just thought that.

The plus point of the mailroom was that it could be entered from the outside, and exited, without passing security at the front of the building. It had its own door especially for the mail to be delivered and collected. There were also no cameras except right at the basement level, where there was a fire exit that led to the street.

Just then, the fire alarm went off and I clamped my hands over my ears to drown out the ringing.

"They must have set it off to distract security," said Adam. "Which way now?"

I pointed to the exit at the far side of the room and Adam followed me. He used his pass again to swipe us out. He shut the door softly, even though there wasn't anyone to see us. I leaned against the building, heaving some air into my lungs while Adam looked around. He ran a hand through his hair, leaving it standing in tufts. After sucking in a decent lungful of evening air, I opened my bag and pulled out the spare flats I carried for high heel emergencies, slipping my feet into them.

"We can't stay here," he said. "Are you north or south?"

"What?"

"Where do you live? North or south?"

"Oh, right, west actually. West Montgomery."

"Let's go." This time Adam tugged me behind him as we cut through back streets, leading us away from the Green Hand building. After five minutes, Adam slowed his pace so we could walk casually. We were still hand-in-hand and it was strangely comforting. My heart rate slowed from its frantic beating to casual fear.

"I planned on getting the bus home. My car wasn't working this morning," I said, suddenly wondering where we were going. Was he really planning on taking me home? Shouldn't we call the police and wait for them to arrive? Or maybe, Adam didn't want anyone to know he had witnessed the murder. He was a witness. My heart rate sped up and I began to babble. "I turned the key and all it did was this little *put-put-put* noise. I think it's dead." I gulped at the words.

"We'll get a cab. Too many cameras, too many people on public transport."

"Right. Yes. Definitely." We walked silently in the dusk. Presumably, anyone looking at us would think we were on an evening stroll, or a date. Adam and me. On. A. Date. When we were a mile from the office, Adam hailed a cab and opened the door for me. I collapsed into the seat, shell-shocked, and looked down at my dress. *Oh yuck*. I'd forgotten about the bloody handprint. I shifted my purse to cover it and stuffed the papers haphazardly inside.

"Where to?" asked the driver, glancing at us in his mirror. Adam held my clean hand in his lap. I kept my bloody hand concealed.

Adam looked at me expectantly so I reeled off my address and we headed there.

By the time we turned onto my street, I was shivering uncontrollably. Adam let go of my hand and wrapped his arm around me, pulling me into him. He was warm and I snuggled happily. Twice in one night. A little bit of me wanted to do a "yay" but the rest of me felt cold and flat and horrified. This wasn't the end of a date. Somewhere in Montgomery were Martin Dean's corpse and his murderers, and I had as much as witnessed it. You don't come from a cop family like mine and not know how bad that sounded.

"You live alone?" Adam asked when the taxi dropped us off outside my place. As far as living arrangements went, I'd majorly scored. It was a three-story brownstone with white trim, owned by my best friend's parents, who had converted it into apartments, which they rented to us. Lily had the first floor apartment, which was the biggest and had the small rear garden. I had the second floor and someone else rented the floor above me. Lily's turquoise Mini was parked out front next to my dead-as-a-dodo black VW. A lamp was on in Lily's living room. I felt relief. At least she was close by. If I screamed, she'd double the noise and bring someone running.

I nodded. "My best friend, Lily Shuler, lives downstairs," I said as I shakily put my key into the lock. After I fumbled it, Adam took the key, unlocked the door and pushed me inside. He hardly said a word on the way over here and didn't seem likely to get chatty any time soon. He followed me upstairs and unlocked the door to my apartment too. In the little entryway, I dumped my purse and shoes, and flipped the light on with a quivering hand. I went straight into the bathroom to wash up, trying not to look at the pink water as it swirled away.

When I came out, and walked down the hallway into the living area, Adam was sitting on my couch.

"Are you all right?" he asked, his concerned eyes running over me as he ran a hand through his hair.

"Not sure." I flopped onto the couch, next to him.

"Have you ever seen a dead body before?"

"Only Izzie, Natalie and Fi," I replied.

Adam gaped at me. "You found three women's bodies?"

"My goldfish."

"Oh."

"Adam, Martin Dean is dead."

"I was there."

"Did those men kill him?"

"Yes."

"They would have killed us." It wasn't a question. It was a fact.

"Probably," agreed Adam. We were quiet for a moment. It was a lot to absorb.

"We should call the police. Tell them what we saw."

"Lexi, you can't call the police. Do you

understand me?"

"Why not? A man just got murdered. We're witnesses." Oh God, maybe they'd make us go into the witness protection program. We'd have to live in some horrid town where no one knew us and I'd never see my family again. Bright side: maybe Adam and I would have to pretend to be married. I was willing to do some very creative pretending.

"Do not phone the police, I'll take care of this." Adam's pocket rang and he pulled a slim cell phone out. He walked over to the window, looking out over the quiet street as he answered it.

"Martin Dean's dead," was the first thing he said. "I saw him get shot... Two of them... No, they didn't see me. They wanted a file... There was another witness. We got out without them seeing us. I'm with her right now." They talked a while longer, Adam giving short, terse answers before hanging up and turning to me.

I had a bad feeling about all of this. "What's going on, Adam?" I asked.

He looked at me for a long moment, like he was trying to decide what to say or whether I could cope. I watched him with scared eyes. He started talking. "I don't work for Green Hand Insurance. I'm a detective with Montgomery PD and I'm undercover in an intelligence op. We've been watching Martin Dean for a while."

"Did Dean know?"

Adam nodded. "Not at first. I spoke to him just before he got shot." He stood in front of me, hands thrust into pockets, looking down with a serious expression. "It's important that you don't tell anyone."

"Why are you telling me?"

"Because I know you're not the ditz you make yourself out to be. I read your file. You're smart and you didn't completely freak out when you saw a dead body. You concealed your presence and knew how to get out of there... and I'm going to make a bet that no one knew you were in the building tonight either."

I thought about the wedge holding the door open so I didn't have to swipe onto the floor, the lack of cameras in the elevator and basement library. The only record of me was leaving the office at four p.m., hours before Dean was killed.

I hadn't been smart. I had been lucky.

"Uh, thanks?" I said, then. "Wait, I've got a file? And you work for the police department?" What else didn't I know about Adam? Maybe he wasn't the cute slash trainspotting loser slash management drone I thought he was.

"Everyone in Dean's office has a file. Yours was the most interesting."

I perked up a bit at that.

"Can't understand why you're a temp. You have a perfectly good degree." I tried not to look really pleased that he knew I was a smarty-pants, but when he carried on, I had to wipe the smile off my face a bit. "You temp in a bunch of different offices. You're a really good researcher and I know you've spent a total of ten hours on the last three reports I've given you combined, even though it's taken you at least a week to turn each one in." Busted again. Though, come to think of it, he had been letting me get away with it. Despite my fear, I warmed to him.

"Why are you telling me all this? Is this one of those monologues the evil dude gives before he kills the girl? And then paints her in gold as some kind of crazy message?" I started to look around without moving my head. I could probably make it to my bedroom, lock the door, jump out the window and flee down the fire escape. Each of my three brothers was a cop. If I called any one of them, the whole of Montgomery PD would turn out in full force and flatten Adam.

Adam had the good manners to look appalled. "No! I'm telling you I think you did a good job tonight and this isn't James Bond."

"I didn't do anything," I protested.

"Exactly."

"What else was in my file?"

"Just the regular stuff."

The fleeting thought that he might have put the lingerie pics in my file pinged into my head and I went a bit pink. "You're really a detective?"

Adam nodded. He was quite good at that. Nice strong chin.

"How long?"

"Eight years."

"Wow." Then, "You're not very good at keeping secrets." Why was he telling me this if he was supposed to be a super secret undercover operative? I thought spies, sorry undercover cops, couldn't tell anyone about their jobs, except their cats and dead aspidistras. My oldest brother, Garrett, had done some undercover stuff and he never said a word.

"I am, but you're quietly freaking out and you'll just dig around until you get the truth anyway, so I'm saving you the trouble and me a lot of bother." Actually, he had a point. I would have dug around, and probably blabbed everything to the police in an

Oscar-worthy scene. "Plus, I don't want you to blab and tell the police then get yourself killed before you can make it to the witness stand." Oooh! He was good at this. No wonder he got to be hotshot spy... and I DIDN'T. Sore point.

He got up and started down my little hallway. "Where are you going?" I asked.

"To get you some juice. You're obviously having some weird internal monologue and I don't want you to dehydrate."

I sank back on the comfy pillows and avoided looking down at my ruined dress while trying to process it all. A few hours ago, I had a dull job and a cute boss. Now I had a cute secret spy detective boss, was witness to a murder (though not the actual act, thanks to the photocopying chore) and... and what next? I just didn't know. My imagination always stopped at the fun bits.

Adam returned with a glass of orange juice and thrust it into my hands. "Drink," he ordered.

"What are you going to do now?" I asked, taking a sip.

"I'm going to stay with you until I'm sure you're okay; then I'm going to file my report."

"Are you sure you aren't going to call the police?"

"Absolutely, and neither are you. My team will deal with this. Keep drinking. I don't want you to go into shock."

I slurped another mouthful and tried to think things through. Was I supposed to go into work tomorrow? Should I go back to the agency and ask for a new assignment? Pull a sick day and stay in bed, wallowing in fear? Decisions, decisions.

"You need to be at work tomorrow," said Adam,

answering my unasked question. "Do everything like normal. Turn up at your usual time—late—" I scoffed at that, but really, he was right. I always ran ten minutes late. "—Work normally. Don't do anything that isn't your normal routine. Don't give anyone a reason to suspect you know anything about what happened. I'll take your statement and you can't discuss it with anyone. Understand?"

"Yes, but why do I need to act like nothing happened?" I asked. "Why are you watching Dean anyway? What was he up to?" I waited while Adam had his own internal monologue. Out of the frying pan, into the fire, I thought as I continued, "C'mon, Adam. You know I'm going to dig anyway. This isn't just about Dean. What else is going on?"

"Fraud," he said at last, watching me closely. "There are millions of dollars in fraud going on at Green Hand and we're gathering evidence for the prosecution. We suspect fake policies are being cashed in."

"And that's what got Dean killed?"

"Maybe."

"Not my report?"

Before I could breathe a sigh of relief, Adam said, "No, your report has something to do with it."

I mustered indignation. "I am not involved in fraud. I'm a temp!"

"I know. We ruled you out already."

"Well... thanks. I guess."

"No problem. We know the fraud is an inside job. Someone is leaking information out of Dean's department and that person is probably connected to Dean's murder."

"Really?" I must have sounded quite incredulous.

I mean, the images of Bob, Anne, or any of the other inmates as fraudsters, corporate spies or murderers weren't exactly the most feasible.

"Yes, really. That's why I was assigned there. To get close to the staff and find out what's going on. Lucky for me, a job came up. The whole transfer was a set-up to get me in."

"So you're staying?" I sipped my juice and felt my eyelids tugging. I yawned and looked at my watch. It wasn't late. There was no way I could possibly be tired. I yawned again and set the glass on the table, blinking hard.

"Absolutely. Listen Lexi, where's the..."

My head swam and I started edging to my feet, pushing my hands against the couch for a boost, barely able to concentrate on what he was saying. "Adam, I don't feel too well," I said. I stood up and swayed. Two Adams reached for me. Then the world went black.

# CHAPTER THREE

The last thing I remember thinking before I passed out was *the bastard drugged me.*

Waking, I stiffened, then cranked one eye open, first ridiculously grateful to be alive, then frightened, because I was alive and Adam had drugged me.

I opened the other eye and looked around, familiarity greeting me. I was in my bedroom, cocooned under my quilt and somewhere nearby, something awful made a hideous shrieking noise. I stuck out an arm, shivering as the cool air hit me and slapped my hand around the nightstand, finally finding my alarm. Fumbling, I switched it off about two seconds before I was ready to hurl it against the wall.

The quilt felt strangely cozy against my skin and just as I was thinking about snuggling under for an extra nap, and that this had all been a really sucky dream, I stopped and peeked under the covers.

Like I feared, my dress was gone and instead, I was wearing my shortie pajamas, The ones with the duck print.

My cheeks heated. It wasn't a dream. It was a nightmare and it was real. Not only did Adam have the audacity to knock me out and tuck me into bed, but he'd also apparently undressed me and put me in my PJs! And, I realized with horrifying clarity, my bra was missing. I froze. Did he get a good look? Cop a feel? Or done some kind of amazing feat of eyes-closed undressing and dressing? My cheeks pinked. Yep. I think we all know the answer to that one. After all, he was a man.

A cursory glance around my room showed me that my dress wasn't just gone, it was missing. Maybe he took it for evidence? I groaned and struggled up on my elbows, feeling like my head was remarkably clear for someone who had been knocked out. It took me another minute or two to realize I wasn't alone in my apartment. Footsteps padded between my living room and kitchen. Someone was humming a song.

Sliding out of bed, I grabbed my short, silk robe from the armchair, wrapped it around me, and scanned the room for a weapon. I grabbed my lamp, popped the plug out of the socket and softly tiptoed to the partially open bedroom door.

Ducking my head out, I shrieked blue murder when I spotted Adam walking towards me.

"You're awake," he said simply, when I got a grip. He smiled and looked pleased.

"You drugged me!" I raised the lamp and bent my knees, ready to spring forward and whack him hard if I needed to.

"I had to." He stood still. I noticed he was drinking from my coffee mug. *Of all the nerve!* "You were freaking out and asking me too many questions and I had to go out. I needed to make sure you wouldn't do anything stupid." See? I said he was distrustful, didn't I? Never believed a word I told him.

"How did you get back in?" I asked.

"Took your key."

"Did you sleep here?" In. My. Bed? My heart thumped.

"On the sofa," Adam corrected.

"Did you take my clothes off?"

He hesitated. "Yes."

"Eyes open or closed?"

"Closed."

I narrowed my eyes. "Really?"

"Well, yours were closed!"

"I am *so* embarrassed!"

Adam's lips curled upwards in a smile. "Don't be. Your underwear matched."

"I know that. I'm just embarrassed you took my clothes off after drugging me. Does the PD offer seminars on that?"

"Of course not. Normally, I'd shoot you first." He rolled his eyes. "Kidding. Coffee? Very nice underwear, by the way. Pink. Cute."

I looked at him like he was a total idiot. "No, thanks."

"It's not drugged," he promised, though he didn't look exactly sorry.

"I'll make my own." As I pushed past him to do just that, he sidestepped and somehow pressed us against each other until I couldn't move. His proximity made my knees weak as I inhaled the scent of limes wafting from his skin. Perhaps if I swooned just a little bit... Hang on! *What was I thinking?* He drugged me and now I was thinking he looked mighty fine? "What time is it?" I snapped, feeling my face beginning to flush. I sniffed again. He smelled suspiciously like my shower gel.

"Seven. You need to get ready for work."

"So do you."

"I'm ready." He was too, smug jerk. He'd already changed his shirt and tie and even shaved. Most likely in my bathroom. I sniffed again. He smelled like my toothpaste too.

"If you'd drugged me a little less, maybe I'd have been ready by now too."

"I'm sorry." Adam replied as he ran a hand down my arm, his eyes sparkling.

"Fine." But I was going to stay mad at him on principle. "Do we have to go?" Wouldn't it be teeming with the police and crime scene investigators? I wanted to ask.

"Yes, we need to look normal, but..." He leaned forward and brushed some stray hairs behind my ear, allowing his fingers to linger on my cheek.

"But what?" I asked, looking up at him, straight into his blue eyes, which were piercing in the early morning light. I wondered what would happen if I stood on my tiptoes, and lifted my chin up ever so slightly... Then, I remembered... I was supposed to be mad at him. And he was still my boss... I think.

"Would you mind leaving the lamp at home?"

I'd forgotten about the dangerous weapon I was wielding, so I handed it to him. I gave him a little push backwards so I could pass him and go into the kitchen to make a rousing cup of coffee—my morning drug of choice.

As I clattered around in the kitchen, pulling out a mug and sugar, and searching through the cabinets for anything edible, I found it hard to stay mad at Adam, if that was even his real name. He hadn't left me alone at the office. He hadn't left me to the mercy of the murderers and he did make sure I was safe all night. That had to count for something when I weighed it against the drugging. But after I thought about that, I decided that the open carton of juice needed pouring down the sink and the open bag of coffee may as well go into the trash too. I'd buy a fresh, untampered bag later.

I showered, with the door locked, and dressed quickly in black pants, a blue blouse and low heels. When I came out of my bedroom, Adam was lounging against the wall, waiting for me.

"Where's my dress?" I asked. "And my heels?"

"I got rid of them."

"Is that legal?"

"Strictly speaking, no." Adam paused as I inhaled crossly. "Do you want things with Dean's blood on them, tying you to the scene?"

"No."

Actually, despite the fact we witnessed a murder, had to escape unnoticed from a building with two psychos in it, and knowing he drugged and undressed me, it was really quite nice to go to work with someone. However, it was mildly embarrassing to run into Lily as she left the building at exactly the same time, uncharacteristically early for her. She ran her eyes over Adam, and then gave me a not very subtle wink, but I got over that pretty fast. He even bought me a muffin and a real coffee on our ride in, seeing as I refused to drink or eat anything unsealed that he might have had contact with in my kitchen, which, unfortunately, meant pretty much everything.

We entered the lobby together, rode the elevator, swiped onto the floor together, then calmly ignored each other as we veered off to our respective desks. My palms felt clammy and I was sure my heart beat loud enough for everyone to hear as I sat in my chair and leaned down to press the power button on my computer, freezing when I realized someone was hovering over me. Bob.

"Hello," I squeaked, straightening up to flash a smile at my co-worker. Bob was a big man, upwards and outwards, with a crop of dark hair closely cut to minimize the bald patch encroaching on his crown. He looked daunting, but as far as attitude, he was easy going, with a laissez-faire philosophy to life, work and everything in between. His official title was "Accounts Manager," but I still had no idea what that even meant.

"Martin Dean was looking for a report from you yesterday," he told me.

"Oh, er, right. I forgot to put it on his desk." Actually it became a big, crumpled mess in my purse while I sat in the closet clutching it. That reminded me... I hadn't seen my purse this morning either. I hoped the PD had a good-sized budget because I loved that purse. On the other hand, Martin Dean was dead, so he probably didn't give a shit about my report anymore. Not that Bob seemed to know that.

I looked around the office quickly. Nothing seemed out of the ordinary. No one seemed upset, or stood in groups, whispering or weeping. No, today looked like a normal day. Somehow, I hadn't even considered that Dean's body wouldn't be found, that no one would know. Hadn't anyone seen the blood?

"He's not in today, so no rush," said Bob.

"Right." I fought to keep the perplexed look off my face.

Bob sauntered out and after a moment, I saw him drop into his chair, pick up the Montgomery Gazette and a pen, to start on what I could only assume was today's crossword puzzle.

Really, it was quite remarkable how normal everything was. I was not a freaked-out, screaming, crying mess. Instead, I was neat and tidy, my blue blouse sprigged with little flowers embroidered on the points of the collar and my hair in a loose ponytail. Adam was tapping away at his keyboard, looking bored. Bob was still sloping off and Anne was pounding abuse on her keyboard instead of touch-typing like a normal person. All around me it was an average workday. Appearances, however, could be very deceptive.

Murder had put me right off my online shopping for the moment, so instead, I looked at the brief Adam had sent me yesterday and pulled out yesterday's notes. I doodled some ideas on my notepad to avoid focusing on my heart hammering in my chest. It took only about ten minutes before I was bored to tears, and another ten seconds before I began thinking about what happened to Martin Dean and his body.

On my "to murder" list, Dean was one of those men who would have occupied the bottom. (Speaking of which, why did no one seem to know he was dead? Where were the press, for that matter? The murder of a prominent businessman in Montgomery should have qualified at least one report.) He might have been the VP of Green Hand, but he wasn't high profile in the community; he didn't attend benefits or dinners, or donate personal funds to needy children's charities. He seemed to enjoy the reclusive life. As far as I knew, he was divorced, had never been involved in any kind of sex scandal and didn't twiddle his expenses. He was usually polite to the underlings (even if he didn't care to learn my name and still called me Lacy), had never even had an inkling to run for mayor, and never caused a stir in his private or business lives. Dean was about as invisible as a man could be in his position.

Last night, Adam mentioned my report, saying that a bunch of them sat on Dean's desk. What had I written? Which report? And what did it have to do with Martin Dean's death? I opened up my "documents" folder and clicked on "reports" to bring up a cluster of thumbnails that represented my saved files. I re-ordered them by date and focused on the ones I'd written in the last month. Those, I surmised, were the most likely to be on his desk

My reports were comprised of burglary trends, new research into preventing electronic equipment theft, some background for a puff piece on a features-style ad for the Montgomery Gazette, and a report on statewide insurance take-up versus theft of non-insured homes. None of them struck me as even remotely interesting at the time, but someone must have considered something in one of them worth killing Martin Dean over. I clicked open each report and skimmed through.

Two things immediately cropped up. One, I didn't have a clue what was worth popping Martin Dean over. Two, my name was watermarked on the lower left corner of every single page! I blanched and slipped down dejectedly in my seat. Then realizing I was being weird, sat up properly again. Acting normal might have been working for Adam, but internally, I felt like a jiggling bowl of Jell-O. I had no clue how I would get through the day. Martin Dean knew something that apparently I knew too. Even though I didn't know what it was. *Life was so unfair!* I wondered if Adam knew which report it could be? I glanced up at him. He was sipping coffee, looking bored and not the slightest bit worried.

I dropped my eyes back to the screen just as something weird started happening. Each file suddenly closed down and disappeared from the folder. Then the whole freaking folder deleted. I felt sick inside. Someone was inside my computer, deleting all my work. I craned my head over the monitor and made some frantic, and probably quite strange, eyebrow waggles at Adam. He just frowned at me and shook his head, before returning to stare at his monitor.

I tried to remember what I knew from the IT helpdesk man, who had been pretty chatty when he came to install software a month ago. All the department computers were secured and loaded with firewalls as well as other ridiculously geeky stuff that stopped people from hacking in. I knew that the IT department could remotely access our computers, so it was possible someone in the building, maybe even on the floor, was deleting my files.

I flicked my hair so I could look over my shoulder. All the suits were hunkered down over their desks with no helpful poster that said 'Yes, I haz UR files!' I casually glanced around once more, then turned back to my now blank screen. Whatever was in the files, someone didn't want anyone to be able to access them ever again.

A light bulb popped in my head. Moving the mouse, I clicked on the little waste can icon. My recycle box had been emptied too. The files were gone.

I pretended to work until mid-afternoon, not even daring to venture out to get a sandwich for lunch, but giving Bob enough money to pick me up a tuna melt. I ate sullenly at my desk, chewing the bland meal until it tasted less like cardboard.

When Adam appeared behind me and spoke, I nearly leapt out of my skin. "We've got a meeting," he said.

"We do?"

"Yes," Adam said firmly. "A phone conference. You offered to take notes."

"I... did?"

He raised an eyebrow at me. Oh! Got it! A ruse! Good thing I catch on quick.

"Right. I'll just get my... notepad."

"Bring your purse. We might be a while."

I logged off the computer, grabbed my bag and notepad and followed Adam out. He motioned with a finger to his lips for me to be quiet. Silently, I followed him into the elevator and then out to the front of the building.

"All my files were deleted this morning," I said, through clenched teeth as we rounded the corner of the building. I couldn't hold it in any longer. "They just disappeared right as I was looking at them!"

"I know. I saw."

"You did? Wait... how?"

"I had remote access software installed on the whole team's computers."

"So... you can see everything I do on screen?" I was smart enough to always delete my browser history after surfing the net, but I tried to remember exactly what I might have browsed during the past few weeks that Adam had been with us. Lots of online shopping, restaurants or bars that Lily and I were thinking of going to, the occasional tickets, blogs, strangely compulsive gossip websites... there were loads of things I would rather my boss didn't see...and all during working hours.

Adam grinned. "Everything."

I changed the subject before I blushed beet red. "Which report were they after? All of mine were gone. I mean, all of them!"

"Chances are, they weren't sure, so they just deleted them all in order to prevent anyone else from reading them."

"Do you think it's the people who... you know..." I bobbed my head and pretended to shoot myself with my fingers.

Adam glanced towards me. "Probably."

"Where are we going?"

"We're going to meet my boss. He wants to know what you know."

"I hope you told him I don't know anything. *Where* exactly are we going though?" I asked as we turned another corner. Adam stopped and I almost bumped into him.

"Get in," he said, nodding to the black car that slid to a stop beside us. It had tinted windows and I couldn't see a thing inside. I was fairly sure my mother had warned me about moments like these. Adam stepped forward and opened the rear door, signaling to me to climb in. Naturally, I stepped back.

"What if I don't want to?"

"I want to keep you alive," said Adam, staring deeply enough into my eyes that I was tempted to swoon. "So, please, get in."

We definitely had keeping me alive in common, so after a quick peek to check yesterday's goons weren't inside, I got in. Adam slid in next to me and gave a blunt "Hello" to the driver. The car drove through the streets, neatly slicing through traffic. No one talked. It was all very ominous. Finally, we drew to a halt in front of a redbrick building downtown and Adam stepped out. He held my hand as I lowered my feet to the sidewalk. The car sped off as soon as the door slammed shut. I followed Adam inside the building.

"You'll be fine," he said. "Absolutely fine."

"Okay," I said with a weak smile.

So far, spying was disappointingly unglamorous. Adam led me through a long corridor, swiping through a doorway, then along another corridor, before turning into a large room with maybe a dozen people. It was pretty quiet as they watched screen upon screen being presented. A few of them glanced our way as we passed them. We stopped at a closed door and Adam knocked before ushering me inside.

The room was tiny, barely bigger than a closet, and a far cry from Dean's plush office. Squashed into it were a table and a few serviceable chairs. A grayhaired man in his forties stood. "Maddox, thanks for coming in. You must be Alexandra Graves," he said to me.

"Hi." I shook his outstretched hand, turning to mouth, "Maddox?" at Adam.

"My real name," he explained. "Adam Maddox.

Most people call me Maddox."

"Special Agent Matthew Miller, FBI. Call me Matt. This is Solomon, our financial and cyber crimes man." He nodded to the corner behind me and I half-turned, inclining my head at the man lounging against the wall. Somewhere between his mid-to-late-thirties, he had cappuccino brown skin that was either a light-skinned black man, a nicely tanned white man, or possibly mixed race. It was impossible to tell in the unnatural light and the shadow falling over him. He sported a few days of stubble and dark hair shaved close to his head. He had intense brown eyes that roved over me.

*Yu-u-um.*

I took a deep breath, my heart pounding a couple of beats faster, and turned away, then back again. "Hi."

Solomon nodded, but didn't speak. I didn't know if Solomon was his first name or surname, and no one said anything to indicate either.

My nose twitched and I turned away, but a big part of me wanted to turn back for another look. Just a little one. From head to toe.

"You've had quite an eventful past few hours," said Matt as he settled back into his chair and undid a couple of buttons of his jacket. Adam sat opposite him and I took the remaining chair, folding my ankles together under the seat.

"It wasn't the average day at work, no," I replied. If he'd asked me last night, I might have sobbed an answer. This morning, I thought I sounded pretty sober and unfazed.

"Maddox said you were very calm, given the circumstances. Got you both out of there, I heard."

"Um, yes, I guess." I wasn't sure if he were praising me, but heck, I'd take it wherever I could get it. Adam hadn't exactly been dishing out any gratitude.

"We're keeping Martin Dean's death quiet for now. It's strictly on a need-to-know basis. Can we trust you to keep this to yourself for the present?" Matt's eyes bored into me. I bet he tortured people with that glare. Or was that the CIA?

"Yes." I swallowed and took a deep breath. "What's going on?"

"Has Maddox explained anything to you?"

"Not in detail."

"Montgomery PD and the FBI are working a joint task force investigating insurance fraud. Green Hand is smack dab in the middle of it, which is why we placed Maddox there undercover. Our leads indicated Martin Dean might have had knowledge of the situation or at least have been able to lead us to those in the organization who did. Maybe even his co-conspirators, but he's dead. If we pull out now, a year's worth of work putting this op into place goes up in smoke. Do you understand?"

"Yes." Wait. Matt seemed pretty convinced Dean was involved.

"Good girl. Now, let's get down to business. The people who offed Martin Dean took a report you were working on. Do you have it?"

Adam Maddox, as I now knew him, answered for me, which was just as well because the "good girl" comment made me twitch. "All her files were remotely deleted from her office computer this morning, sir, before we got a chance to copy them. But Lexi has copies on a flash drive."

Miller nodded. "We'd like a copy. We need to know what you were working on that was so important someone had to kill Martin Dean for it."

"Uh, Matt, are you, um, sure that it was my report that got him killed?" Now that I'd gotten the chance to read my most recent files, I was still convinced that there was nothing in them worth killing Dean over.

"It seems highly probable. Do you have the memory stick on you now?"

"No, it's..." I was going to say, it's at home, but something inside me told me to keep that quiet. I didn't know these people and they hadn't shown me any badges. Adam didn't say where it was, so neither would I. "It's elsewhere."

"Maddox, Solomon will go with you and Miss Graves to get the memory stick."

Adam flicked a glance in Solomon's direction, which I wouldn't describe as a happy one. "No need for Solomon to come, sir. I'll retrieve it." I followed his gaze. Solomon returned my stare, his face blank. I made a sincere effort not to flinch, keeping my eyes steady and even until Matt spoke again and I turned back to him.

"All the same, Solomon goes with you. As of this moment, we consider Lexi to be a target. She's the only one who's seen the file."

"Which file is it?" I asked.

Matt's jaw moved about and his lips creased together in a thin line. "That's the thing, Miss Graves. We hoped you could tell us."

I shook my head. "I don't know. I've worked on a few reports for Dean."

Matt nodded, brushing his jaw thoughtfully. "We can't offer you twenty-four hour protection at this stage."

"Am I in danger?" I asked, because what I construed from Miller's comment was, *you'd better think of something quick before you get shot.* Not exactly reassuring.

"Possibly. If Dean's murderers assume you know something, they may try to have you erased." And there it was. The threat of getting whacked along with the proviso that the FBI and Montgomery PD could do nothing to stop it, if I didn't work with them. Not the warm and fuzzy promise that I was seeking. As far as coercion went, it wasn't subtle and it wasn't kind.

I gulped. "My name is watermarked on every report."

"Then they'll conclude you know something, even if you don't know what it is. We could consider protective custody."

"Sir, if Lexi stops going into work, someone may surmise that she does know something. We don't know how dangerous that would be or how badly they might want to find her."

I chanced a glance at Maddox as he defended my corner, fully aware that Solomon's eyes were boring into my back. I wondered if he ever spoke.

"What are you getting at, Maddox?"

"Have Lexi go into work as normal, sir. Let her do everything that is normal. That offers her the best chance in case someone, or anyone, assumes that she knows something. No one knew she was in the building that night. I checked; there's no record of her after four p.m., which was hours before Dean was killed. Plus, she's been at Green Hand for a couple of months. People like her. No one would suspect her."

"Suspect me of what?" I frowned.

"We need eyes and ears in the department. People don't talk to the boss. They'll talk to the pretty temp." Adam leaned towards his boss and flashed a look at me, his eyes sparkling like the sapphires I hoped to wear one day. But more importantly, he called me pretty.

"You're talking about swearing her in, Maddox." Matt's tone was thoughtful, inviting even, rather than simply a warning, and my heart gave a little leap. I could go on as normal, maybe I wouldn't even have to testify and my life would stay just that—mine.

"She can do it, Miller. You've read her file. She's smart. Like I said, people like her. She has easier access to gossip and co-workers than I do."

"And what if she stuffs up? Blabs to the press, or her friends? What if someone offers her a bribe?"

I coughed, and not particularly politely, seeing as my reputation was being shredded faster than a duck in Chinatown. "I can't be bribed, sir." I knew I couldn't. It was simple: my price would be way too high. Plus, who would believe this? If I told my family, the whole of Montgomery PD would know. If I told Lily, I'd be putting her at risk, and I'd rather lose my new Kate Spade purse than do that!

"Do you understand what we're asking you, Miss Graves? May I call you Lexi? Your surname is..."

"Depressing, I know. And yes, I think I understand and I can do it." How that slipped out of my mouth, I'll never know. It was probably the adrenaline racing through my system. Or stupidity. Hard to tell.

"We're asking you to potentially rat on your colleagues, snooping through their desks and making notes of your conversations with them. We'll ask you to view everyone you work with as a suspect, and to investigate anything you may find suspicious. You might even have to lie to them."

I remembered the time I lied to Lily, saying the strapless, red, mini dress she'd fallen in love with had just sold out during a sale, when I'd actually hidden the last one on the plus-size rack, where she would never look. To be fair, it didn't suit her and I was trying to be nice. "I can do that," I said with absolute confidence.

"Good. Maddox will brief you. I look forward to your first report."

"You're not seriously putting Blondie on the case?" The voice came from behind me. Cool, disembodied. I resisted the urge to turn around, and confront the hulking presence of Solomon, while shouting *"Blondie?"* indignantly. Miller's eyebrows rose in the silence that followed. He refocused on me, clearly waiting for some kind of answer.

"Thank you, sir. I, uh, won't let you down," I said, my jaw firm. The insult sealed it for me. Unnatural blondes were not incapable.

"If you let me down, it's because you're dead," said Matt, and there wasn't a hint of warmth in his voice this time. "Maddox, get Lexi's statement; then you and Solomon take Lexi home and retrieve the memory stick. Whatever is in those files, I want to know about it. Yesterday."

# CHAPTER FOUR

"Where to?" asked Solomon, as we exited the building an hour later. He slid a pair of sunglasses on, hiding his beautiful brown eyes, and took the keys from the waiting driver, who nodded at us and walked away. Maddox took the front seat without bending to the time honored tradition of calling shotgun, so I slid into the back and fought hard not to stick my tongue out at the back of Solomon's head.

The "Blondie" comment still cut deep. Blondes were supposed to have more fun; gentlemen were supposed to *"lurve"* blondes if Marilyn was right. And here was a Neanderthal who thought my hair color meant I couldn't compete with the big boys. We'd soon see about that, I decided resolutely.

"My place," I mumbled, my head still ringing with the thought that I was now an undercover operative. Just how cool was that? It almost made up for the heart-stopping moment of finding a corpse, a moment I'd relived in less than glorious detail as I gave my statement. It was almost as good as snuggling up to Adam... Maddox (what did I call him now? I wondered) in a dark closet.

Solomon, clearly the strong, silent type, drove us to my apartment without a word. He didn't even ask where to go, as he zipped through the traffic, ultimately pulling into my driveway and parking beside my VW.

Lily's car was absent, which was fine with me. How could I explain arriving home with not one, but two hunks? One of whom she already thought I'd spent the night with! Even worse, I had no plausible explanation and I couldn't tell her the truth. I could tell her some brilliant lies though, I thought, mashing my lips together so I didn't giggle.

I unlocked the door, and both men followed me up. Inside the apartment, they slipped past me, Solomon neatly picking me up and placing me to one side, before they fanned out, checking through every room, opening and shutting doors, their weapons drawn. I must have been sleepwalking before, because the guns made it lethally real now. Not to mention that they thought it necessary to check through my apartment.

This wasn't a game.

"All clear," said Maddox. Solomon nodded in agreement. "Come through, Lexi."

"What were you doing?" I tossed my keys onto the slim console and followed them into the living room.

"Checking to make sure no one was waiting in your apartment," said Maddox.

"Like whom?" I asked as Maddox raised an eyebrow. "Oh, like someone who wants to kill me?" My voice rose a notch. "Oh dear God, someone wants to kill me!" Perhaps, I really didn't consider my offer to snoop around at work carefully enough.

"Is she going to get hysterical?" asked Solomon, whom we both ignored, though the timbre of his voice sent a shiver down my spine. I wasn't sure what to think of him.

"Adam, why didn't you do that last night?" I asked.

"Didn't need to last night. I got to thinking," he told me, "whoever deleted your files this morning might realize you copied the files. That's why we can't be too careful." Maddox walked over to the big bay window and looked out, his head sweeping from side-to-side as he surveyed the street below. He turned back to us, looking at Solomon for a moment, who had settled onto the couch and was flicking through my TV guide. "There are two men in a car outside, watching the apartment. They're ours. Is there any other way in?"

I shook my head. "The only other door is downstairs in Lily's apartment and her garden backs onto the other gardens, so there isn't an alley. Only an acrobat can get onto the fire escape from below."

"Good. That'll make it easier to keep watch. Do you have any plans we should know about?"

"Lily will be home soon, then nothing. No, wait..." I rolled my eyes as I remembered I *did* have plans. "I forgot. I'm going to my parents' tonight for dinner."

"Are they far?"

"Twenty minutes."

"Good. You should keep up with your usual routine. Maybe I should go with you," Adam mused.

"I can't really turn up at my parents' with a

strange man." Solomon laughed at "strange" then covered it up with a cough. I glared at him. "I mean, I'm already bringing Lily. It would be weird to bring a man they've never heard of before. Besides you're PD and undercover; and my whole family is PD." That statement was close to being literal. My father had retired a few years before. Out of my four siblings, three were currently serving officers. Even my sister-in-law worked dispatch and that was just my immediate family. They could smell a rat at a hundred paces, and probably shoot it dead at fifty.

"I suppose so." Adam sat on the armchair across from the sofa and opened the backpack he carried with him. He spread a thick stack of slim manila files on the coffee table and asked for my cell phone, which I handed over. "I've programmed in our numbers, mine and Solomon's. You can call anytime," he said, handing it back. I didn't think he might go for a "No, *you* hang up first" type of chat.

"What's all this?" I pointed to the files.

"Our co-workers. There's a short profile on each one featuring their backgrounds, families, hobbies, and other information including their recent bank records. They all seem clean from what we've determined. No unexplained large transactions, no unexpectedly lost family members, or criminal connections. You'll need to read all these and familiarize yourself with the histories of the people you work with."

I hovered in the doorway, watching Solomon move around the room, allowing me a better look at him. As he checked the view from each window without a trace of emotion or interest on his face, I checked out his body.

What? I have a pulse and he was extremely nice to look at.

"Why do you need all this information?" I asked Adam as I tore my gaze away. It was like going from chocolate dessert to chocolate cake; the view was just as tempting whichever way I looked! Seemingly satisfied, he returned to the armchair.

"Like I said before, there's a leak in the department. Someone is involved selling information or part of a fraud ring. Greed is our best estimate for motive. Money or blackmail is the most common reason for the average citizen to turn bad, hence the reports on your colleagues."

I tried to imagine anyone in the department trading secrets, or being involved in criminal activity, but it was impossible. They were all so mundanely dull.

"And you don't have any idea who is involved?" I asked. "At all?"

Adam shook his head. "We have ideas, but now that Dean is dead, it's thrown us. It could have even been him, in which case, we definitely need to catch his killers to get to the rest of the ring. Or maybe Dean uncovered something about someone in the department that got him killed. We don't know what information they are concealing or leaking, who's leaking it, or who's buying it. We just can't get close. Everything points to major fraud, but we don't have enough evidence to narrow down any of our leads just yet."

"But you've got all that spyware on the computers."

"There haven't been any suspicious messages or documents emailed. Nothing is going through the office machines."

A thought occurred to me. "When you joined us and we had that team building day... The one where you confiscated all of our cell phones..."

"We bugged them," Adam admitted without any more prompting. "Recording and location transmitters."

"So you've been listening in on every call any of us made since then?" I paled thinking about my argument with my occasional friend-with-benefits, boy-toy, Mike, three weeks ago when he wanted to come over after a couple of months of no contact. I just wasn't into him anymore, even though it had been fun and he had more than just scratched the itch that needed, um, scratching. Mike became more than a little rude when I suggested we stop... scratching. How mortifying. Still, at least, I had come out of it with my dignity intact. I hoped.

"Yes, and nothing there either. No coded messages or anything suspicious."

"I hate to ask you the obvious, but are you sure the leak is from our department?"

"Absolutely sure."

"Where's the memory stick?" asked Solomon suddenly. The TV guide landed on the coffee table with a resounding slap.

"Sorry, got somewhere to be, have we?" I retorted smartly, but he just stared back. We glared at each other, and I was sure I saw the faintest shadow of a smile. It seemed Big Bad had a sense of humor.

His eyes ran over me. "Yes, actually."

"Oh, right." Crap. He probably had to go save the world, or single-handedly take down the fraudsters while Adam babysat me. His tone was clear: I was holding him up. "I'll get it," I said.

The memory stick was exactly where I left it in the top drawer of my dresser in my bedroom, so I grabbed it and returned to the living room less than a minute later. Adam and Solomon were talking in hushed tones, but they stopped when I entered. I dropped the memory stick into Adam's open palm.

"Has this got everything you worked on at Green Hand?" he asked. I nodded and he passed it to Solomon. "Thanks, Lexi. We'll get the team working on this. The reason for Dean's death is in there somewhere."

Downstairs, I heard the door open and slam shut seconds after Adam's phone beeped. "Your friend is home," he said, after checking the screen.

"Was that the men outside?"

"Yes."

"Are they staying?"

"No. They'll do spot checks."

"I'm going to go," said Solomon, pulling my attention to him again as he stood and stretched. I expected him to crack his knuckles, but thankfully, he didn't. Instead, he stuck the memory stick in his jeans pocket and strode out of the apartment without a backwards glance.

"Quite the charmer, isn't he?" I said, when the door shut and I was sure he couldn't hear me.

"Solomon's okay, just not the conversational sort."

"Is Solomon his first name or last?"

"Last, I think. Why?"

I shrugged. "No reason. I need to get ready. Can you stay for a while? Or do you have to go?" I suddenly felt nervous at the idea of being in the apartment on my own. Knowing that Martin Dean's murderers were out there was bad enough, but Adam's team being concerned that they might come after me was worse. What if they hadn't checked the closet properly and someone was lurking on the floor? What if there was a bomb hooked to my oven? Oh God, what if...

Adam took a steady look at the panic creeping onto my face. "I'll stay. Shall I make coffee?"

I remembered last night and pulled a face at him, just to remind him that I was not happy about that. I'd probably never accept a drink from him again. "None for me, thanks. Help yourself. Hey, can I see your badge?"

He grinned. "I thought you'd never ask." He loosened his tie, undid the top button of his shirt and pulled out on a chain until his badge appeared. I've seen plenty. It was legit.

"Thanks."

"No problem."

I flicked through my wardrobe, looking for something nice to wear for my dinner that was warm. It might be summer, but my parents' house was always cold enough to hang meat. Adam was standing in the hallway, sipping his coffee and asking the occasional question. My work clothes wouldn't quite cut it, so I settled on a knee-length skirt and matched it to a pink top. Smart, but still feminine, and unlikely to upset my mother who had a "dress-nice-for-dinner-or-don't-eat" policy. I liked eating.

"Maybe I should stay here?" I said, straightening up after I laid the clothes on the bed. "I already got out of work early. I don't want anyone to follow me to my parents' house."

"Remember what I said about being normal. You had plans to go to dinner tonight and you need to stick to them. Nothing out of the ordinary. Nothing that would raise a red flag if anyone is watching you."

"Even leaving work early?"

"As far as anyone knows, we were on a conference call on the second floor all afternoon."

"Huh. How would I know if anyone is watching me?"

"Most likely, you wouldn't. We'll have a team keeping an eye on you over the weekend. Keep your cell phone with you so we'll always be able to locate you. You don't have to worry, Lexi, I promise." Adam placed his mug on the console and stepped through the doorway towards me. He laid his warm hands on my shoulders. I found myself gazing up at him in a way that, so far, I'd only ever imagined in three very exciting dreams. In every one of those dreams, he leaned down and kissed me. He dipped his head, just as I tipped upwards on my tiptoes, our lips parting as our mouths moved closer.

Then a fist hammered on my door. We flew apart, my heart pounding.

"Lexi? Are you home?"

"Lily," I whispered in Adam's ear. "Am I home?"

"Of course you are. Go answer the door."

"Be right there," I called, stepping past Adam, whom I was rapidly starting to think of as Maddox now, to take the few paces to the door, then across the hallway to let her in.

"Hello," Lily cooed, her big blonde curls bouncing around her shoulders. "I didn't know you'd be home early. Do you want to leave before the commuter traffic?"

"Sure, I guess."

"I'll just go... oh, *hello*." Lily's eyes widened as I heard Adam step into the hallway, out of my bedroom. Her eyes zeroed in on the casually undone shirt and loosened tie. She brushed past me, extending a hand to him as she flashed "tell-me-everything-later-or-die" eyes. "We didn't meet properly this morning. I'm Lily, Lexi's best friend, neighbor and confidant."

"Adam Shepherd, Lexi's boss," said Adam, his cover firmly in place.

"Hello Adam Shepherd, Lexi's boss." She paused, lips pursed, waiting for him to say something. She had a knack for doing that, and making the silence so uncomfortable that you'd be willing to say anything just so it would stop. Adam, apparently, was a tough nut to crack. "Are you doing some extracurricular activities?" she asked, when he stayed silent.

I rolled my eyes.

"No." But he smiled this time. "We're just going over a few things for next week."

"On two consecutive nights?" Lily cast a glance at me that was full of suspicion. "Lexi is very, very dedicated. Hit me up when you're ready, Lex. I'll wait downstairs." She sashayed out with a flick of her hair.

"She does not believe we're working," I said as I returned to my bedroom closet. I rifled through to find the low-heeled, pink, peep-toe pumps I wanted, my eyes ready for any strange wires or bomb-shaped objects. I found the pumps shoved in a protective plastic box at the back of the closet.

"That reminds me, you need to read the files."

"But there's loads," I pointed out. "It will take me all night to read them and I can hardly take them to my parents'."

"Skim through them later. You can read the rest over the weekend."

"Thanks. And, Adam?"

"Yeah?"

"I really can do this. I won't let you down."

~

Lily has seriously questionable taste in music, but seeing as she was driving, I didn't have a choice. Several Celine Dion tracks later, we turned onto my parents' street, sliding into a space right outside the house.

My parents had lived in the same house throughout my life and it always looked unchanged. The colors were my mother's choice, white siding with yellow trim. My mother thought it looked like a daisy; I thought it resembled an egg. Out front, the house had a neat lawn, edged with rose bushes and surrounded by the smartest picket fence in Montgomery.

Five children had grown up in this house; five kids skinned their knees racing bicycles on the street outside. Four of us had favored a quick exit out of the bathroom window to escape via the porch roof, and only three of us had ever been caught. Three of the five grew up in my father's footsteps to become cops. One graduated summa cum laude from Harvard and became an accountant. And one of the Graves' offspring earned an okay degree, had a flirtation with the Army, and eventually, found a career that sucked. Guess which one I was.

But before nostalgia could hit me harder than the rumor of a designer sample sale, I locked my eyes on the shiny, black Mercedes parked further down the street. It belonged to my sister, Serena. If we were really, really lucky, her husband, Ted Whitman the Third, would be with her. Oh, happy, happy day.

"I didn't know Serena was coming tonight," said Lily, without enthusiasm.

"Me neither."

"You know, I have a bottle of vodka in my bag. We could play a drinking game where every time Serena name drops or rags on someone, we take a shot."

"We'll be drunk in minutes," I replied, a spark of hope igniting the evening. At least with Lily beside me, putting up with the perfect Serena wouldn't be so bad, but I still had to ask the obvious, "Why do you have a bottle of vodka in your bag?"

"Seemed like a good idea," said Lily, grinning. Before we'd even closed the car doors, the front door opened and Serena tapped her foot impatiently as she blocked the entrance while we walked along the path.

"Alexandra," she sighed. "Lily. How nice."

"Serena." I dropped a kiss on her proffered cheek. "And it's still Lexi." Oh, the conversation that never got old. Serena was five years older than I, the only girl for years until our mother accidentally got pregnant, resulting in little, ol' me. I think it stuck in Serena's craw that not only was she no longer the only girl, in a basket of boys, but she also had to compete for attention. Consequently, that just seemed to make her aim for, what would be to mere mortals, stupendously unachievable goals, but which she nonetheless always attained. Top university? Check. High flying job? Check. Closet full of designer clothes and a perfect figure? Check. Husband by thirty? Check. Gorgeous house with its own gym? Check, effing, check.

"Can't believe you're forty this year!" squealed Lily as she threw her arms around my sister's stiff neck. I sniggered because age was the one thing Serena had on me and didn't want.

"I'm not," sniffed Serena. "I'm only thirty-four." The formal façade slipped back onto her face. "Come through. The folks are in the living room."

"Is Ted here?" I asked, pausing to trace the crude shamrock with a finger. It was a testament to our Irish heritage, and had been carved in the doorjamb at some point in our childhood. Ted Whitman the Third was about as much fun as Serena. They had been married for six years, but I'd never had any cause to hang out with them. Serena was too perfect for me, and I was too, well, embarrassing to hang out with, according to Serena. She only ever invited me to their house with strict conditions attached, which was fine by me as I preferred to get in and out in thirty minutes flat.

"Of course."

"Yay," said Lily flatly, giving me a poke in the ribs and pulling a face as Serena turned her back.

"I'm glad you're here," Serena said. Lily raised her eyebrows at me. I shrugged: news to me. "We have an important announcement. It'll be nice to catch up. I'm sure Mom and Dad are dying to know what's new in your life too."

Lily stuck her tongue out. I pulled a face right back at Lily as Serena strode away, her heels making little clip-clop noises on the wooden floor before they got muffled by the rug. Serena was uncharacteristically jovial. I mouthed, "*What's got into her?*" But Lily just shrugged.

"Come on," she said, grabbing my arm. "Maybe she's moving to Argentina."

The Argentineans should be so lucky.

As we entered, Ted was in the middle of a story that made Dad discreetly yawn into a tumbler of whiskey. You would have thought I was Santa bearing presents the way he launched himself across the room, wrapping me up in a bear hug. In my ear, he whispered, "Do you need to go somewhere urgently? Fishbone in the throat, perhaps? Emergency appendectomy? Is that your cell phone ringing with Lily reporting that a pipe burst in your apartment?"

Lily squeezed into the doorway. "Hi!" she said, beaming, and Dad sighed, moving to embrace her too, repeating the same thing in her ear as she giggled.

I waved to my older brother, Jord, the youngest of the boys. He took a moment to turn from Ted, wave at me, and look Lily over from head to toe, winking at her before turning away, and frowning at whatever Ted was droning on about.

"Hello, Officer Tasty," whispered Lily under her breath. Her crush on Jord started in high school and had never waned. They flirted, but never went any further. Despite Jord's reputation as a skirt chaser, he knew better than to start something with Lily, only to ditch her. None of us would put up with that. It had been suggested more than once that we might even prefer Lily to him, but those reports were unconfirmed.

I nudged her side with my elbow.

"Yum," she said, licking her lips as she watched Jord.

I rolled my eyes and leaned into my dad, whispering in his ear, "You said yes when Ted asked you if he could marry Serena."

"My greatest regret," Dad whispered back, releasing me so he could spin me around, exclaiming loudly, "Look! It's Lexi!" and cutting Ted off in the process. He pointed to my head for extra effect.

"We can all see that, dear," said my ever-tolerant mother, who, for the record, loved Ted to bits because he was so smart and successful. The rich bit helped too. The latter certainly helped Serena accept Ted's prematurely receding hairline. "Lily, darling, looking lovely as always. How are your parents?"

Lily plastered a bubbly smile on her face, the kind she always adopted when talking about her cold, indifferent parents. "Fine! Thank you!"

"Where are they these days?"

"Australia."

"How... sunny."

My friendship with Lily was set the day I met her, but our parents didn't exactly get along. Lily's parents were rich, slightly standoffish and traveled frequently, often working abroad for long stretches, as they were now. They were nothing like Lily, who was warm and funny and had about as much ambition as I—plenty, but no idea where to direct it.

Mom fussed over us, seating Lily and me as far away from Ted and Serena as possible. It made me realize how much wiser she'd gotten in her old, sorry, advanced age. We used to tease Ted mercilessly and she wouldn't let us anymore. I think Ted missed it. Normally, he went bright red every time he saw Lily, and today was no exception.

"Garrett and Daniel are due any minute," said Mom, her eyes flitting over the table as she added brightly, "We have a full house tonight."

My father is a retired cop, as were his father and their brothers and sons. My oldest brother is Garrett. MPD, as a whole, thinks it's hilarious to have a homicide cop called Detective Graves, but I heard it makes victims' families cry. Then there's Daniel, who's also a detective with a different team and also working his way up. Serena skipped the becoming a cop urge, as well as the urge to marry one. Finally, the youngest of the boys, Jord, is a beat cop and happy to be one. A recent incident involved his elbow being used a little too enthusiastically during an arrest last month. It resulted in bumping him down to traffic duty, as well as gave him a leg up to bi-weekly anger management classes. I hoped Garrett and Daniel were bringing their wives and kids. Jord rarely ever brought anyone, which was fine with Lily, because to her, our family dinners meant he was virtually her date. Even if he didn't realize it.

Garrett arrived first, letting himself in, before returning to usher in his wife, Traci, and their three children. I blinked when I saw their t-shirts. Traci's read "COP WIFE." Their children, Patrick, (the Teenager), Sam and Chloe, wore t-shirts that read "COP KID." Two of them were visibly embarrassed and the third couldn't read yet.

Traci gave me a friendly hug and smoothed her blonde hair behind her ears. Married young, Traci had been in my life since my mid-teens. She was a friend, a sister and sometimes employer, offering me cash for babysitting favors.

"Nice shirts," I said, running my eyes over them.

"I know. Right? Garrett thinks they're great."

I raised my eyebrows. "Okay."

Traci punched me lightly on the arm. "Enjoy

them while you can. They may never be seen again."

Garrett gave me a quick hug before helping Chloe in. I wondered if he knew about my dead boss and had to bite my lip to stop myself from asking him.

Traci went into the kitchen to help my mom, and Daniel arrived with his wife moments later. None of us had ever fathomed how Daniel persuaded Alice to marry him, much less how he bagged her in the first place. She was smart, magazine cover pretty, a dedicated runner with a body to match, only a few years older than I, and the mother of his two little children, Ben and Rachel. There is nothing wrong with Daniel. He's an all round nice guy, a dedicated cop and a good husband, which must have gained him entry into her league, after all, great guys like Daniel are hard to find.

When everyone was crowded into the already stuffed to bursting living room, Serena perched on the big leather couch next to Ted. She gathered his hand into hers and beamed. Realizing she was being ignored, her sharp whistle pierced the air and called us all to attention. I made a quick check to see if she had any notecards because she had a habit of giving presentations, rather than news; but whatever she had to tell us, it was apparently going to be short. *Hallelujah!* Garrett caught my eye and winked, clearly thinking the same thing.

"I'm pregnant!" Serena exclaimed and everything else was lost to the sound of my mother shrieking and the chorus of congratulations. Lily dutifully squealed and clapped her hands while Dad and I exchanged concerned glances. He was definitely thinking what I was thinking. There was only one thing worse than Serena and Ted—Serena and Ted breeding.

"Yay," I said feebly, as the thought of their progeny entering the world dawned on me. "Marvelous."

"And we want you to throw the baby shower, Alexandra. And be godmother," Serena added to sweeten the deal.

Huh? Lily elbowed me.

"Thank you," I blurted, instead of *Why me*? A baby shower? I've attended my share of them, but I'd never thrown one. I had a sneaking suspicion that Serena had terrified everyone else so I was her one last hope to hostess a good shower.

"Thanks, Alexandra," said Serena, cutting off my protest before it even began. "My friend, Jane, threw a fabulous pink-and-blue themed party for our friend, Alison. We hand-painted sleepers with non-toxic fabric paint and did baby jar shots. Non-alcoholic, of course. I'll give you a list of names and a date."

"How lovely. Grandma O'Shaughnessy will be so excited!" squealed my mother, a smile spreading across her face as she contemplated a sixth grandchild to add to the existing brood. The mention of Grandma O'Shaughnessy sent shivers through the room. "Alexandra would love the challenge. It's not like she's busy with her little temping job," she added.

I scowled and pinched my nose to stop my nostrils flaring in annoyance. Oh, how I wished I could have said I was now a super secret agent on the trail of a murderer. Except, so far, I'd done nothing but hide in a closet—*mmm*, nice memory of Adam there—and hand over the memory stick, as well as agree to snoop on everyone I knew at work. Nope, I couldn't say that. I had to keep my mouth shut and take the jibe, crossing my fingers that Grandma

O'Shaughnessy wouldn't be planning a visit anytime soon. She was ancient and mean and probably born that way.

"No problem," I smiled sweetly, elbowing Lily in the ribs. If she thought I was tackling this alone, she was so wrong. "So, when's baby due?"

"In three months. A fall baby," Serena clarified, just in case I was challenged at working out the season. All the same, I had to count backwards on my fingers. Serena was in her sixth month and none of us had noticed a bump. Now that I thought about it, it explained the flowing tops.

"I'm very happy for you both," I managed, my smile echoing the size of my mother's, who was already chirping about clothing and knitting. I could have been wrong, but I didn't think she could knit.

"I think we should have a celebratory drink," interjected Dad, ambling over to the door. I suspected self-medication was about to occur.

"Non-alcoholic," chirped Serena, and I wondered if her unbearable perkiness was going to continue throughout the entire pregnancy, and if that was really an improvement on her normal self. Personally, I couldn't wait until she got cankles.

"Double shots for the rest of us," said Dad, under his breath, but I'm pretty sure only I heard. Mostly because Mom and Serena were squealing something about cribs and whether drop sides were really a safety threat or not. Apparently, it was something worthy of a lot of debate, given Traci's and Alice's contributions.

"Let's go." I nudged Lily and we slipped out of the room, following Dad down the hallway into the kitchen. He was pulling a bottle of emergency slash celebratory champagne left over from Christmas out of the refrigerator while simultaneously downing a shot of whiskey.

"To the next generation," he toasted us as he poured another one.

Lily knocked him on the elbow playfully. "Not ready to be a grandpa again, Mr. Graves?"

"Not ready to be a father," grunted my dad.

"Oh, Dad, you'll be just fine." It's the rest of us that will suffer the most, but I decided not to share that. Gosh, I'm a good daughter.

I sat with Dad to watch the news while Serena filled in Traci and Alice about her plans for the nursery. They were far better qualified than I to discuss the intricacies of cribs and onesies. Serena was even receptive to the name tips from Rachel, who thought the names, "Pumpkin" and "Toodles" sounded great for a girl or a boy. Now as I thought about it, and after seeing her talk to Rachel, maybe Serena would make a good mother. And Ted probably would continue to work late at the office until the child was eighteen, so the chances of him or her being ruined by his input and influence were low.

"How's anger management?" I asked Jord as he wedged himself onto the sofa, squashing me between Dad and him. Lily gazed at Jord in unbridled adoration. I kicked her shin.

"It's amazing. I love it." He gave me a Cheshire cat grin before stretching his long legs all the way under the coffee table.

"You're not supposed to love it," I told him. "You're supposed to feel remorseful, bare your soul and promise to never do it again."

"To hell with that mumbo-jumbo shit. Ow, Dad,

sorry, okay?" said Jord as Dad reached around me and lightly cuffed his ear without saying a word. "No more swearing, got it. Anyway, the chick who takes the class. She's got hooters like…" As Jord extended his hands, cupping them, Dad coughed politely right before my mother walked past and smacked him over the head with a magazine. "Ow! Jeez, Mom! No wonder I have anger issues. Anyway, the view makes the soul-bearing stuff just about manageable."

"Poor you. How you suffer."

"I do," Jord agreed. "Tomorrow night we're going to talk feelings again. We have to talk about the event that brought us there and how we feel."

"Yeah? How's that going?"

"I was pissed off and that punk deserved a broken nose," said Jord decisively. "He was lucky I was off balance."

"You might want to adjust your story before tomorrow night," I suggested.

"No worries. I plan on squeezing a tear. She's big on hugs for the ones that cry. I've been practicing my sad face in the mirror."

I sighed at his dedication and shook my head. Asking a Graves man to bare his feelings was like asking a hungry lion to play nice with the stray dog that just fell into its den: it wasn't going to happen. They'd rather just get messy.

"Jeez Louise, would you look at that," said Dad, nodding at the scene that flashed onto the screen. The local news channel ticker flitted across a screen crowded with onlookers. We watched as a covered stretcher was loaded into the back of the Montgomery morgue mobile, as it was known locally, before the anchor came back into view, recapping the event. *Ron Harris,* said the caption underneath, *forty-two, killed in a hit-and-run,* then a number for any eyewitnesses to call in. "What kind of asshole plows into someone and leaves them to die in the street like a dog?" Dad asked, with a shake of his head.

"Dunno, Dad."

"Bad karma will come."

I cut a sideways glance at him. "You been reading one of Mom's magazines?"

"No. I saw it on one of those psychic shows on television."

"You need to get out more."

"Tell me about it."

"You need to put your shoes on, open the door and leave the house and do all the stuff you couldn't do when you were a cop."

"Funny, Lexi. Funny."

"Don't forget your keys."

After a dinner of my mother's baked salmon, new potatoes and greens, topped off with chocolate cake, I went in search of Garrett and caught him sneaking a cigarette on the back porch. He hid it guiltily behind his back when I slipped through the sliding door, pulling it closed behind me.

"I'm down to one a day," he said, returning the cigarette to his lips when he saw it was me. I drew in a lungful of tar, as well as other carcinogenic gases.

I put my hands in the air. "I'm not judging," I said. Then coughed.

"A year ago, it was twenty a day," Garrett continued. "I'm nearly there. I'll quit soon."

"Good for you, Gar'. Do you know a detective named Adam Maddox?" I asked, framing the question as casually as I could.

"Sure. Maddox worked homicide a while."

"Brown hair, blue eyes, about six-one?"

"That's the one. Why?"

I thought about that for a moment. I didn't want to say anything about what went down at Green Hand, so instead, I said, "Oh, a girlfriend wanted to know."

Garrett raised his eyebrows. "I don't know him too well myself, just in passing, but word is he's a workaholic. Nice guy, though. Doesn't take any shit. Gives respect where it's due."

That was all I needed to know. Just that he existed. That it wasn't some weird ill-fitting part of the puzzle and the whole taskforce thing wasn't some elaborate joke, or the real fraud enterprise.

"Thanks. Listen, there's something else, but I don't want you to tell Mom or Dad."

"Go on."

"I want to get a gun permit." It just occurred to me today when I saw Adam and Solomon's weapons drawn as they searched my place. I couldn't rely on my lamp for a weapon to scare people away—unless through laughter—and, truth was, I couldn't close my eyes without seeing the blood seeping from the hole between Dean's eyes. I was scared, and I had ample reason to be.

"What for?" asked Garrett.

I shrugged nonchalantly. "Just thought it would be interesting to shoot again. Maybe put in some hours at the range."

"If Mom gets another cop in the family, she'll never hear the end of it."

"No chance of that."

Garrett took his last couple of puffs and stubbed

the cigarette out with his foot. He turned to me. "You sure that's all you want a gun for?"

"Yep," I said, plastering a smile on my face. "That's it."

"If you're in any kind of trouble, you can tell me. A man, or whatever." Garrett gulped, looking uncomfortable. He gave me the guy talk occasionally when I was a teen, about not trusting them and the best way to kick them in the balls if they got too frisky. He never quite understood that I pretty much only had one thing on my mind then. It was possible I was worse than the boys! "I can cuff 'em and lose the key," he offered.

I figured that might come in useful one day. "Thanks, Garrett, but it's nothing like that," I said. "Raincheck?" It was about a murderer, and there was no way I was going to tell my brother that.

"You bet. Come down to the station this week and I'll go through the forms with you. I can take you out to the range too. You used to be a good shot. You'll pick it up again."

"Thanks."

~

"Sorry the evening was such a bust." I placed the bag of leftovers on the backseat of Lily's Mini and slammed the door.

"No, it was great, Lex. You know I love coming here."

"Even though you had to listen to baby talk all night?"

"I now know more about babies than I ever learned at school, so it's been educational." Bless Lily, she always looked on the positive side of things even after listening to Serena's hideously endless narratives of her friends' ghastly birth stories, which sounded like "Alien" versus "Predator" mashed up with a Disney ending. "Although I might not have sex for a while," Lily finished thoughtfully. She skittered around to the passenger side, leaving me to wedge myself into the driver's side. I had skipped the wine and Lily had helped herself to my dad's whiskey upon hearing the breech birth story.

After adjusting the seat, and the mirrors, I pulled out, and both of us waved to Mom and Dad, as I aimed for home, my mind full of Adam Maddox and the hidden room downtown stuffed with the taskforce's equipment.

I hadn't heard from Maddox, as he'd told me to call him, all night, even though I obsessively checked my phone. I thought about calling him, or sending a message (or seven), but super cool undercover operatives just didn't do that, did they? I even watched the news with Dad just in case Martin Dean's murder popped up, but there was nothing, not even an accident report or a faked suicide. Maybe the body just hadn't been found yet and no one knew where the murderers had taken him? Maddox and I were the only ones who had seen Dean dead, and overheard the murderers' plan to move his body, but unfortunately, they hadn't left any GPS maps with a big arrow pointing to the dumpsite. For all I knew, Dean could be swimming with the fishes. Clichés aside, his death would have to be announced soon. I didn't know much about Dean's personal life, but I figured someone must be missing him.

Even my brothers didn't have any police gossip when I gently prodded them. According to them, murder was currently unheard of in Montgomery and even though I knew differently, I didn't press any further, just in case they got suspicious and I blabbed everything.

This was my one shot at proving myself, and that I was much more than just a temp.

## CHAPTER FIVE

When we got home, I didn't see anyone watching over our building, but I slept a little better knowing Maddox had someone spot checking my apartment, if not simply observing. After a restless night, filled with nightmares of the murderers opening the closet doors and finding us, I was determined to take the snooping business seriously. The joint taskforce seemed to have nothing, as far as they said, and I had no doubt that they'd picked Green Hand Insurance apart as soon as Maddox placed his call; but I wanted to look over the scene of the crime too.

Dominic, Dean's assistant, didn't budge all morning, giving me plenty of time to think about my next move. I knew I needed to get inside Dean's office and take a look around. Even though I wracked my brain, I couldn't work out what was so interesting in the reports I'd written. If, however, I could find out what Dean had been doing in the hours leading up to his death, I might find a clue.

As soon as I saw Dominic move away from his

desk, I picked up a stack of papers and made my way to Dean's office.

"Hey, Lexi," said Vincent Marciano, the company accountant, his head popping over the cubicle wall as I passed his desk. Vincent was about as far from an Italian stallion as a man could get, but he strove to adopt the swagger and supreme self-confidence that he was every woman's fantasy. Unfortunately, that also made him resistant to subtle brush-offs that fell short of screaming and mace, but since he did co-sign my timecard, I had to be nice.

"Hey," I said, holding up my papers, deflecting whatever silly comment he was about to make. Vincent was probably harmless and might even have been sweet if he didn't try so hard, but he had an annoying habit of always getting in my way when I was in a hurry. I think he just wanted to talk to me. I hoped it wasn't because he had more than a friendly interest, because there was no way *that* was happening. I was taught never to be cruel unless necessary and I really didn't want it to be necessary. "Photocopying," I said, flapping the papers.

"Waits for no man," Vincent finished, chuckling at his joke.

"You know it."

"Want to get coffee after work?" Vincent called after me.

"No can do," I said, glancing over my shoulder to give him an apologetic smile. "I'm meeting a friend after work." Instead of veering off to the photocopy room, I walked past Dominic's desk and down the short hallway, as if I owned it. Then, with a backwards glance to check that no one was watching, I opened Dean's door and slid inside, shutting it softly behind me.

I placed the papers on the console by the door and darted forwards. My first stop was Dean's desk. I rifled through the neat stack of paperwork on the desk, noting that it was a smaller pile than two nights ago. None of my reports were in the stack, but there was a bunch of papers from accounts, some memos from the call center below us, and a few spreadsheets. I discounted them all after a quick scan and moved to the orderly line of Post-it notes that spanned the side of the desk, adjacent to Dean's phone. It was the usual stuff—calls to return, questions from Dominic regarding Dean's travel to a conference next week, confirmation of a dinner reservation, a credit card bill. I sneaked a peek. A two hundred and forty-six dollar balance, plus a home address. Nothing stuck out as being out of place or unusual. In fact, as I glanced down, there was no blood stain where Dean lay dead either.

With a frown, I returned to the desk. A selection of newspapers were folded across the top portion. National titles and the Montgomery Gazette, all new. I knew Dominic placed them there every day because I had to run out to get them a few times when he was too busy. I checked the diary printout that I knew came from Dean's Outlook calendar, also managed by Dominic. It also had today's date and I guessed Dominic had updated it and left a printout just in case Dean came in. I wondered if Dominic was in the loop on Dean's demise. I guessed not.

Next, I tried the drawers. The top two were locked so I was surprised when the third one easily slid open. There wasn't much inside. A couple of candy bars, a spare tie and one of those miniature

Japanese sand gardens, complete with a tiny rake, that was supposed to help de-stress busy minds.

The door opened abruptly and I don't know who was more startled. Dominic or I.

"What are you doing in Mr. Dean's office?" he asked.

I bent toward the files. "I made a mistake in my file and I wanted to get it before Mr. Dean saw," I lied. "It's the pie charts, you see. I put in the wrong numbers." I grabbed a file and held it up. "Here it is!" I plastered on a grin.

"Mr. Dean doesn't allow people in his office," said Dominic, crossly, his hands braced on his hips.

"Yes, sorry. Won't happen again," I said, nudging the drawer closed with my leg as I skirted the desk. I crossed the floor quickly and grabbed my papers from the small table. "I'll be off," I said, walking back to my cubicle without a backward glance, hoping no one besides me could hear how fast my heart was beating. Halfway there, I dropped the file that I swiped into a trash basket under someone else's desk.

Maddox caught up with me after lunch (chicken mayo, courtesy of Bob), and isolated us into a meeting room. "I saw you go into Dean's office," he said, folding his arms across his chest. He didn't look thrilled, but he didn't look too upset either.

"I went to get some paperwork," I said. "And Dominic wasn't around."

He raised his eyebrows at my lie. "Our people went through it already. The files were gone when they arrived."

I groaned and dropped into a chair. "I saw. None of the files on Dean's desk were mine. Dominic must have put new ones there. You find out what they're so interested in yet?"

"No. Our techs said nothing stood out when they pulled the files from your flash drive and it's not like we can ask Dean."

"Didn't you bug his phones?" I asked, a light bulb popping on in my head.

"Sure, but he didn't use his personal cell phone, his BlackBerry or the office phone, so we didn't pick anything up, only what I overheard. The call he got that night went to a burn phone that he concealed. We traced it back, but it was made from a burner too."

"What about DNA?"

"Nothing. The killers wore gloves. They were both bald, so no hair. They took the gun with them and we don't have his body to do an autopsy, or run a ballistics report on the bullets. They were extremely careful."

My head shot up. "You don't know where his body is?"

"Not yet. We've searched his house, his garage. Nothing. Either he's been dumped somewhere or..."

"Or what?"

"Or they've still got him."

"Eugh!"

Maddox shrugged. "He'll turn up."

"So... you have nothing."

"Not exactly *nothing*. You were in his office. What did you see?"

It was my turn to shrug. "Everything looked normal. Fresh newspapers, new diary page and a bunch of sticky notes. I couldn't get in the top two drawers of his desk and there were a few candy bars and things in his bottom drawer. Nothing that said,

'Hey, I'm in the fraud biz!'" I thought about it some more. "Oh, and no blood on the carpet."

"We already replaced the blood stained section."

"That's fast. It took my parents' carpet people days." I shook my head. "Don't ask. So... I didn't see anything unusual. Is there something I should be looking for?"

"Not in there."

"What else am I supposed to do?"

"Just keep your eyes and ears open," said Maddox. "Don't do anything to attract attention." His eyes flickered to the open top buttons of my shirt. "And don't do anything dangerous."

"Ten-four," I said.

"And when your day's over, just go home, like normal."

Nothing exciting happened all afternoon, which was disappointing, and no one was in a talkative mood, so my snooping went downhill fast. I left right on the dot of home time and drove without incident, my VW having decided to come back to life that morning. Lily hammered on my door five seconds after I kicked off my shoes and I let her in.

"Okay," she said. "What gives? You were acting really weird last night and I've seen two guys in your sex-famined apartment in the space of two days."

"Wait. How do you know about the second one?"

"I saw him when he left yesterday. Mrs. Crichton next door asked if you were a masseuse and if she could book Mr. Crichton in."

"Yuck. Nothing's going on. What did you tell Mrs. Crichton?"

"I said they must be your brothers." Lily took my hand, putting on her best pout. "I'm your best friend and I will never forgive you if you don't tell me."

"Nothing is going on," I protested, but at the same time, I put my finger to my lips and motioned to the floor. Ever since Maddox had mentioned our cell phones were bugged and our work computers were being monitored, I had a sneaking suspicion that he might have installed some kind of bug in my apartment too. It wasn't so farfetched, coming from a man who drugged me. I walked through the living room, turned on the television and went back to where Lily waited, confusion etched all over her face. "Listen, I'm going to have dinner, maybe a bath, then an early night. Let's talk tomorrow."

"Sure, sweetie. Maybe you're just tired," she replied, contorting her face into a WTF? expression. I opened the door and we both slipped out. I followed Lily downstairs to her apartment and flopped onto her couch.

"Okay, my weirdie friend, what was all that about?"

"I think my apartment is bugged."

"No shit? Why?"

I couldn't contain it any longer. My subconscious had been nagging me to tell somebody. I told her everything. When it happened, I was determined to tell Lily nothing, especially after the warning I'd received; but since she lived in the same building as I, to my mind, that put her in danger too. Plus, even though Garrett had confirmed Maddox existed—short of running his badge—and that he would help me get the gun permit, I still wasn't okay with the whole "trust no one" thing. I thought I was being realistic about it. If Martin Dean could get shot in the head and chest, then disappear without a trace, it could happen to me too. I wanted someone close to me to know and start looking for me if the worst happened. A very sobering thought for a Friday night.

"No. Way," she said when I finished explaining. "And I thought I had a rough couple of nights working the door for happy night at Mulligan's last weekend."

"I don't know why you still work there."

"No one gets shot in the head there and I get free drinks."

"Point taken."

"You should come hang out next Saturday."

I hated Mulligan's. It was loud and crowded and I always got groped. On the other hand, I liked free drinks, which they always poured with generous measure. "Okay," I agreed.

"So what's going to happen now? Are you going to keep working at Green Hand?"

"I guess. No one fired me."

"Always a plus."

"And I hate my temp manager."

"Word. Your boss, Shepherd, Maddox, *whatever*, is a fox though." Lily snapped open a bag of marshmallows and we sat together, munching on them. "You know what I want to know?"

"What?"

"Where Dean's body is."

"Me too."

"Do you think it's intact?"

"Huh?"

"You know..." Lily mimed chopping her hand up and down across her body.

"Oh, yuck! I hope so."

"Why? It's not like he's going to need it."

"What do we call the other one?"

I thought about Solomon. How could anyone categorize Solomon?

"Prince of Sexy Darkness?" suggested Lily.

"Too much of a mouthful."

"Huh-huh," giggled Lily and I rolled my eyes. "How do you know they haven't already been through Dean's place?" Her eyes opened wide. "Maybe his body is there."

I shook my head. "Nope. Maddox said the cops went through the place. No body."

Lily looked disappointed. "So why are we looking?"

"We're fresh eyes. We won't look at things the way cops look at things. We might get something that they missed." I sounded a lot like Maddox.

"Cool."

We cruised past Dean's house and I parked a block away under the shade of a massive oak tree. If we were lucky, no one would notice my car parked there. If we were *really* lucky, it wouldn't be covered in bird poop by the time we got back.

Lily had wrapped herself in a knee-length, black, trenchcoat and slim-fitting black pants as a concession to fashionable burglar chic. Fortunately, I noticed the black beret in her hands and tossed it back into her apartment as we left. Me: I went for a far less conspicuous jeans and fleece, zip-up jacket. I tucked my hair back in a low ponytail that swung as we walked. Walking around my apartment to change was no problem. If it were bugged, they'd expect to hear footsteps. I left my cell phone behind and no one followed us here, so far as I could see from my every-ten-second-mirror-check, so I figured we were safe from prying eyes with regard to law-breaking.

Martin Dean's house was a large, white, two-story stucco with a detached garage. The front was protected by six-foot tall, iron gates and an equally high brick wall flanked by green shrubbery. I tried the gates, but they were firmly shut. An electronic keypad recessed in the wall offered no clues as to the code. I hadn't seen an automatic gate opener on Dean's desk, so I figured he must have kept it in his car, wherever that was.

"Now what?" asked Lily as I shook my head.

"Let's try around back," I suggested, scanning our surroundings to see how obvious we were being. Fortunately, all the other houses were behind walls and gates too, ensuring we weren't being observed. Favorably for us, the wide road was quiet. Everybody was either working late at the office or settling down to their family dinners, rather than jogging, walking dogs, or whatever the well-to-do folk of Bedford Hills did in the evenings. My stomach rumbled. I wanted dinner too.

We walked around the side of the property, seeking entry, without any luck. The walls were just as tall here too and smoothly plastered without any footholds. Besides, even if we did scramble up, I had no idea what would meet us on the other side. At the back of the property, we struck gold. The gate seemed to be some sort of service entrance that led to the garage and it was open just wide enough that we could turn sideways, suck in our stomachs and slither through.

"Nice," said Lily, looking around as we walked cautiously along the path, poised to run should a salivating Doberman suddenly appear.

On one side of the path was an indoor pool, and a long stretch of neat lawn that separated us. In front was the four-car garage with a pitched roof, and just beyond that, the house.

We made for the house, ducking across a neat patio with a cluster of furniture covered in tarpaulin. It didn't look like Dean entertained outside very much. A large expanse of glass in sliding panels revealed a living room, complete with a grand piano. I moved past it, careful not to fog up the glass by breathing on it as we headed for the only door.

"DNA," said Lily, wisely, before scrubbing at the window with her sleeve. At the kitchen door, we paused and I tried the handle. "I knew you were going to break in," she said.

"It's not a crime if no one sees you do it," I replied.

"Very true," she agreed.

"Besides, it's open." The handle turned easily, and without any resistance, the door opened. Also, now that the owner was dead, technically maybe it wasn't even committing a crime. Besides, how could Dean file a complaint? Through a medium?

"Prints," said Lily, sliding on a pair of slim leather gloves. I scrabbled in my pockets and found wool mittens, cumbersome, but fingerprint-proof. They would have to do. I pulled them on and wiped the door handle clean.

"Where to first?"

"Here, I guess. I keep all my bills and important stuff in a kitchen drawer."

"Do you?" Lily's brows knitted together.

"Don't you?"

"No. I have a box file for tax, a binder for bills,

and a shoe box for credit card statements."

The shoe box was very fitting, seeing as Lily's credit card slid through more shoe stores than not. All the same, I felt a little chagrined that she was apparently a lot neater than I. I resolved to go to the stationery store and buy some binders. Or filch them from the office.

I opened drawer after drawer, but apparently, Martin Dean was a neat freak too. All I got were knives, forks, and kitchen implements I couldn't even name, never mind own.

"Maybe he has a study," said Lily, poking her head into the pantry, then pulling out. "This is a big house."

"Okay, let's look." A thought hit me. "You think it's theft-alarmed?"

Lily chewed her lip a moment, looking thoughtful. "Maybe. The door was open. No one leaves a door unlocked, even in a nice area like this."

"Maybe the police forgot to lock it when they left?" All the same, we agreed it was better to just be quick than get arrested. Leaving the kitchen, and ignoring the breakfast nook, we walked down the hall, taking a few seconds to duck our heads into the living room, then into a formal dining room.

"This is a really nice house," said Lily. "Imagine having a place this big all to yourself."

"Your parents' house is this big," I pointed out. I knew their house currently stood empty while Lily's dad was posted abroad, but Lily preferred her own small apartment to living in their sprawling house. Her parents were loaded, but she never got an attitude about it.

"I know, but it was never really home. They

always moved about so much, except for the last few years of school. Oh, here's the study. It's so..."

"Neat," I finished, taking in the large mahogany desk, inlaid with a leather writing pad. Except, the leather chair behind it wasn't empty.

It was occupied by Martin Dean.

Lily screamed and grabbed my arm. I jumped and screamed too. After a moment, we both clapped hands over our mouths and stared, bug-eyed, at my dead boss.

I moved to take a step closer, but Lily clung onto me. So instead, I strained forward, taking in his ghostly gray pallor and his slack, still-open eyes. He wore the same suit as when I found him dead in the office. He didn't smell good.

"Is he dead?" asked Lily, her voice shaking.

"Yes."

"Still?"

"Ye-e-es."

"Maybe we should call the police?"

"How could we explain being here?" My heart raced, and I felt the creeping onset of panic.

"Maybe we came to visit?" she suggested.

"Maddox said the police swept the place already and there wasn't a body then. They might think we brought it... him." I flapped a hand at Dean. "Let's search and get this over with."

"You take the desk. I'm not going near a corpse."

"I don't want to go near a corpse either!"

"You already found him dead once!"

And it seemed pretty damn mean that I had to find him dead a second time.

"Okay, I'll take the desk," I said with a sigh.

Lily walked shakily over to the bookcases flanking

the near side of the room and I crept towards Dean, half expecting him to jump up and shout, "Punk'd!" any moment. I'd probably die of a heart attack if he did that. As it was, he stayed completely dead while I moved towards him, edging my way next to him. A set of drawers occupied each side of the desk. I opened all of them in turn, poking through the papers with my mittened hands. I didn't find any death threats, demands for money, blackmail notes or confessions, which was a trifle disappointing, given that I at least had the corpse. And boy, oh boy, was he too close to me right now. All the time I was going through his drawers, I expected an icy hand to land on my back. Or worse, my ass.

"Here's something interesting," I said. "It's an address book. Oh, it's new. There's nothing in it. Sorry."

Lily peered from across the room. "I got nothing," she said. "Lots of books on tax, accountancy and biographies of business leaders. Yawn."

I moved my attention to the top of the desk, crossing around so I wouldn't have to stand hip to corpse with Dean.

There was a hole in the desk for power cords, but no laptop or PC, which I found interesting. There was a small, black notebook that I flicked through, but it was a jumble of numbers, and nothing that made any sense. I put it to one side, because it was an oddity and oddities were what undercover operatives look for. A leather pen holder held an assortment of pens and pencils. I fisted them in one hand and shook the pot upside down, but the only things that fell out were a few paper clips and a little notepad. I put the pens and paper clips back, almost screaming in frustration at picking each one up in my wooly, mammoth paws, and picked up the notepad, turning it over. It wasn't a notepad at all, but a little matchbook. It was black with a single flame. No name or phone number. I opened it, just in case something was written inside, but there wasn't.

"Uh-oh, we've got company," said Lily, flattening herself against the wall. I dropped to the floor, despite the wooden blinds at the window, as the electronic gates swung open and a community security vehicle maneuvered inside.

"Time to go!" I pocketed the notepad and the matchbook, and we half crawled, half ran for the back door, shutting it behind us just as the doorbell rang.

"Given that Dean isn't exactly going to answer the door, I think we should run," I said and Lily nodded enthusiastically. We sprinted for the rear exit, arms and legs pumping, nearly getting ourselves stuck in our race to squeeze through the half-open gate at the same time. We slunk around the side of the house and crossed the road, trying not to hurry as we walked back to my car. I risked a glance over my shoulder and saw the security guard standing at Dean's door, before he started to walk around the house.

"I don't think he saw us," I said, pulling out my key fob and beeping the car open. We slid in on either side and I rested my hands on the wheel for a moment. I pulled my mittens off and stuck them in my pockets.

"I can't believe we found your boss!" Lily exclaimed. "Do you think we broke the case?"

Occasionally, Lily wasn't the sharpest knife in the drawer. "Nope. I just think we found the body."

"We have to tell someone."

I nodded. "I know. But I can't tell Maddox without admitting we broke into Dean's house."

"Won't he be pleased? You found Dean and he didn't!"

I wasn't sure he would see it that way. "Don't know," I said.

"So leave an anonymous tip. People do it all the time."

"You'll have to call. I don't want the line picked up by Traci." I wasn't sure if my sister-in-law was even on duty in the dispatch office at the moment, but I didn't want to risk it.

"Fine. Do you have a burn phone?"

"No."

"All undercover agents have a burn phone," protested Lily.

"I don't. I have a two-year plan."

"Never mind. It was just a thought." Lily pulled the seatbelt around her and buckled up. "I know! Swing by my manager's office. He's always got a drawer full of phones people leave at the clubs. We'll use one of those."

"Cool." I switched the engine on, pulled a three-point turn and drove back the way we came, heading to Lily's manager's office. The lights were off when we got there, after fifteen minutes of speeding, but she let herself in with a key, and turned off the alarm. She rooted around in the lost property box, producing a little cell phone with two bars of battery life remaining. She dialed 911 and placed a call, adopting a weird accent and telling them there was a dead body. When she gave the address, she dropped the 'h' on Hyacinth, and hung up when they asked her for details. Lily tossed the phone back in the lost property box, and reset the code on the door.

"Didn't sound like Traci," she said as she locked up, pushing the handle to test it.

"Good. What was up with the Australian accent?"

"That was British!"

"Oh!"

"That was totally Lara Croft."

"Um, okay."

We dived back into my car. "What now?" asked Lily as she turned down the collar of her jacket.

"Pick up a pizza and go home? Spend the evening looking really innocent while bleaching our eyeballs so that I don't see a corpse every time I close my eyes."

Lily was quiet for a moment, then, "Sounds like a plan."

Lily dialed, using her own phone this time, and ordered a large margherita, a side of garlic bread, and a tub of ice cream. We picked it up and went home. In Lily's apartment, we finished off an open bottle of red wine and munched on the pizza.

"You think they found him yet?" she asked, diving in for a third slice.

"Maybe. Maddox will tell me in the morning if they did."

"You think he's going to drop by on a Saturday?"

In all the excitement, I had forgotten it was Friday night and that I wouldn't be in the office in the morning. Normally, it would be a blessed relief. I would go out, shake off the office cobwebs, with my nails painted, wearing a pretty dress and hit the bars with Lily, if she wasn't working, or maybe with Traci or Alice if they could get a pass out. Or I would have a nice night in front of the television, facemask on, nail polish ready and a bunch of snacks by my side. My third option was spending the evening with one of my brothers, or, on rare occasions, babysitting. Serena, funnily enough, never fit into my plans and that was a mutual thing. As it was, I'd veered out of my routine and started the weekend with a B&E after fleeing the scene of a crime. I was fairly certain tampering with a corpse would never stick, seeing as I hadn't even touched Dean.

But the thought of Maddox dropping by was a little weird, and, if I really thought about it, quite nice. It was sweet that he had checked up on me several times through the past couple of days and even offered to come to my parents' with me. Although I was still a little cross about the whole drugging thing.

However, he hadn't mentioned anything about stopping by, but then, I doubt he thought it was necessary as long as someone else was keeping an eye on me. Maybe I was reading too much into it because I liked him. He was good looking, and he had a cool job and danger didn't scare him. I liked him a whole lot more now than when he was just my new, annoying boss. I'd take an excuse to hang out with him quite happily, so long as the conversation avoided dead things and the possibility of me being next.

Thinking about Maddox made me think about Solomon. Tall, brooding, quiet Solomon. I wondered how he spent his weekends; if he hung out at home and did normal things. I couldn't imagine him dragging out a lawn mower on a Saturday morning, or tending a garden. I also couldn't imagine him stripping drywall, or painting, or cooking or going shopping at the mall. I was fairly certain he could do all of those things, because men like Solomon could do anything. It just didn't fit with the image in my mind of him disappearing off on some kind of commando mission at the drop of a hat.

"I don't know," I said. "I guess if Maddox wants me, he'll find me."

"Hope you're naked when that happens."

"Lily!" Still, I had a hard time struggling with how that could be a bad idea.

She stuck out her tongue and changed the subject. "You want to come to my spin class tomorrow to work off the pizza?"

"Is the hunky instructor going to be there? The one with the dreadlocks?"

"Anton? Yeah. He's the only reason anyone goes." Lily sighed.

"Count me in."

# CHAPTER SIX

My bedside phone woke me at what felt like the crack of dawn. I stuck a hand out from under the covers and grappled for it. I knocked it out of the charger first, forcing me to lean over the edge of the bed to search for it on the floor. I found it, hit "answer" and pressed it against my ear as I shuffled back under the covers.

"What are you doing?" asked Serena, her condescending tone barely spared from becoming a sneer.

"Hello to you too," I said, stifling a yawn.

She cut right to the point. "We need to talk baby shower."

"Aren't I supposed to be planning it?"

"You are, but I want to make sure you get it right. I have a scrapbook of ideas and a list of places you need to scope out for the venue."

"How thick is this scrapbook?"

"Seventy-six pages." My brain winced. "It's divided into boy, girl and neutral. We don't know what it is yet though."

"So we just need to look at neutral?" I asked hopefully.

"No! We need to look at everything because maybe we'll do a boy/girl theme with neutral elements. We need to decide on food and drinks. I'm thinking mocktinis."

"What's a whattini?"

"A mocktini. It's a cocktail, but without alcohol."

"Won't you be the only pregnant one there?" I asked, because it seemed unfair that the rest of us should be punished for Serena's nocturnal activities.

"No, there will be other ladies from my birthing group. Ted and I are doing Lamaze."

"Did you find your way out yet?" I joked. I could almost imagine Serena wrinkling her forehead trying to decide if I were sassing her, or really just as thick as she thought.

"Very funny," she said, with a sigh. "We'll need to decide on five hors d'oeuvres, three mocktinis and games."

"There are going to be games?" I wondered if we could do a murder mystery. It seemed appropriate.

"Of course. It's traditional."

"We're not doing the melted chocolate in the diaper one," I said, putting the kibosh on the grossest game known to adult women, bar dating. "Anything but that one."

"That is not a problem," said Serena, in agreement for once. "We'll probably do a crafts table instead."

"Are babies into crafts?"

She thought about it. "I don't know. We've only signed the baby up for Mandarin, classical music appreciation, and baby ballet so far."

Sheesh. Poor kid. "Don't babies love all that finger-painting stuff?"

"It's not exactly Ivy League," Serena pointed out. "Plus, we've already passed womb Beethoven, so classical appreciation is the next stage; the ballet is to encourage fluid movement; and given the state of world affairs, Mandarin immersion is essential from birth. Maybe we'll do art appreciation, too. Thanks for the suggestion."

"Whoa! Back up! Your baby's not even born yet and it already passed a class?" Boy, did I ever feel like a failure. At this rate, the baby would probably earn a decent salary before I did.

"Ted and I want to be *very* proactive parents. So, can you meet me at Alessandro's at one and we'll go through the scrapbook?"

I thought about all my other plans for the day. Spinning with Lily to assuage last night's pizza guilt, maybe some yoga for the wine guilt, and shopping to cheer me up after all the guilt. On the other hand, Alessandro's was pretty nice; the type of place where ladies lunched and men took their dates when they wanted to impress them. They served the best lasagna in the world, the waiters were polite and deferential, and everyone was smart and pretty. I didn't go there a lot because it was pricey and I was on a temp's budget, but Serena was on a first name basis with most of the staff.

Serena sweetened the deal. "Lunch is my treat and we can get the dough balls you like for an appetizer."

"See you at one."

Hanging up, I glanced over at the clock and realized I had scant minutes before Lily would come knocking at the door. I got out of bed with a groan, padded into the kitchen to add fresh grounds, which I'd scrounged from Lily to the coffee pot, and then into the bathroom to brush my teeth, wash my face and tie my hair into a high ponytail. As a concession to Anton, the hot instructor, I added a slick of mascara and a swipe of lip gloss before putting on my yoga pants and a stretchy top that was starting to look unforgiving around the middle. Just as I laced up my sneakers, Lily knocked on the door and I let her in.

Despite our late night, Lily was impossibly perky. Dressed in knee-length, stretch pants and a short, cropped top, she displayed as much toned flesh as she could get away with. She'd matched the look with a sports watch and a cute headband in stretchy material. There wasn't a pimple or eye bag on her flawless face, but I loved her anyway.

"Ready?" she said.

"Ugh."

"Excellent. Let's get that coffee to go." She rooted through the shelves and pulled out two travel mugs, prepped our coffee, and dragged me out the door, leaving me just enough time to grab my tote bag.

An hour and a half later, I felt like I was probably going to die. I'd gone from half asleep to feeling enthused about the class—especially when Anton bent over to pick up his class registration list and flaunted his taut buns—to all of my muscles screaming for mercy.

"Maybe I should go back to the beginners' class," I said, staring at the ceiling from my prone position on the dressing room floor. It seemed less embarrassing to pass out in here, should I need to, than in the gym lobby. Two skinny women stepped over me without breaking stride and carried on around the bank of lockers. Lily held a hand out and hoisted me back up onto my Jell-O legs.

"No way, you just need to go more often. I spin three times a week."

"You're a headcase!"

"You still got through the class," Lily pointed out. "You weren't the first to wimp out."

"But now I might *die*."

Lily flicked water from her bottle at me. "You will not die."

"I might not be able to move for the rest of the weekend. I hate Anton. He's a sadist."

"Go home and take a bath and a nap. You'll feel better, I promise. Do you want to come to Body Pump tomorrow?"

"I don't know what it is, but it sounds horrible."

Lily drove me home while I muttered and winced, as I massaged my aching muscles. My thighs had stopped screaming, at least, but I felt, literally, like my legs had turned to rubber.

I never "got" the exercise thing. I did it because I had to, because I was starting to feel the spread and I needed to fit into my clothes; but no amount of exercise could make me love it. Maybe if I saw the effects faster and had a bod like Lily's, I'd appreciate it more, but as it was, exercise and I enjoyed, in the loosest possible sense, a love/hate relationship.

"Have you heard from Maddox yet?"

"No, I kind of expected him to call last night, but nothing."

"Maybe he called while we were out," said Lily, turning the Mini onto our road. "Did you check your cell phone before you went to bed?"

Actually I hadn't. I'd crawled up the stairs, thrown my clothes on the floor; put my pajamas on inside out, and fallen asleep. "Want to come up and find out?"

"You bet."

We were both disappointed when I let us into my apartment and the answering machine didn't have a flashing light. My cell phone didn't show any messages either. "Maybe later," said Lily. "Maybe he's been to the morgue. Or maybe he's got loads of paperwork."

"Maybe." Or maybe I wasn't as useful to Maddox as I hoped. Maybe I didn't have a part in this investigation at all. Maybe they were just humoring me so I didn't poke my head where it didn't belong… like at Dean's house. I wondered if they'd found the body yet.

"You want to go shoe shopping?"

"I do, but I have to meet Serena at Alessandro's. We're going through her baby shower demands."

"You mean, inspiration?"

"Nuh-uh. Definitely, demands."

"I'm going to check out that new club downtown later. Pecs. The one with the topless waiters."

I brightened at that. Rumor had it all the waiters were part-time male models. The place was crammed opening night, so we didn't get in. Life was full of disappointments. "Okay," I said. "I have a great dress to wear."

"It's going to be packed with women. We could go to O'Grady's afterwards, if we're going slutty."

"No, my brothers might be there and they'll tell my mom." The last time I'd been there, I'd worn a cute, little, black dress and was happily chatting with a really nice, smart guy wearing a hundred-dollar shirt when my brothers muscled in and he escaped. Turned out, Daniel had been present at the guy's bail hearing for assault a month earlier and the guy was pretty dumb to choose to hang out at a cop bar after that. My mom got on the phone the next morning and tried to set me up on a date with the twice-divorced son of one of the classmates in her evening French cooking class.

"Yeah, bad idea," agreed Lily, who knew the full extent of my mortification. "Maybe we could try somewhere different. I know the girl working the door at Paradise tonight. I bet she could get us in free."

"Great."

I let Lily out, then showered and washed my hair, quickly blow-drying it before fastening it back into a high ponytail. This time, however, it was smooth and sleek and my face wasn't bright red from all the exertion earlier. I picked out a beige shift dress with black panels on the sides, black pumps and finished it off with a cropped, black jacket. I fished a nice purse out of the wicker basket sitting on the floor of my closet and got my tote, transferring my cell phone and wallet. In doing so, I noticed the matchbook and the little black notebook I pilfered from Dean's house.

I opened the notebook, peering at the rows of numbers inside. They seemed to be divided into sections, the long rows of numbers further separated by slashes; but other than that, none of it made sense. They didn't look like any number sequence I'd ever seen; not phone numbers, bank accounts or dates; and there was page after page of them. I did, however, recognize Dean's cramped handwriting.

Once, when Dominic was overwhelmed, he had asked me to type up some of Dean's notes and this was clearly the same hand.

Glancing at my watch, I realized I didn't have time to sit and ponder the numbers or I would be late. I stuffed the notebook and matchbook into my dresser drawer, snatched my purse, and hurried to meet Serena.

By the time I got to the restaurant, Serena had already arrived and was seated at a window table that overlooked the street.

"You're late," she said, glancing up from the menu.

"I couldn't find a parking space." Serena's Mercedes was parked directly outside, but I had to circle the block three times before finding a space, then hike back to the restaurant on my three-inch heels. Now in addition to my residual spinning aches, my feet were also sore. I slid onto the seat opposite her and picked up my glass of mineral water, taking a sip.

"Well, you look nice," she said. "I had my fingers crossed that you wouldn't turn up in jeans."

"You sound like Mom." I don't think I've ever seen Serena in jeans. She's very much a skirts and dresses, no matter the weather, kind of woman. In summer, it's linens and cottons with neat little pumps; in winter, wool and tweed with long boots. Today, she wore a flared skirt in raspberry pink with a loose fitting, white top, as a concession to the neat bulge rounding out her belly. A thick scrapbook lay on the table ominously between us.

She picked it up, flipped to the page she wanted, and after running her eyes over it, passed it to me. I took it and placed it on the pristine white tablecloth. Serena, apparently, had thought of everything, from colors and fabric swatches to recipes and images she had neatly clipped from magazines. I kept my thumb on the page she marked and flipped through the book.

"You did all this when you found out you were pregnant?" I asked. Serena had always been a bookish sort, but more of the read-and-auto-transcribe-a-textbook type. Somehow, I couldn't imagine her sitting on her living room floor, surrounded by baby magazines, eagerly clipping and gluing into the scrapbook.

"A couple of years," she replied and her eyes closed for a moment. "We've been trying for a while."

In an uncharacteristic moment of sisterly bonding, I reached across the table and held her hands in mine. "I'm sorry," I said. "I didn't know."

"Well, you wouldn't," she sniffed. "You have your own life."

"I would have still come with you, if you needed someone to go to the hospital with you, or, you know, stuff." I didn't know what stuff, but I would have found out.

"Thank you, Alexandra. It didn't quite get to IVF, though we talked about it. The baby is natural," she finished proudly. God forbid Serena should ever have to get help for anything, even her martyred ovaries.

We both looked a bit sick then. Serena: because she was pregnant. Me: because I had a mental flash of she and Ted getting it on. "So, tell me what you want," I said, steering the conversation away from Ted in the buff. Humping.

Serena looked equally relieved. "I thought you

could host it here. Alessandro's has a private room upstairs that would be perfect. Mindy Laws had her shower here last year."

"Do you really want to have the shower here after Mindy?" I had no idea why she and Serena remained friends. Even by Serena's standards, Mindy was a spectacular bitch. She was mean too.

Serena's mouth twitched downwards. "No, she'll never let me forget it." She took out a pen and a neat, little, leather notebook and crossed Alessandro's off the list. "Where else could I have it?"

"What about at your house? You have lots of space."

"Ted hates messes."

"Ted's not invited. We can clean up before he gets home. Garrett, Daniel and Jord could take him to a bar."

"Ted doesn't like bars."

I made a mental note to get Jord to take Ted to a strip bar. "The boys can work it out."

"I suppose I could hire a cleaning crew."

"How about instead of ducks and baby animals, we do a spa theme?" I suggested, after scanning the page and flipping to the next. "It'll be totally original."

Serena wrinkled her nose. "It's not very babyish."

"It's about you! Everyone could get manicures and pedicures or mini facials. We could do a whole spa theme with those mocktini things you want, and cucumbers, and…healthy stuff." I trailed off, running out of ideas.

"Well…"

"Mindy will go crazy that she didn't think of it."
That clinched it.

"But we can still do games?" Serena asked.

"Yes, we can still do games. It'll be very grown up and chic, but with traditional elements. You could change the way people do baby showers in Montgomery." And I'd get pretty toenails too. "Plus, if we do it at your house, the venue is free, so we can splurge on the fun stuff. You could ask Alessandro's to cater. They wouldn't say no to you."

We paused to order, lasagna for me—corpse or no corpse, I was hungry—while Serena took a long time to discount anything with shellfish, soft cheese and nuts. She finally settled on a half portion of lasagna with a side salad, no dressing. If this was what pregnancy did to women, I'd probably starve before the first trimester was over.

"Can you arrange everything?" Serena asked as she passed me her credit card. "I don't have time. My workload is huge. I was lucky to get today off."

"You don't take Saturdays off?"

"Not usually, but I figured, what the hell, the pregnancy has probably cost me the partnership anyway, I may as well take a Saturday off. They'll probably give it to that asshole, Jeff Walters, even though I've worked seventy-hour weeks for years." Her jaw stiffened.

Sheesh. I never heard Serena swear. She seemed to shake herself, and the mask slipped back into place.

"They're not going to promote someone over you," I said with certainty.

"Sure they will. They've done it to every other woman in the practice. I thought if I worked harder than anyone else, if I put in my hours, worked more weekends, they wouldn't be able to pass me up. But since I told them I was pregnant, it's Jeff that my boss takes golfing, and Jeff whom he takes to dinner."

"You hate golf," I pointed out. "It's a silly sport."

"It's not the golf. It's the corner office and the salary."

"Why don't you leave? If they're going to screw you over anyway? Why not just leave first?"

"Did I mention the salary?"

"Yeah. Right after you mentioned how they screw over every woman in the company who dares to have a baby. Why don't you set up your own practice? Everyone needs an accountant."

Serena tilted her head to one side. "I never thought of that. Ted would hate it."

"Ted hates everything."

Surprisingly, Serena laughed. "He is a little uptight."

I wisely kept my mouth shut because Serena saying Ted was a little uptight was like saying Kim Kardashian's marriages were a little short-lived.

Relaxing while the waiter delivered our plates and refilled our glasses with mineral water—Serena nixed the wine—I contemplated my sister. Serena had always known exactly what she wanted in life, and had gone all out for it. I was as surprised as anyone when she moved back to Montgomery, but by that time, she was already engaged to Ted. He was her college boyfriend, had a job here, and she was interviewing, finally settling on her current employers, and rising swiftly through the ranks. I knew she worked hard, but the crazy hours were a blow to me, not to mention her pinched lips when she talked about them possibly firing her for the pregnancy. There was an awful lot I didn't know about my sister.

Thinking about her number-crunching made Dean's notebook flash back into my mind. I was sitting opposite a person who loved number puzzles.

"Serena, I want to ask you a question about numbers."

She paused, a forkful of salad halfway to her mouth and arched an eyebrow. "Numbers?" she said. "Do you have a tax problem?"

"No. It's more of a puzzle. I've got a list of numbers and I need to know what they mean."

"Tell me about the list." The fork disappeared into her mouth.

"Well, it's divided into sections which might mean something and the numbers are varying lengths, split into four parts. Eliminating dates and phone numbers, and I doubt they're bank account numbers, I have no clue what they could be."

"Do you have the key?"

"Huh?"

"It might be an encryption and all keys have encryptions. Is it a work thing?"

"Sort of. It's a project I'm working on and I'm supposed to work out what they mean." It wasn't strictly a lie. The notebook was so odd, I had a hunch it could mean something. Solomon's insult snapped into my mind. *Blondie* could work it, I thought with determination. "Why would someone use an encryption?"

"It's pretty standard to keep things secret. The numbers might be names or words, represented by digits. If you find out the key, you can work out the code."

"That's kind of paranoid."

"Only if they aren't out to get you," said Serena.

Someone had definitely been out to get Dean, that much was clear. If he were up to something that he didn't want anyone to find out, like say, oh, *insurance fraud*, an encryption sounded like a good idea. There was a chance I might have really found something useful. There was a first time for everything! Also: Solomon could suck it.

"So how do I find an encryption key?"

"It depends on how complicated it is. It might be as simple as working out the most obvious letters, like the vowels, and guessing from there. Or it could be that the numbers equal a movement of places up or down the alphabet from a specific point. That's if it's a simple, manual, alphabetic code. Some encryptions are machine-made, and unless you have the same equipment, you won't be able to crack it."

I had to hope that Dean couldn't access anything like that and would have to opt for a simpler code. That would make it easier to decipher.

"You're talking about hundreds of possible combinations," continued Serena. "And that's just for words that make sense. Names are tougher. And it could be a number-for-number encryption. It could be as simple as each number moving, say, two places up from where it's supposed to be. I've seen that on fraud before."

*Great.*

"I don't suppose you could ask whoever made the codes?" she asked.

Not without a medium. "No. He's... out of town."

"You're smart, you'll crack it."

I looked up from where I'd been stabbing the lasagna, red sauce oozing out of the tine marks. "Thanks," I said, trying not to bristle at the sudden, unexpected praise. If my sister believed in me... I smiled.

"Now about this shower." Serena curtly slipped a typed sheet of paper out of the scrapbook and passed it to me. "Here's the list of invitees. I have the stationers on standby. The web address is on here. All you have to do is finalize the location—which will be easy now, as it's at my house—and time, and get them to print it. They will mail everything."

"When's the date?"

"Next week."

"Next week!"

"Keep your hair on. Everyone got a save-the-date months ago."

"You sent save-the-dates for your baby shower!" I thought about it. "I didn't get one."

"I don't get many days off. I have to be organized. And you're family."

I got my notepad and pen out of my bag and looked sadly at my lasagna, which was probably going to get cold while I took notes. Given the time constraints, there wasn't any grace period for messing about. We had to get military about this; it was better for Serena to give me her list of demands so I could work like hell to fulfill them. If not, I'd be forever known as the sister who ruined her first, (and let's hope, only), child's baby shower. "Tell me everything you need."

~

An hour later, I left Alessandro's with a full tummy, a splotch of creamy sauce on my shoe, (no explanation how it got there), a thirty-six point list of Serena's instructions for her imminent baby shower, and a prepaid reservation for catering the shower next week. God-parenting had better have its perks. I was hoping for a regular supply of daintily drawn cards on which I was depicted as something benevolent like an angel, a tiny, nice-smelling child to supply snuggles, and a profound respect from Serena for my nurturing throughout its life.

I suspected it actually meant I would be expected to donate extra special birthday and Christmas gifts, regular babysitting, as well as contributions towards its college fund.

Instead of heading straight home, I swung by the police department and asked for my brother. Garrett helped me fill out the gun permit and told me he would call me to set up some practice time on the range. He told me to pick out a gun when I found one I liked. I gave him an IOU babysitting voucher and drove home.

Turning into my parking spot, I jumped in my seat when I turned off the engine and spotted Maddox stepping off the porch. Drat. I really should have tried harder to get the splotch off my shoe. On the plus side, however, I looked great. I grabbed my purse and exited the car. I was mindfully standing up and sucking in my stomach, while pushing back my shoulders, which had the added benefit of making my boobs momentarily bigger.

"You look nice," said Maddox, smiling. "Pretty. Go somewhere special or are you moonlighting at another office?" That was twice now he'd called me pretty. Not that I was counting.

"Thank you. I've just been to lunch at Alessandro's." I couldn't return the compliment. Maddox was not a man you called pretty. Sexy, however, would work. Gone were the suit and tie, replaced by black jeans, boots that were well worn and a button-down shirt in a soft jersey. He hadn't shaved this morning and dark bristles covered his chin. He looked delicious, especially when his eyes darkened. "A date?"

I thought about teasing him, but instead, I said, "With my sister."

"Oh." I could see the mental cogs turning as he thought about my file. "Serena? You have a big family?"

"Yep, lots of us Graves and yes, I've heard every joke about all the ones in the cemetery."

Maddox followed me into the building and up the narrow stairs. "So, to what do I owe this pleasure?" I asked, glancing at him over my shoulder. I could hear music, something with a fast beat, thumping through the wall from Lily's apartment.

"I thought you would want to know that we found Martin Dean last night."

I turned away and kept my face steadily impassive as I unlocked the door. "Oh?" I said, holding it open for Maddox to step past me.

"You don't seem surprised," he observed.

"I already knew he was dead," I countered. I dropped my keys on the console and sauntered into the kitchen, reaching into the refrigerator for Cokes. I passed one to Maddox and he snapped the tab and took a sip.

"We found him at his house," said Maddox, and I felt his eyes on me as I walked into the living room and sat. Maddox dropped onto the couch, next to me. "In his office chair, would you believe? Kind of fitting for Dean."

"I thought you already searched the house."

Maddox watched me closely, his face impassive too. I wondered what was going on behind his all-knowing eyes. "The local security guard got a call about someone sneaking onto Dean's property."

"Did the caller say whom?"

"No. The guard went to investigate, but saw nothing."

I shrugged and tipped my head back to take a swig from the can. Not exactly ladylike, and my mother would probably have thrown a fit, but I was out of clean glasses and it never occurred to me to buy straws.

"Then dispatch got an anonymous call from an Australian woman saying there was a body," Maddox continued. He leaned forward, elbows on thighs, the weight of his glance making me recoil. "You wouldn't know anything about that, would you?"

"Me? *Nooo*. I can't do accents. And Lily can only do British."

"Dispatch sent out a squad car, and eventually it got to me. There was Martin Dean, dead as a dodo, seated upright in his home office."

"Guess that solves the mystery of where his body went." I smiled brightly.

"Guess it does, though the two snoopers are of interest. They might have something to do with the body reappearing after we swept his house."

I decided it was better to steer the conversation in a different direction. "So, where do you think they've been keeping Dean all this time?"

"The M.E. thinks he was put on ice."

"Pardon?"

"Refrigerated. He hadn't fully thawed when we got him."

"That's... creepy." I made a note to scrub my kitchen later.

"I got to wondering. What if the snoopers had nothing to do with the body turning up? What if they found something? Something that would help the case."

"Like what?" I thought about the notebook and the matchbook in my bedroom. I had a feeling the notebook had a lot to do with the case; the matchbook I wasn't so sure about. I'd only taken it because I forgot to put it down when the security guard came to investigate.

"Could be anything. Now we have the body, we have new leads to follow up. The ballistics report is on a rush."

A knock sounded on the door, and before I could ask Maddox to explain what that meant, Lily stuck her head inside.

"In the living room," I said, leaning back to wave her in.

"Oh, hey," she said, flinching when she saw Maddox.

"Lily," he said by way of a greeting. He gave her a long, hard look.

"So..." Lily said, pursing her lips like she was about to whistle her innocence. "Just came by to see how the baby shower planning went."

"My sister, not me," I said to Maddox, just in case he thought my file missed something. Then to Lily, I said, "We're doing a spa theme."

"Very cool. Am I invited?"

"If you bring a gift."

"No problemo."

"So what did you two get up to last night?" Maddox interrupted.

"Nothing," Lily said quickly.

"We went out for pizza," I said, because we *had* done that. Except for all the bits I left out, it was the truth.

"Yeah, *pizza*," Lily echoed, folding her arms defensively.

"Make any calls?"

"Maddox said the PD got a tip off from an Australian lady and they found Dean's body," I said in a rush, my voice edging towards helium pitch.

"I only do British," said Lily.

"I thought as much." Maddox smiled, and for a moment, the three of us did the quiet version of a Mexican standoff. Then he got to his feet, stepping past Lily and me. "I'm glad you're both okay. I have some stuff to do, but I'll come back later. I have a few questions to ask you, Lexi."

"What if I'm busy later?"

"Are you busy later?"

Lily shook her head and mouthed "no." Then made kissy faces. Maddox half turned his head to look at her and she stopped. He frowned.

"No," I said.

"Then I'll bring dinner. See you at seven."

Lily barely contained herself while Maddox let himself out. She flopped onto the couch beside me, taking his place. "Tonight is totally a date," she said.

"It is not a date."

"Did you see him inviting me?"

"No."

"And he's bringing dinner?"

"Yes."

"It's a date," Lily decided, nodding. "Hey, the corpse thing was a close call."

I mimed zipping my mouth shut and waving my

hands round until she froze, then nodded. But she was right, it was a very close call indeed. Except I thought Maddox knew all along it was us. Part of me was very happy that he came by to check up on us. On me, because, now I thought about it, he knew Lily was home, but still waited to talk to me, instead of her, which was unexpectedly nice. If he were tracking my cell phone with its apparent location device, he could have come by Alessandro's and interrupted lunch, but he didn't. He waited. And now I had a date, too.

"You don't mind me blowing off O'Grady's and Paradise?"

"For a night with a sexy cop? No."

"What do I wear to a not-a-date at home?" I asked.

"I feel a fashion show coming on."

Dear God.

# CHAPTER SEVEN

Maddox turned up at seven sharp, strolling into my apartment as if he owned the place, with a bag of something delicious-smelling in his hand. Fortunately, I had just finished dressing in jeans and a silky, pale blue top, my hair still tied in the ponytail, but this time, with a sparkly band, given the potential dateness of dinner.

"Come in," I said and he grinned. He hadn't changed. He still looked great.

"You should lock your door."

"The one downstairs was locked."

"No, it wasn't."

"Huh. Maybe Lily forgot." I tried to summon up worry at that but couldn't be bothered. Maddox was in my house. With food. That was infinitely more interesting right now. I would realign my priorities later.

"Remind her." Maddox paused, like he was trying to decide whether he should tack on another warning to that or not. Evidently, he decided for, because he said, "There are two killers out there and someone else with an interest in you."

"Is that why you're here? To look after me?"

Maddox smiled in that sexy way of his, the one that made my stomach flip and beckoned me to follow him to the kitchen. It was a good job I hadn't known he was undercover, or that he looked even sexier with stubble, or I'd never have gotten any work done at the office. I padded barefoot behind him, eyeing the rear view. Very nice. He said, "Next time someone walks in when you're not expecting it, it might be one of them, not me. Their intent might be the same as mine."

That flattened my daydream. But then... "And what's your intent?" It came out a little more breathy than I intended. Maddox turned, stepping closer and my breath caught in my throat. He reached behind me, and for a moment, I thought he was going to wrap his arms around me, pull me in close and... then he stepped back, two plates in hand and winked before moving around me to set the bag on the counter.

"I intend to feed you," he said.

Well, that worked for me too. I stood to one side and watched as Maddox unpacked the containers he'd brought and served them onto plates. He was opening my drawers and extracting knives and forks. "Do you have wine?" he asked.

"Red or white?" I'd made an emergency run to the supermarket, just in case. I also had a new carton of orange juice, coffee, eggs, milk, croissants for the morning—not that I planned to ask Maddox to stay the night, perish the thought, but you know, better safe than sorry, which was why I wore matching underwear and shaved my legs—and fruit.

"Either."

I uncorked a bottle of red and carried it through the living room, along with two wine glasses, setting them on the coffee table beside the plates. I was glad he'd chosen not to use my small, dining-for-two table because this seemed so much less formal. Maddox scrolled through my iPod, set an album to play, and we sat side-by-side, eating the spaghetti marinara. It was companionable. Nice. My mother would have asked where the tablecloth was. And the candles. I resolved to buy candles.

"This is good," I said.

"It's my favorite take-out spot. Best Italian in Montgomery."

"Can't argue with that."

"You like Alessandro's? You went there earlier with your sister?" he prompted.

"Uh-huh. It's Serena's favorite, but I like it too. You ever been?"

"Sure."

*On a date?* I wanted to ask, but I didn't. I tried to imagine Maddox in a suit and tie, date smart, not office-wear smart, clean-shaven, smoldering across the table from me. I had to stuff a forkful of pasta in my mouth to mask my sigh.

"You lick your lips anymore and you're going to lose them."

I hadn't realized I was doing it. "Just getting rid of the sauce," I mumbled.

Maddox leaned in, stopping just an inch or so from my face, and his eyes fluttered down to my lips, then back to my eyes. When I didn't move, but for a slightest parting of my lips, he closed the last little bit of distance, and his lips brushed mine, briefly, then again, longer, enough to make my blood rush as I leaned into him.

"Got it," he said and kissed me again. This time, I was certain there was no sauce left.

Holy chick-a-bow-wow.

We finished our meal, talking mostly about food, and cleared the plates. When he sat down again, I poured another glass of wine for each of us. "What are you doing Sunday?" he asked.

"Nothing much." Traditionally, I went to dinner with my family, but since Mom and Dad retired, Mom started taking a bunch of adult ed' classes and that meant Sunday dinners moved to Thursday night. For the past couple of Sundays, I did laundry and tried to enjoy my last hours of freedom before my Monday-to-Friday sentence at Green Hand Insurance began. Now that Dean's body had been found, it suddenly occurred to me that maybe I didn't have a job anymore. A fleeting moment of sadness passed through me. Also: poor Dean. "What happens Monday?" I asked. "Now that Dean's been found?"

"Next week I'll announce Dean died over the weekend. Things will go on as normal for a while. We still have an investigation to run."

"And what about me?"

"Try not to break in anywhere."

It was my turn to smile enigmatically. I stacked the plates and retrieved the tub of ice cream from the freezer, adding bowls and spoons to the counter before I pried the lid off.

"Here let me," said Maddox, taking the scoop and running it under warm water. He slid his arms around me and grasped the tub, cutting through the ice cream easily.

"Are you distracted?" I asked as his lips nuzzled my neck.

"No. Totally on the ball."

"You scooped ice cream onto the counter."

"Maybe a little distracted," he said, his hands spanning my waist before he turned me around. My arms went around his neck as he kissed me, slowly at first, then eagerly when I responded. "Sprinkles," he whispered.

"Do we *need* a safe word?"

Maddox laughed. "No, do you have any sprinkles?"

"No."

"Chocolate sauce?" he murmured against my lips.

"Kinky."

"For the ice cream."

"No. All out." But I'd definitely get some now. Sauce, that is.

"How do you live?" he asked as he moved me aside to clean up the spilled ice cream and fill the bowls. He carried them back to the living room so we could curl up on the couch.

As it turned out, apparently non-date-dates weren't sacrosanct anymore.

Solomon turned up first. He strolled in as casually as Maddox did and we sprang apart like guilty teenagers who shouldn't be snuggling on the couch. His eyebrows rose when he saw the wine glasses, half-empty bottle and empty bowls. "You should lock your doors," he advised me.

I turned to Maddox. "That's your fault. You lectured me on keeping my doors locked, then you didn't lock the door."

"But I'm here," he pointed out.

"You're just relieved Solomon has honorable intentions."

"That'll never stand up in court," said Solomon, taking the armchair and looking pointedly at the wine.

"Would you like some?" I offered. It wasn't like he looked like he was about to leave.

"Please."

I got up to get him a wine glass, hearing them speak softly as I entered the kitchen. I was tempted to eavesdrop, given that it was my apartment and thus perfectly reasonable, but I decided that was probably rude. Also, I couldn't hear them too well.

I grabbed the glass and went back, hoping that I was interrupting and they would just continue—they didn't. As I set it on the table and poured for Solomon, I passed it to him and his fingertips grazed mine. He took it with a nod and sipped.

"So... what are you doing here?" asked Maddox in a not-so-agreeable tone. He relaxed against the back of the couch, his wine glass in one hand, while he slung one leg across his thigh. Sometime during the evening, his boots had come off and now lay under the coffee table. He couldn't have looked more at home. I wondered what Solomon made of our cozy evening and why he was gate-crashing.

"I was in the neighborhood and saw your car outside. Thought there might have been trouble."

Funny. Solomon hadn't entered like he thought there was trouble. I thought he was more curious as to why Maddox's car was outside when he hadn't expected it to be. And, come to think of it, why was Solomon driving past? Somehow, I didn't think he had drawn stakeout duty.

"What's the real reason?" I asked, seeing as he was crashing our not-a-date and deserved short shrift.

"I heard you applied for a gun permit today." He sipped the wine. "That's good."

I never expected that. "How did you know?" I asked.

"Why did you apply for a permit?" asked Maddox, equally surprised. His eyebrows drew together as he waited for my answer.

"To keep myself safe from men who walk into my apartment unannounced," I snipped, looking at them both pointedly.

"You don't need a gun," Maddox replied.

"Possibly true, but rather safe than sorry."

"This will be over soon. If you don't feel safe, I can get a car to watch you twenty-four/seven," said Maddox.

I'd already heard plenty about how tightly Montgomery PD was stretched. A car seemed like an unnecessary expense to me, but I was grateful he offered. "I appreciate it, but no thanks."

"You really don't need a gun," he continued. "Guns are dangerous."

I bristled. "You think I'm some silly little woman who can't handle a gun?"

"No! Any idiot can handle a gun."

"Oh!" I took a large swallow of wine and glared at Maddox.

"Sorry, I didn't mean that. I meant..."

"I know what you meant. Look, don't worry about it. My brother Garrett helped me with the paperwork."

"Do you need someone to take you to the range?" asked Solomon, interrupting our cross silence. "Can you shoot?"

I relaxed at his words. Here was someone who wasn't telling me I was a danger to myself, even if I were blonde. And he didn't try to patronize me. I was just surprised it was Solomon. When we first met, I got the impression he thought I was a ditzy temp. Blondie, he had said. Perhaps I was wrong. Then again, I wasn't sure I could surmise anything about Solomon. "Thanks for the offer, but Garrett is taking me, and yes, I can shoot, but I haven't in a while." Not since Army boot camp, but that was a story for another time. Or never.

"Garrett Graves is your brother?" Maddox frowned, like he was trying to match a name to a face.

"He's my oldest brother. The surname is a clue, huh?"

"He's a lot..."

"Older than me, yes. I was an accident." My parents had always been perfectly nice about it, but I was an accident. Occasionally, my family referred to me as the Graves' Hiccup; a complete surprise, but an amusing one. "He's a detective too. You might know each other." I already knew they did.

Lily seized that moment to stroll in.

"Come in," I said, "It's open house tonight."

"Cool," she said, ignoring my tone. "I just came to borrow a..." Her eyes flickered around, drifting over Maddox to Solomon, then settling on the coffee table. "A bottle opener," she decided.

"It's in the kitchen. What happened to yours?"

"Can't find it."

Great. The first time I'd had a not-a-date in months and it ended by being crashed by my not-a-date's scary colleague and my nosy best friend. I might as well give up now. I would have to capitulate and accept one of my mother's blind dates. How bad could that be? On second thought, best not think about it.

I rose to get another glass. By the time I returned to the living room, Lily had pulled out my desk chair and positioned it opposite the couch. I poured and handed the wine to Lily who accepted it with a "Thanks."

I dropped onto the couch, about as far from Maddox as I could, and she flicked her eyebrows at me, then looked at Maddox as well as Solomon. "This is nice. Cozy," she said. Then to me, she asked, "How was dinner?"

"Very nice."

"Ice cream?"

"Would have been better with sprinkles," I said. *Or if you two hadn't shown up*, but I kept that to myself.

"Do you have any coffee?" Lily asked.

I narrowed my eyes. We fell silent again, the four of us simultaneously taking a sip of wine. I didn't know about the others, but I was unsure of how the conversation would proceed at this point. I knew how to escape bores on bad dates via faked desperate phone calls (usually performed with weeping by Lily), making polite small talk and never seeing them again; I understood all out lust, and my personal favorite, building suspense that ended in rampant sexscapades. This, however, fit into the "none of the above" category.

I sighed and took another sip, but still no one moved. From the corner of my eye, I saw Maddox and Solomon exchange glances that ratcheted up to the glare level as every second passed. Maddox looked annoyed; Solomon looked amused and far too relaxed.

"So, I told Lily everything," I said to diffuse the tension.

"What?" said Maddox, his head whipping round to look at me. I waited for Solomon to say something too, but he just looked Lily over. She did some kind of jerky "Whassup?" movement with her head, while widening her eyes at him, daring him to give her attitude. I'd seen her do it to mouthy patrons when she worked the club doors. It was all posturing, sass, and don't-mess-with-me, wrapped into one move. Solomon didn't say anything, but inclined his head slightly my way, waiting for an explanation.

"It seemed prudent to tell someone," I said, avoiding Solomon's eyes and directing my comment into the middle of the room. "And Lily won't say anything."

Lily mimed zipping her mouth, locking it, and throwing away the key.

"How much paperwork will this take?" asked Solomon.

"Plenty," replied Maddox.

"Good job I didn't hear anything."

"Me too," agreed Maddox with a sigh.

"While you're all here and pretending not to hear anything," I said, glossing over their attempt at teamwork, "I found something odd that you may as well take a look at. Adam, you said to look for something out of place; and well, I found something out of place."

I walked through to the bedroom and picked up the matchbook, ignoring the notebook and my thick pad. I'd filled the pages with scribbled combinations that I worked on during the afternoon and discounted. I promised myself I would mention it soon, but I wanted to have a closer look at it before it wound up in an evidence locker somewhere.

"It's a matchbook," I said, when I rejoined them. "I haven't seen matchbooks in ages and usually they have a club or bar name or a website, a phone number, that sort of thing. But this has nothing. I just thought it was odd."

I handed the matchbook to Maddox, who looked at it, turning it over and opening it, then passing it to Solomon who did the same thing. I took it back and handed it to Lily without thinking. "I can't think of anywhere that still has matchbooks."

"That's because you don't go out enough. I know what this is," said Lily, turning the matchbook over and smiling. "So old school, right? Just like the movies! It's for a club called Flames. You see the flame insignia?" She tapped it with her forefinger.

"I've never heard of it."

"It's not exactly well known," said Lily. "It's a members' club. Did you say you found this in your boss' office?" she asked, blinking at me.

"On his desk," I said slowly, which strictly speaking, wasn't a lie. I just didn't specify *which* desk. Lily suppressed a smile, though her eyes widened and she opened her mouth to say something before clamping it shut again. "What?" I asked.

"Flames isn't your average club," Lily said.

"I can't imagine Martin Dean in any kind of club."

"You'll struggle to imagine him in this one. Flames is a sex club."

I blinked. "Pardon?"

"A sex club. You know... PVC and leather,

paddles and spanking. Dominatrixes and stuff like that."

"You have got to be kidding me." I spanned the distance between incredulous and appalled in three seconds flat.

"'Fraid not. I've worked the door there a couple of times. It's very exclusive."

I turned to Maddox. "I wonder what else Dean hid in the closet."

"Oh, he's definitely not in the closet if he's going to Flames, or even out of the closet," Lily continued as she flipped the matchbook over one more time and then passed it back to me. "It's a couples' club. Men can only go if they bring a woman with them. It ensures there's always the same amount of women and men, and it stops lecherous, loner weirdos getting in. Someone has to vouch for every member or guest. Your Martin Dean would either have been the guest of a woman, or he'd have sponsored a woman to get in."

"And they... do stuff in there?"

"No! That's illegal," said Lily, catching my intimation with a grimace of her own. "Whatever they do when they leave is up to them."

"Why did you never tell me about this?"

"It never came up!"

"It should have!" I protested. This was exactly the kind of juice Lily should have given me. However, there was something more interesting that superseded that. "So now we have a mystery woman," I mused. "Maybe part of the fraud?"

"Or someone who just likes to get spanked." Lily shrugged.

I chanced a glance at Maddox, then Solomon.

Maddox looked intrigued. Solomon looked bored. However, he could have been jumping with glee inside. It was hard to tell.

"I want to check it out," I told them.

Lily blanched. "The spanking?"

"No!" I gave her a look. "I want to know who Martin Dean let it all hang out with. I never got the impression he had a lady friend."

"It's worth a try," said Maddox. "But you should leave it up to us."

Lily flicked a glance at him. "Mmm, yes. They'll like you in there."

"Do you know the owners?" I asked Lily, ignoring Maddox's paling face. "Can you find out if Dean was a regular?"

"Sure. If that's okay?" she asked out of deference for the equal number of law enforcement versus nosy parkers in the room. Maddox nodded and Lily pulled out her cell phone and dialed, waiting while the line connected. "Hey, is that Jane? It's Lily. I know. Forever, right? Listen, I have a quick favor to ask. I know this girl who's seeing this guy and, to cut a long story short, we think he's no good. And here's the kicker. I'm sure I saw him when I worked the door at Flames. Yeah. I want to warn my girlfriend off him, if he's regular with another woman. Can you run his name against the door list for me? It's Martin Dean. Sure, I'll wait."

We waited breathlessly for Lily's friend to make her checks. Then Lily's eyes widened and she gushed a little to her friend while agreeing to switch a shift. When she clicked off, we were waiting.

"So, here's the thing. Martin Dean was a regular for the past year and he was always with the same woman. Seems they were pretty hot and heavy too. Her name is Tallulah Smith." Lily cramped her fingers into bunny ears around the name. "Sounds fake to me. It's not unusual. Not everyone wants to bare it all while they're, uh, baring it all. We're lucky Dean didn't care. My friend, Jane, said he's a watcher not a doer."

I met Maddox's eyes, trying not to think about what that meant. "This is the only way of finding her if she knows something."

"I have to get into that club," he said, nodding. "We need to find her. I don't think you should be part of this."

Lily coughed and cast a look at me. "You're going to need a woman to get inside," she reminded him.

"Me," I said.

"No way."

"Where else are you going to find a woman?"

"Where indeed?" Solomon smiled.

"And I just took tonight's door duty so I can put you on the guest list." Lily grinned. "The club is a once-a-month thing. This is the only chance you'll get before next month. Doors open in an hour."

"And your boss already knows I'm working with you," I said, with a pleased smile as I watched Maddox's mental cogs turn.

Evidently, he decided he didn't want to miss the opportunity because he said, "Fine. We'll poke around, see if anyone knows who this woman is, then we're leaving. As soon as we get a name, or our eyeballs on her, we'll leave and someone else can pick her up. We'll put a wire on you. Solomon can listen in from the car."

"I'll find you something to wear," said Lily with a

pleased clap of her hands.

"Can't I just wear a dress?" I asked.

Lily stifled a giggle and shook her head. "Oh, honey, no. You have nothing suitable. Trust me."

Ten minutes later, Lily and I stood in my bedroom. Lily had run downstairs, rifled her closet and produced a garment I can only describe as...

*Ohmygodtherewasnowayiwaswearingthat.*

Made out of a stretchy material, it was cut into a sleeveless halter-neck and ended around four inches below my butt. Worst of all, it appeared to be about ten inches long in its entirety. Hello, my old friend, Spandex.

"What am I supposed to wear under that?"

"Two Band-Aids and a thong."

"This is a joke right?" I asked, putting my hand up it. I think I saw a spark.

"Sweetie, this is practically Puritan for Flames. Wear a strapless bra and a thong," she insisted.

"A bra and hotpants," I countered, wincing at the thought of the fabric slithering up my thighs.

Lily blew out an exasperated breath. "Oh boy. You're not going to know where to look tonight."

"I don't see you telling Adam to wear a dress barely larger than a t-shirt."

"He's in black jeans and a shirt. He looks fine. The stubble is a nice touch. He'll fit right in."

"Major double standards."

"Tell me about it."

I ushered Lily out the room. After a long moment of holding the tiny dress in front of me and rethinking the plan, I exhaled long and hard. It would only last for an hour and we'd be out of there. How bad could it be? I changed quickly, pulling on the hotpants and a strapless, black push-up bra that squished my boobs up front and center. Then I pulled on the dress and smoothed it over my hips and thighs. I finished the look off with a pair of hooker heels borrowed from Lily that I hoped to God I would never have to wear again.

With my hands on my hips, staring into the mirror, I was sad to say that all the workouts and the Saturday spinning had paid off enough that I didn't have to worry about not holding back on the pasta at dinner. I just didn't think this was the moment I had worked towards, as opposed to say, having Maddox undress me and do naughty things that I would really, really enjoy.

I looked again at the hemline, already inching to my upper-thigh, despite my attempts at stretching it. I didn't want to leave the bedroom, much less go into the wide world wearing this get-up. What if my mother saw me? What if someone who knew my mom saw me? Like a TV reel in my head, I could see the car crash news now: the Graves' Hiccup spotted in full-on slutwear, cruising the streets of Montgomery, temping replaced by a life of vice. My mother would have to cancel her adult ed' classes; my father would lock and bolt the door; my brothers would probably arrest me for my own good; and Serena... Serena would point out that she had a different surname now and pretend not to know me.

I took a deep breath, reminding myself that I was dressing like a skank to get a lead on our victim and hobbled into the living room, where I was met with silence.

Maddox gulped. Solomon leaned back in the armchair. He had one long, lean leg slung across the other, and his eyes ran over me darkly from head to toe. I didn't know if he liked or loathed what he saw—and he really was seeing too much, given that the Spandex clung to every curve like a second skin—but I tried not to care.

"Jeez," breathed Adam, his eyes having a hard time leaving my boob area to look at my face.

"I can't believe I'm going to leave the house looking like this." This was also going down in my dating life as possibly one of the weirdest dates ever.

"You should have worn the thong," said Lily. "Now let's go slut up your face."

Music to my ears.

# CHAPTER EIGHT

I strained to hear the brief, not so happy, conversation between Maddox and Solomon, barely audible from the bathroom where Lily gunked up my face. After a swooping layer of black eyeliner and retro red lips, and my hair rearranged to loose, we tripped back to the living room, where it was decided that Solomon would wait outside Flames and monitor our wires, listening in on everything we said and heard. The moment wires were mentioned, the four of us spent a couple of uncomfortable (for me) minutes assessing my costume. Every time I yanked the hem down, one hand holding the top up, I was less sure that it qualified as a dress. Maddox didn't seem to mind until he saw Solomon looking long and appreciatively, and scowled at him.

"There's nowhere you can put a wire on her," pointed out Lily. "It'll bug out."

"It'll fit in her bra," said Maddox, seriously studying that region under the pretext of a technological emergency. At least, I think that's what he was doing.

Solomon looked at the piece of kit in his hand, then to my bra region, and finally met my eyes. He smiled. I lost the ability to think for a few precious seconds as my breath quickened.

"I'll fit it," said Maddox, holding out his hand to Solomon.

"Where did you get that?" I asked, proffering my hand. I didn't wait for an answer. "I'll fit it. Just tell me what to do," I said, trying not to think about Maddox's hands in my bra. Or Solomon's. Certainly not both at the same time! I bit the insides of my cheeks before they could flush as red as my lipstick.

A couple of instructions later, and the wire was transmitting and tucked, by my own hands, into the right cup, away from the sound of my heartbeat.

Solomon handed a similar one to Maddox, which he tucked under his t-shirt, fastening it to his chest with a piece of tape. After a couple of "One, two, one, twos," we were happy they were working. Some creative shuffling later (me alone in the kitchen, Lily generously offering to help Maddox) and they were switched off until needed.

Lily zoomed off to change while we went through the plan. A short time later, she reappeared looking like an Asian dominatrix in a tight, rubber dress and a black bobbed wig, her lips blood red and her face pale. "Trust me, I will not look out of place," she said at my raised eyebrow. "I'm going to head out. There's a parking lot for employees. You'll be on the guest list under fake names and I'll wave you through. I'll text you if Tallulah comes in." She clattered out, her spike heels sounding like daggers on the stairs as I wondered what else she had in her closet that I didn't know about.

We gave her an hour's head start before I jettisoned the hip-length cardigan I'd wrapped around myself in favor of a jacket. We clambered into Solomon's car, and I crossed my fingers that none of the neighbors would happen outside and see me dressed like a prostitute, despite the long coat thrown over me, as I climbed into the Lexus with two men.

Solomon drove without speaking, steering the sleek car with ease through the light evening traffic and pointing it downtown. He pulled into a space half a block from the club fifteen minutes after Lily said the doors opened.

"Seriously? You expect me to walk in these things?" I asked, pointing at the heels.

Solomon twisted around and looked down at them, his eyes running up my legs before fixing on my eyes. I shivered. "Can't you?"

"Not a half block. These are "get-in-a-car-get-out-of-a-car-and-pose" shoes." They were also "flat-on-your-back-heels-over-your-head" shoes, but I decided putting that image into Maddox and Solomon's minds probably wasn't the best idea. Lily, however, would have thought it was marvelous.

"I'll drop you outside when we're ready. You need help switching on the wire?" Solomon asked.

"No. I'm good." I wriggled out of my coat and placed it over my front, shuffling to get my hand inside my bra and switch the wire on. When I noticed Solomon watching me in the rearview mirror, I stuck my tongue out, just a little bit. He laughed, which surprised me into smiling. "Is it working?" I asked.

Solomon stuck an earbud into his ear and said, "Say something."

"C cup," I said.

"It works."

"Try mine." Maddox switched his wire on. "Eyes forward," he said.

"Not as flirty," said Solomon, "but it works."

"Safe word?"

"Scarlet."

"Done."

"Pardon? Safe word?" I asked.

Maddox twisted in his seat. "In case we get any trouble. Just work 'scarlet' into a sentence and Solomon will be alerted that we need help. It's not a typical conversational word, but it's not so crazy that it would make anyone suspicious."

"Okay. Scarlet it is."

Solomon extracted a passport-sized photograph from his jacket pocket and passed it to me. "This is a recent shot of Dean. Find someone who recognizes him and can point out Tallulah."

I took it and slipped it into the tiny purse I carried. It was just large enough to hold my lipstick, a few dollars, my cell phone and bank card. "Anything else?"

"That's all for you." Solomon checked the traffic, pulled out and drove the half block before swerving to the curb and letting us out. "I won't be far," he said, quickly glancing at me. I think he was trying to reassure me.

Flames' entrance was an anonymous black door set into a brick wall. A small emblem of a flame on the front was the only clue. Maddox gave the handle a tug and it opened. With Maddox in front, we walked up the stairs to the booth at the top where Lily waited. Before we could say anything, she checked our fake names off the guest list, stamped the backs of our hands with a flame stamp, visible only under the blacklight wand she waved over top, before signaling we could go in. The tuxedoed hulking wall of a doorman opened the door for us. I didn't even have a chance to ask if she had seen our mystery woman before she turned to a woman in a leather trenchcoat who entered right behind us.

Throbbing techno music assaulted us as soon as we entered and a sea of scantily clad bodies, both male and female, paraded in a wave of human flesh. Lily was right. My bra, hotpants and skintight dress combo was positively overdressed compared to the buttless chaps, skimpy lingerie, PVC and rubberwear, stomach-roilingly worn by both sexes. I could see dancers on a far stage performing, their movements fluid and spry as they dipped and swung around poles. A small dance floor divided them from us. Beneath the sparkling disco ball, couples gyrated, their hands freely roaming the places that should not be groped in public.

"Montgomery has a wild side," I said against Maddox's ear and he shot me a bemused glance.

"Let's start at the bar," he said, nodding in the direction of where I assumed he could see the bar over the small crowd blocking the way. As we pushed past, hands seemed to find their way onto my butt, brushing over my thighs and arms, each receiving a sharp jab from me.

As we proceeded, I turned and saw a woman bent over a chair, which wouldn't have been interesting at all, if not for the Victorian-costumed woman spanking her enthusiastically with a ping-pong paddle.

I stumbled and Maddox caught me, yanking me

past the line of the onlookers. "Make mine a double," I said.

"I think a man just groped me," said Maddox, worried lines furrowing his forehead.

"Everyone just groped me," I muttered. Somewhere, not far away, I imagined Solomon smiling.

The bar was several people deep. When I felt a hand on my arm, I jumped, expecting another groper, but instead found Lily. "Your table is ready," she said, her Geisha lips pursed. She cracked a whip. I blinked. *Where had my friend gone?*

"Our what?" I wheezed as she recoiled the whip.

"Your reservation is ready," she repeated slowly, flashing wide 'get with it' eyes before beckoning us to follow her to a small booth. As we sat down, I realized I could see across the small dance floor to the corridors that sprang off at the far end: the bar and the "entertainment" areas. We had an excellent view of the club. I sent Lily a mental pat on the head. "Your waitress will take your drinks order shortly." And with that, Lily was gone. I noticed no one dared grope her and the one hand that did get too close got a sharp sting from her whip.

"Can you imagine you-know-who in here?" I said to Maddox as he edged closer to me, his forearms resting on the table. He clasped his hands together. I felt grateful that he blocked me mostly from viewing the club, even if I were tempted to peek. Montgomery was a lot more exciting than I gave it credit for, I decided, when a man in a rubber mask and hotpants stalked past. "I wonder what Dean wore."

"I'm trying not to think about it."

"Do you think he was a rubber man or chaps?"

"Jeez."

"PVC must get pretty hot in here." I mimed peeling it off, my tongue making a wet, popping sound.

"Sounds like you know what you're talking about."

"Me?" I shook my head. "Heavens, no."

"Maybe he wore a rubber thong like that guy." Maddox nodded and I shuddered the moment my eyes hit on the skinny man in, yes, a rubber thong, incongruously paired with a pair of dress shoes and black socks.

"I didn't need to see that."

"No one does."

A woman in a black tutu with a frilly apron and an impossibly small-waisted bustier, which she was nearly popping out of suddenly blocked out our view. "I'm Ruby. Can I take your order?" she asked, before blowing a very large bubble of pink gum, which deflated after a loud pop. She sucked it in and gave us an expectant look.

I pulled the photo of Martin Dean out of my little bag and placed it flat on the table. "Actually. Maybe you can help me. Do you know this man?" I asked. Okay, it wasn't subtle but I bet my tiny dress that if anyone would recognize our man, it would be the waitress.

Ruby studied it for a moment. Her jaw stiffened and she glanced at me, then somewhere across the room, and back again. "I'm not sure," she said finally, looking from Maddox and back to me with suspicion. "What'll it be?"

Instead of a flash of uncertainty, I thought she sounded pretty definite. I rooted in my bag, pulled out a folded twenty and slid it next to the picture. "How about now?"

Ruby palmed the money in a smooth movement and it disappeared. "Yeah, he's a regular. I don't see him tonight and he's usually here by now. What did he do to you? Get a bit too frisky in the dungeon? Boyfriend gonna spank him back?"

"Uh, *no*." The idea of Maddox spanking anyone had not crossed my mind until that very moment. But now... I thought about Solomon snorting as he listened. This was a bad idea. Now, he would really think I was stupid. I took a deep breath and persisted, "Actually, I'm more interested in the woman he came with. What can you tell me about her?" Also: what was Dean into? And what was the dungeon? I *had* to ask Lily. Frankly, I had so much to ask her, I should make a list.

Ruby glanced up, quickly looking around the room, then pulled out her pen and pad. "You gotta order drinks," she said, her voice rising above the thump-thump of the track playing.

"Are we being watched?" asked Maddox.

She smiled brightly like we'd just complimented her. Definitely the right question. "You betcha. My boss likes to make money not small talk."

"Okay. Let's discuss the cocktail list..." I picked the menu off the table, adding, "and the woman."

"She's about my height. Red hair in a bob, though I think it's a wig. A lot younger than him," Ruby said, tapping her pen on the cocktail menu as though giving advice.

"Is she here tonight?"

"Yeah. I saw her ten minutes ago."

"Where?" I asked.

"She was at the bar. There was another guy with her. Not that dude." She nodded at the photo. "She's with a short guy."

"What did he look like?"

"Kinda average. White guy. Thirties, maybe. I wasn't really looking. You don't here, ya know. Unless, you... *ya know.*"

I got her point. I didn't want to "ya know." I darted a look at Maddox. Not in public anyway. "Where'd they go?" I asked.

"I dunno." She tapped her pen on the pad impatiently. "C'mon guys, you gotta order or I'll get in trouble."

"Martini," I said, placing the menu I held on the table, right over the photo, which I palmed just as smoothly.

"And a beer," added Maddox.

She jotted our order down. "Coming right up," she said, turning on her heel and sashaying away, her hips wiggling like nobody's business.

"We need to find this woman," said Maddox.

"And the guy," I said. "You think he's here for the spanky-panky? Or is he part of the gang?"

"I'm not sure I want to guess." All the while Maddox talked, his head was facing me, but I could see his eyes roaming the room. "I don't see her," he told me. He relaxed, resting his back against the padded upholstery of the booth.

Ruby, the waitress, returned, cutting off his view and we waited while she lay down cocktail napkins and our drinks. As she slid my martini in front of me, she whispered, "I just saw the woman go down the hall towards the ladies' room. The guy was with her. Not the one in the picture, the one she's here with tonight. I think he's new. He had that look about him." She looked pointedly at us. Yeah, okay, so we stuck out.

"Thanks," said Maddox as he slipped her enough money to cover the drinks and a tip. At this rate, the waitress was going to be our best friend the whole night. Not that I planned on staying that long.

"The sooner we find this woman and find out what's going on, the better," I said, after taking a sip of my martini.

"Whoa. There's no 'we' here," said Maddox. "We find this woman. You go home. We take her in for questioning."

I raised my eyebrows. "No way! You wouldn't have gotten in here without me. And you're sure as hell not getting into the ladies' bathroom." Hah. Take that, Maddox. I got up, grabbing my purse, but before I could slide around the other side of the booth, Maddox caught me by the wrist.

"Fine. I'm coming with you," he said. "I'll wait in the hall. Don't approach her. Just make sure she's in there, then come out as soon as she leaves. I'll catch her outside."

"Okay." We walked hand-in-hand to the narrow hallway that veered off, away from the dance floor, towards the bathrooms.

Just as we entered the hallway, I caught a flash of red hair by the door to the ladies'. I hurried forward, teetering in the stripper heels. A groping couple peeled away from the wall, blocking our view momentarily, and we stepped past them, avoiding eye contact when they turned to assess us. Behind them, the hallway was empty. A thought occurred to me. I really, really hoped I wasn't about to walk in on the red head and her new man doing the nasty in a public restroom, but my nosiness won out. Plastering on my game face, I ducked inside the bathroom and walked forward, hips about three inches ahead of my icked-out face and pulled-back shoulders, poised to leave the moment I heard any humping.

"Hello?" I called.

I pushed the first stall door and it opened, clanking against the stall divider before swinging shut again. Empty. I tried the second, then third. At the fourth, I got something. No woman in a red bob, but the lid of the toilet tank was slightly askew. I stepped inside and looked closer. I could see small scrape marks around the edges. The lid hadn't been moved by accident, but worked off. I peeked inside, but couldn't see anything except water and the flush mechanism.

Stepping out of the stall, I looked around. No one was in the bathroom and there weren't any security cameras.

My reflection in the mirrors frowned back at me. There was only one reason someone would have fiddled with the toilet tank on a club night, other than to fix it. It was the perfect place to hide something small.

I left the bathroom and rested my back against the wall, next to Maddox, leaning in to talk to him. "No one's in there," I said. "But I think something was hidden in one of the toilet tanks—the lid was off—and whatever it was, the red head's got it."

Maddox scanned the hallway towards the dance floor and didn't say anything about how farfetched my idea seemed, which gave him extra points. "She didn't come back out this way," he said, turning to look the other way, past me. He jerked forward, stepping past me, and jogged along the hallway. I followed him through an "Employees Only" door at the end, and saw a dark blur then a flash of red. Someone squealed. A bang, barely audible over the pumping music, rang out and Maddox broke into a run as a rush of light suddenly lit up the room as the exterior door opened and banged shut.

I barreled as fast as I could on high heels out of the emergency exit moments after Maddox. The cold night air blasted over me as I found myself on a small iron platform, one story up. I just had time to look down, see Maddox jump the last few steps off the fire escape and race into the alley, swallowed up in the darkness.

I turned, my arm knocking the door, and it banged shut. An alarm sounded inside, probably alerting someone that a door had unexpectedly opened. I sighed and looked down. Maddox was off chasing someone, and I had no hope of keeping up in the heels. I gave the door a hopeful tug, but it was shut tight.

Shivering against the cold, I wrapped my arms around myself and tutted. The only way forward was down, unless I wanted to wait for whomever to come and investigate the door opening. Clinging onto the railings, I made my way down the rickety fire escape, my spiked heels catching in the steps' iron mesh surfaces. As I hit ground zero, I pulled a face and groaned. I landed in something soft on putting my foot down. Typical. Maddox got to run after the bad guy. I got to stand in garbage, wearing a hooker dress.

Looking around me at the litter-strewn dark alley, the overflowing dumpster probably the source of the disgustingly ripe smell, I knew I was stuck. Running into the dark would be as stupid as standing still. My best hope was to make my way to the front of the club and find Lily, or wait for Maddox to pick me up there.

I took a couple of steps forward, stumbled, and with both arms flailing to steady myself, I tripped and landed palms down. "Oh, great," I mumbled in annoyance as I peeled my hands off something dark and sticky. I hoped I hadn't cut myself in the fall because God knows what was breeding in this alley, seeking a human host.

I rocked backwards, crouched on my haunches and took a deep breath, preparing to wobble back to my feet. I brushed my hands against my hotpants, my dress somewhere around my hips. I looked for something to grab onto and help me up.

My breath caught.

A pale leg protruded across the alley. Not a mannequin, not a fake limb, but something fleshy and undeniably human. Worst of all, it wasn't moving. I followed the line of the leg, past a limp knee to a scrap of fabric and higher up until I saw her face.

There was no way the red head was ever going to talk. She sat like a ragdoll propped against the wall, her fists clenched to her sides, her red wig slightly askew. Blood trickled from her mouth and dripped onto her top. Her chest bore an unmistakable bullet wound, leaving the flesh puckered around the hole. I froze, unable to move, but unable to look away. She was dead.

"Deep breaths," I whispered, trying to focus on breathing in and out as my stomach heaved and I turned away.

Maddox would not be a wimp. Maddox would look for a clue. I steeled myself as I turned back to her. Yep. Still dead. I edged closer and looked over her, when I noticed something jutting out of her hands. I reached forward gingerly and grasped the object, giving it a little tug. It slipped through her still warm fingers. In my hand, I had a small silver key ring, no fob. Flicking through them, feeling awful, I guessed the keys were to her house, her car, and two smaller ones, probably locker keys. I forced myself to check her other palm, and this time, I found a single small key. I snatched my hand back and stared at her.

God. I'd just robbed a body. Sort of.

Something rustled behind me and I glanced over my shoulder in alarm, expecting to find the shadow of her murderer looming over me. Nothing. No Maddox. No mystery man. No Solomon. Now would be the perfect time for Solomon. What was the safe word again? I scrabbled through my memory, gulping.

"Scarlet," I whispered, hoping the receiver picked up my voice. "Scarlet! Very, very scarlet," I squeaked.

The shivering took on a life of its own, and feeling sick to my stomach, I straightened up, subconsciously yanking the dress hem to a more appropriate length.

My hunch about the red head was right. Whatever happened to Martin Dean, she knew something. Maybe she knew who killed him, or what he was involved in. I looked at the single, solitary key in my hand. Perhaps he had trusted her to look after something for him? We were just too late.

Instinct kicked in and I moved the opposite direction from Maddox, to what I felt sure was the front of the club. Tripping and stumbling as I came out of the alley, I staggered into a wall of a man and almost shrieked. My fists reflexively moved to sucker punch him until I looked up and saw it was Solomon.

Throwing myself at him, I wrapped my arms around his waist and held on, relief washing through me. After a moment of him standing still and I feeling too relieved to be awkward, he put his arms around me and held me close to him. My head rested against his warm chest as his hand stroked my back. Slowly, the violent shivering stopped.

"I heard gun shots through the wire," he said. "I was looking for you when you said the safe word."

"Back there. The woman we were looking for. Tallulah. She's dead," I gasped into his shirt, clutching the material in my fingers. I had no idea how my hands ended up inside his jacket and chose not to care. He was warm, familiar... he wasn't going to shoot me. "Shot," I squeaked, blinking rapidly at the recollection of her face, frozen in death. "Someone shot her."

The back-stroking didn't stop, even as he asked, "Maddox?"

"We saw someone and he chased after him. He isn't armed! Maddox that is. Maddox isn't armed and the other guy has a gun!" Panic streaked through my voice as I babbled.

Solomon maneuvered me towards the building and detached himself, which was quite a feat given my limpet-like grip on him. Holding me by the arms, he bent his head and looked into my eyes. "I'm sure Maddox is armed. He'll be fine. Stay here. Don't move," he ordered, "I'm going to check." He took off down the alley, returning a couple of minutes later, his demeanor sober. "Let's get out of here," he said, folding me into him, only his presence stopping my knees from buckling. "Backup's on its way."

The Lexus was parked in an alley a hundred feet away. Solomon deposited me inside and went in search of Maddox. I sat huddled in the front seat, feeling cold and exposed in the skimpy garments. More than anything, I was just frightened. I scoured every shadow for the whites of a killer's eyes, every nook for a crouching figure, expecting the mystery man to leap out at any moment, his gun aimed at me. In his other hand would be Maddox's severed head. I squeezed my eyes shut.

So when the door opened, I jumped a mile. But instead of a murderer, it was Solomon. Not that his presence stopped my shivering that started up again with a vengeance. He closed the door and slipped off his jacket. Reaching over to me, he wrapped it around my shoulders. I pulled it close, and for a moment, I just closed my eyes, with my head bowed, my knees knocking together. The jacket smelled of him, fresh with the faintest scent of spice and warmed by his body heat. When I opened my eyes, he was still sitting there, just waiting patiently.

"Is Maddox okay?" I asked, afraid of what he might tell me.

"He's fine. He's waiting for the police." Solomon slipped the key in and the engine turned over. "You don't need to be part of that."

I glanced at his shadowed face. "But I found her."

"And you shouldn't have."

"I'm part of the crime scene."

"And Maddox is the police," Solomon pointed out. "I'm taking you home. No arguments."

I was too shaken up to protest. "Okay," I whispered. Reaching inside my top, I pulled out the wire, switched it off and held it until Solomon gently took it from me and pocketed it. He pulled the seatbelt around me and buckled it, making sure his jacket was still tucked around me.

Solomon turned the heat on and pointed the vents at me, warming me up. He drove slowly out of the alley between the buildings and didn't turn the lights on until we hit the street. We rode in silence all the way home. He parked outside my building, shutting off the engine and walked around to open my door.

Still stunned, I took his hand and held onto it as he followed me to the door, and stayed behind me as I walked up to my apartment, opening the locks like a robot, thoroughly attuned to doing it automatically.

"I'll be okay from here," I said.

"All the same, I'd rather make sure."

I stepped inside and held the door open for Solomon to pass through. I followed him into the living room and sank onto the couch. I pulled off my ridiculous shoes and tossed them into the corner; then I shrugged off Solomon's jacket and folded it over the arm of the couch.

"I've gotta get out of this," I said, waving a hand at my outfit. It seemed puerile, after seeing the dead woman, for me to be dressed up, like I was playing undercover spy in a game. More than anything, seeing her dead eyes drove it home that this wasn't fun. It wasn't a break from real life. It wasn't pleasurable anymore or something to entertain Lily with or to stop me from being bored at the office. Someone was killing people and it was too close to comfort for me.

I took a deep breath, swore I wouldn't cry in front of Solomon and retreated to my bedroom. I peeled off the dress and hotpants, tossing them into the hamper. Something dropped to the floor and I blinked at the noise, then looked down. I'd forgotten all about finding the keys. Stooping down, I picked them up, and for a moment, just held them while trying not to break down. I wanted to pull on my jammies and crawl into bed, squeeze my eyes shut and pretend it was a nightmare, but I couldn't do that with Solomon waiting in the living room. So, instead, I pulled on jeans, a sweatshirt and thick socks and went into the bathroom to scrub off the makeup and wash my hands.

I took my time, half expecting Solomon to leave, but when I returned to the living room, he was waiting for me. Sitting half reclined in the armchair, one leg slung casually over the other, his hands folded behind his head, he looked utterly at ease.

"I'm feeling better," I said. "You really don't need to babysit me."

"I know," he said, but didn't make any gesture to leave.

"Beer?" I suggested, because I sure as hell needed one. The wine earlier and the sip of martini weren't enough to fortify me. Ethanol would probably have worked, but I was fresh out.

"Sounds good."

I padded out of the living room and opened the refrigerator, skirting past the leftovers tub from my mother to reach the beer. Maddox's and my plates were by the sink, but I would deal with those in the morning. I pulled out two bottles for Solomon and me, snapping the caps off before walking back into the living room. I flopped onto the couch, passing a bottle to Solomon, as I took a long swig on mine. I was really tempted to chug it.

"Tell me what happened," said Solomon when I opened my eyes again.

I told him about seeing the woman, then checking out the bathroom and finding the toilet tank lid askew, but she was already gone. I told him Maddox spotted them heading out back and followed the couple out to the alley when we heard the shot. "If we assume Dean was part of the fraud, and she was his girlfriend or something, he must have given her something to hide," I said, "But I don't know what. It must have been really small."

"Or in a waterproof bag," suggested Solomon.

"I guess. Whatever it was, Dean didn't want to keep it at home or at work." I took another swallow. "You heard everything the waitress told us. Any clues?"

"Not one."

"This sucks." I pulled the keys out of my jeans pocket and passed them to Solomon. "These were in Tallulah's hand when I found her and this little key too. I don't know why I picked them up. I just did."

Solomon examined them and came to the same conclusion as me. "House and car keys. I'll let Maddox know to look out for her car. It's probably parked nearby. What are the smaller keys?"

"You tell me. Maybe a locker?"

"Too small."

I straightened up. "Could it be something useful?"

"Maybe."

"You think Lily is okay?" I felt bad for leaving her behind, even though I knew she had her own car parked in the employee's secure lot and planned to drive home alone anyway at closing time, long after we were gone.

"Maddox called while you were in the bedroom. The club's been shut down and everyone has been detained. Your friend is still there."

"I've seen two dead people in a week," I said, draining my bottle. "Have you seen dead people?"

"Too many."

"Oh." It was probably best not to dwell on that. "Is Solomon your first name or last?"

"Last."

"What's your first?"

He looked at me for a long time. Just when I started to regret asking, he said softly, "John."

Maddox arrived an hour, and two beers, later. After a brief discussion in hushed voices in the hallway, Solomon left without saying goodbye, although I didn't have the energy to be irked, and Maddox walked in.

"How're you holding up?" he asked, sitting next to me and pulling me into his arms.

I held up my bottle and gave him a lopsided smile. "Marvelous," I said with a hiccup, then a yawn. The fright had worn off and sleep beckoned. I hoped I wouldn't dream tonight. "What happened?"

"I saw the guy and ran after him, but he gave me the slip so I walked back to where I left you, but you'd gone and Solomon was there. The body you found was Tallulah, Dean's girlfriend."

"I guessed. She was shot." Of course, he knew that. He'd seen her. I just couldn't get past it.

"The crime scene investigators are doing their thing and Montgomery PD are questioning everyone in the building. Lily won't be home for a while, but I had someone check on her and she's okay."

"Why didn't you stay?" I waited for him to say,

'because he wanted to be with me.'

"I didn't want to blow my cover."

*Oh, well.*

"Did you see who shot her?"

"Barely. White guy, shorter than me. Almost certainly the same man the waitress saw."

"So that narrows it down to, what? Forty percent of Montgomery?"

"Yeah."

I thought about that for a moment. Whoever this guy was, he would be almost impossible to find, given our vague description. I doubted anyone in the club saw anything, except maybe the waitress. Everyone else was concentrating on the performers or bumping and grinding on the dance floor. If he were an average guy, no one would have paid him a second glance. Our best witness was dead. For the second time, I thought about the keys.

"I found keys in her hand and gave them to Solomon."

"He said. Maybe she was getting ready to go back to her car or..."

"Maybe she thought she could fight the guy off?"

"With just her keys?"

"It would be the only weapon she had." I made a jabbing motion.

"Some weapon," said Maddox.

I uncurled my legs and walked into the kitchen, pouring myself a large glass of water. Maddox followed me and leaned against the doorjamb, waiting.

"You know, a key could have been hidden in the toilet tank," I said. "It's small. It wouldn't be damaged by the water. If Dean trusted her and he knew she could only hide something in there if he were with her, and could only pick it up if she had a guy, him, with her, he might have had her hide something," I babbled. "He might figure it was safer than keeping it at home or the office."

Maddox nodded. "Sounds plausible. I'll check with the M.E. to see if her hands were wet when they got to her."

"That wouldn't matter," I pointed out. "She could have dried her hands on her dress or a paper towel."

"Why didn't her attacker take the key with him, if that's what he wanted?"

"Maybe we disturbed him?" I suggested. "It could only have been seconds between her getting shot and you running outside."

"I didn't even see her. I just took off after him. He could have grabbed it from her."

"Maybe she wouldn't give it up. Maybe she knew he would kill her if she gave it to him. Maybe she was bargaining?"

"There wasn't a lot of time to bargain," Maddox pointed out.

"Not by the time they were outside," I said. I drank the water and turned to pour myself another glass. I didn't want a hangover in the morning on top of everything else. "Maybe she was bargaining the whole time? 'I'll get you the key—if that's what it was—and you let me live.' That sort of thing."

"But she had her keys in her hand."

I smiled. "The guy didn't go into the bathroom though. He waited outside, like you did. Tallulah could have gone in and switched the keys. She could have put the mystery key on her keyring and given him a different one. One of them wasn't on her keyring. Or maybe she just wanted to confuse him."

"Why would she do that?"

"Bargaining still, or to confuse him," I said. "He might not have known what he was looking for. Or maybe she didn't know Dean was dead yet."

"Maybe."

"Maybe she wouldn't give up the keys," I continued, even though I started to think we were talking in circles now, "so the murderer had to kill her too. What if he was going to grab them when we came out? He'd have to take off when he saw you."

"If that's true. He'll still need the key. It's a long shot."

"What would he need to do to get the keys now? If that's what he wanted all along?"

"Normally, they'd go with the body to the morgue. The M.E. would put all the effects together for the next of kin, if we don't need it as evidence. If it's evidence, it goes to the evidence locker."

"So... if he hasn't gotten them already, there's no way he could get the key now Solomon has them?"

"It's unlikely," agreed Maddox. "You did right picking them up."

It didn't feel right, not one bit, plucking the keys out of Tallulah's dead hands.

# CHAPTER NINE

I had no recollection of crawling into bed and passing out. When I woke up, Maddox was clattering around in the kitchen, singing softly and a large glass of water was on my nightstand. I rolled my thumping head to eye the pillow adjacent to mine. No indentations. Despite that, my jeans had magically disappeared, but my sweatshirt was still in place. I changed into clean jeans and a fresh top before dragging a brush through my hair, and tumbling into the bathroom to splash some water on my face.

"I made scrambled eggs," said Maddox when I wandered through, yawning, noting the reappearance of my jacket on the rack in the entryway as I passed by. "And tea. You don't have a lot of food. What do you eat?"

"Food that people bring mostly," I said. "You... stayed over?" *Again*, I stopped myself from saying. Strangely, I didn't mind that he'd stayed. It was nice having company. Definitely reassuring after last night.

"Yeah. We made passionate love, then fell asleep.

You were an animal." He watched my mouth drop open as I tried to remember any shenanigans, then laughed when my eyes continued to flit. "You fell asleep on the couch, so I put you in bed. I slept on the couch."

"Ah."

"I didn't want to leave you on your own." Maddox thrust the plate of eggs at me and added two slices of toast.

"Thanks." I wasn't sure if I was thanking him for breakfast, or taking care of me. Both, I thought. It was pretty considerate, given everything we'd been through in the last few days. I would have felt horrible waking up to an empty apartment. I wondered if Lily was okay and if she were downstairs yet.

He gathered up his own plate and the mugs, nudging me towards the living room.

"Sorry for passing out on you," I said.

"No need for apologies. Two bodies in one week is cause for a good drinking session."

"Never again," I moaned as my head thumped when I sat at my small dining table. Normally, I squashed it into the corner of the room, a nod to civilized eating that satisfied my mother, on the rare occasions she came over. Today it seemed nice. Nicer still with Maddox.

"Bodies or drinking?"

"Both."

"I have an ulterior motive for staying over," Maddox confessed. "I need to take your statement and I didn't want to drive all the way home, then back again."

For some reason, I hadn't really thought about

Maddox having his own home, much like I couldn't imagine Solomon living in a neat, one-family unit. I wondered how Maddox decorated it, and what he liked. "Where do you live?" I asked.

"Harbridge," he said.

"Alone?" I asked.

"Is this your way of asking if I'm a mommy's boy?"

"Are you?"

"No, I have my own place. I even do my own laundry."

"I bet your mother is proud."

"She is."

I shoveled the buttery eggs into my mouth, swallowed, and demolished a piece of toast, washing it all down with a hot gulp of sugary tea. Finally, I pushed the plate to one side and slumped in my seat.

"How's the head?" asked Maddox. He munched a slice of toast and a little butter caught in his lip. I thought about licking it off.

"It's okay. I didn't drink that much."

"It was probably the shock."

"Probably," I agreed, waiting as he ate his breakfast. When he finished, I took our plates into the kitchen and refreshed our mugs. "Let's get this over with," I said and Maddox retrieved his notepad and a digital recorder.

An hour later, Maddox was gone, my statement on tape. He said he'd type it up himself and make sure it remained confidential until the investigation was complete. Tallulah, as we still called her, would also remain a confidential case until then. At some point, I would probably have to testify, but I tried not to think about that. I hadn't actually *seen* either murder, just the immediate aftermath. I hadn't even seen Tallulah's murderer up close, so my testimony wouldn't be the concrete evidence a prosecutor could use anyway.

I cleaned the kitchen, phoned Lily and left a message before going back to bed for the rest of the day. My phone rang a couple of times, but I let the answering machine pick up the messages. One was from Lily, saying she was fine, and the police had been very nice, and she was staying in bed to catch up on sleep. The other was my mother asking if I knew where to get a belly-dancing outfit. I didn't.

I wanted to enjoy a day in bed too, but instead of sleeping, my mind whirred with possibilities. Finding the bodies had been horrible, but I couldn't help thinking about the key, the numbers in the notebook, and the missing money. I wanted to know what was going on under my nose.

I had the urge to call in sick on Monday and spend another day hiding under my quilt, but my commitment to work seemed to have increased tenfold, now that I had the discovery of two bodies under my belt. A day of wallowing had taken me from fear to anger to resolute determination to find out what the hell was going on.

Looking in the mirror, I couldn't believe that two nights ago, I had been a half-dressed slut, and today I looked... well, pretty damn stylish in red pants, a cream blouse and cute, two-tone heels. I got up early to blowdry my hair, sweep it into a ponytail, grab my beige tote, and leave. Downstairs, all was quiet in Lily's apartment so I figured she was still asleep. Not me though. I had murderers to catch, and today, I planned on talking to everyone in the office.

As I rode up the elevator with three call center monkeys, I added a quick chat to their supervisor to my list. My reasoning was pretty simple, someone had passed the fraudulent claims through the department and I wanted to know how, as well as who. I suppose I could have asked Maddox, but somehow, I thought he probably wasn't telling me everything, given that I wasn't PD or FBI. I was just a blonde temp who had the unfortunate habit of being in the wrong place at the wrong time.

After logging on and ensuring Maddox wasn't around yet, I decided to start with Dean's assistant.

"Hey, Dominic," I said, coming to a stop in front of his desk. Behind him, the doors to Dean's office remained firmly shut.

"Hey," said Dominic, looking up and checking out my ensemble. For a couple of weeks, I thought Dominic was on the other team, then I was informed that he was in the metrosexual camp. I still had no idea what that meant, except he seemed to enjoy fashion and gossip, and had an eye for the ladies. He was single, kinda cute and an efficient guard dog to Dean's office, which he pretty much ran when Dean wasn't around. I had a hard time envisaging him putting together a multi-million dollar fraud scheme, even if he managed Dean's personal diary and correspondence closely.

"Dean still not back?"

"No." Dominic leaned forward. "I'm kinda worried, you know. I have to book his travel and hotel for next week, and he's so particular, but I can't get in touch. Do I book it? Or wait until he gets back?"

"Book it," I said. So what if Dean would never

use them? It was company money. Besides, I wasn't supposed to know he was dead.

Dominic nodded, so apparently, I'd given the right answer. "I'll book everything he had last time. He didn't complain."

"Does he ever take a girlfriend with him?" I asked.

Dominic frowned. "Not that I know of. I don't think he even has a girlfriend, but he wouldn't tell me, I guess. Why?"

"Just wondered." Come to think of it, I hadn't seen any photos in Dean's house of Tallulah or anything else feminine around. Maybe she didn't stay over, or he was just super tidy. Whatever their relationship was, he clearly trusted her to do more than just spank him.

"I can't imagine Martin getting romantic. I don't think he even stretches his expenses. You would not believe what some of the secre... uh, executive assistants in the building get asked to do."

"Like what?" Clearly, I'd caught Dominic in a gossipy mood.

Dominic leaned in. "Flowers, chocolates, jewelry. And not just to their wives." He winked and I tried to look appropriately scandalized. "You remember when David Bernard got fired?"

I shook my head.

"Oh, right. It was before you started. Bernard got a little frisky with his accounts. A meal here, drinks there with clients. Then a meal here, a champagne there with his girlfriend... both of them. Dean clamped down on the expense account after that, and even he isn't exempt."

"So you'd say he's pretty honest with money

then?" I pretended to examine my nails and look disinterested.

"Yeah. Between you and me, he's got a big mortgage and some expensive habits, but he draws a good salary and his pension package is one nice kiss-off. Sally-Anne, in accounts, told me."

"How do you know about his expensive habits?"

"I opened his Amex a couple times."

"Anything naughty?"

"Oh, you!" Dominic laughed. "Martin Dean is a man's man. Imported cigars, a tailor, racing cars, fine wines and some seriously old whiskey for ten thousand bucks."

"Wow. I don't get the cigars or whiskey thing, but I'd like a tailor. He must make a good dinner guest," I mused.

"Honey, you don't need a tailor. You'd make a paper bag look good." Dominic waved a hand over me. "Loving the outfit today. Very retro. Very foxy lady."

"Oh, shush." I preened anyway.

"I hate to ask, but do you have time today to do some typing for me? I have to type up Dean's notes from the executive meeting, and I still have to organize next month's brokers conference. It's a bore of a chore."

"Sure. Hand it over."

"You're a star." Dominic handed me a blessedly slim file and blew me a kiss as I retreated to my own desk.

Okay, so far as I could see, Dominic did not have one mean, murderous bone in his body and now I knew a little more about the big boss. Ten thousand dollar whiskeys needed a good salary to keep up; and after seeing his house and the location, I already knew it was pricey. Now I knew the mortgage cost a pretty penny too. I could imagine Dean wanting to grease the wheels with a little extra. He did have a lifestyle to keep up. An expensive one. The only thing I hadn't gotten was any information on his personal life. Who did Dean hang out with? Who were his friends? And what was the deal with Tallulah? On first glance, she didn't seem like the type of woman Dean would take home to meet his mother. But she was clearly the type of woman he possibly got it on with regularly, given the waitress' comments and what Lily gleaned from her colleague.

I checked Maddox's desk, but he still hadn't come in yet; so I dropped Dominic's typing on my desk, swiped off the floor and took the elevator down to the call center.

A burst of noise hit me as I entered the room. Row after row of people, like robots penned behind desks, wore headsets as they carried on one-sided conversations, their fingers flying across keyboards to dumb terminals. I looked around, spotting the nearest supervisor and walked over, waggling my fingers in greeting. I knew Scott from Green Hand's summer party and he always made a point of saying hi to me.

He looked up from his screen as I approached and smiled. "Hi, Lexi. What can I do for you?"

" I just have a couple questions about claims. Just something that cropped up while I was typing up a, uh, report on the claims process."

"Is this about the new process they're testing?" Scott sighed, leaning back in his padded chair. He was in his late twenties and still dreamed of escaping the call center pen. I took Lily to see him play guitar with his band a month earlier and had a strong suspicion he'd taken a fancy to her, making him the best person for me talk to right now.

"Oh, no, I don't think so. Did something change recently?"

"Yeah, a bunch of claims were siphoned off through another branch. They should have come to us because they're in our area, but there was some kind of test being run on a sample."

"What kind of test?"

Scott shrugged. "I don't know. I keep expecting to get the reports, but this test has been running for nearly a year. It's a real pain. It sounds a lot more streamlined, so I was hoping we could use it here too."

"How is it more streamlined?"

"It just cuts a lot of the red tape we have to wade through. It's supposed to be some kind of service that collates everything for the customer so they get their claim payout faster."

"I don't follow."

"Instead of us having to chase down the police reports or the fire department, this service sends out automated requests and faxes the reports in, getting them on the system. It could cut our case time by thirty percent and the customers get their checks faster."

"That sounds pretty good."

"I know, right? I've been trying to get a report of the progress, but when I called the Boston office, no one had even heard of it. Maybe they pulled the plug already, but I'd like to at least look over the report and see what happened. I asked Martin Dean about it, but he said it was confidential."

"You want me to ask Dominic about it?"

"Oh no. You know, I'm not sure I was supposed to have said anything. I guess I'll find out eventually. So, what was your question?"

"I just wanted to know what happens when you get a fraudulent claim."

"That's easy. We get people trying it all the time. First, we check them against the claims register internally, then externally. We don't insure people with prior fraud convictions, but sometimes they slip through the net; plus, we have to log every claim so that two policies don't pay out on the same compensation request. That's fraudulent too. If it's damage, we usually need a proof of purchase or some evidence thereof. Sometimes we send out an investigator, especially in the high cost claims, to check that everything looks okay. Basically, if there's a problem, we have to get more information before we can pay out."

"What kind of information?"

"Receipts. Home photos with the claimed item in. Statements from householders. Those sorts of things."

"Burglary and malicious damage, too?"

"Yes and fire damage. We need crime and fire reports along with receipts. We need to make sure the householder wasn't at fault, or caused the damage themselves to try and get some quick cash, or an upgrade on their TV, or whatever. Our car insurance department, that's the Boston office too, had a problem with a hit-and-run gang writing off cars a while back. All over-insured junkers. It was in the news about two years ago."

"I think I remember that." It had been a pretty big

deal. The gang had claimed more than a quarter million dollars before the insurers got wise. It wasn't just Green Hand Insurance that was targeted; it had been a statewide problem.

"Do you need anything else?" asked Scott.

"No, that's it," I said. "Thanks. You've really helped out."

"Anytime, Lexi. Let me know if you hear anything about that test process."

"Sure."

"And say hi to Lily from me."

"I will."

I chewed on Scott's comments as I waited for the elevator. When I stepped in, lost in my thoughts, I looked up to find Maddox, so I made a point of looking at my watch.

"I had a briefing," he said.

I imagined Maddox wearing briefs and flushed. "Hot in here," I said. He looked at me oddly as the doors closed. "Did you know Martin Dean liked to drink ten thousand dollar whiskey?" I asked.

Maddox whistled. "Must be some nice stuff."

"Are you a whiskey drinker?"

"No. Beer is my poison."

"Dean had some expensive habits." As we glided up, I repeated what Dominic told me. "Do you think his salary could have supported that?"

"Maybe. We didn't see any red flags on his financials. Not much in the way of savings though."

"What about his pension? Dominic said it was good."

"Basic would be my opinion, and a nice kiss-off from Green Hand when the time came," said Maddox, confirming roughly what Dominic had related from Sally-Anne in accounts.

"I wonder what he planned to live on when he retired. He must have had..." I counted on my fingers, "nine years to go? He didn't sound like a man who could live on a basic pension, despite the extras, and Dominic said his mortgage was hefty."

"I agree," said Maddox as the elevator shuddered to a halt and the doors opened. I caught him by the sleeve, halting him before we could enter the office. "I just spoke to Scott in the call center downstairs. He said there was a test process for streamlining insurance claims. It seems like it was some kind of secret program. I think it sounds fishy."

Maddox frowned. "I haven't heard anything about this."

"It's supposed to be running out of the Boston office, but Scott said when he called, they hadn't heard anything about it."

"I'll look into it. Good work, Lexi."

"Thank you. Did you hear anything about Saturday?" Somehow, I couldn't say "murder" without getting a lump in my throat.

"I'll get a report later."

"Will you tell me about it?"

"Yes."

The door opened then and Bob plodded out, nodding to us on his way to the men's room.

"Back to work," said Maddox, his voice business-like, and I followed him through the doors, splitting off to head towards my desk.

After completing Dominic's typing and ditching it on his desk, I went in search of Anne, but she'd gone home sick, so I stopped by Bob's desk.

"Hey, Bob."

"Hi, Lexi." He looked over one shoulder, then the other one, and beckoned me closer. "You any good at cryptic crosswords?"

"I'm craptic at cryptic."

"Too bad. I'm stuck on eight down. What can I do for you?"

"I heard something about a new secret insurance process that Green Hand was testing. You hear anything about it?"

"Nope. Who told you that?"

"Overheard some gossip."

"Probably just that. Your contract up or something?"

"Or something." It was a rolling contract, but once Dean's death was announced, who knew? I quite liked Green Hand. The work was easy, the people were nice. I might not be so lucky on my next assignment.

After taking a look at Bob's crossword, I gave up and went back to my desk. I had clues, but I didn't know what to do with them, so I got stuck into typing something else Dominic had sneakily slipped onto my desk, a Post-it with a smiley face on top, and I mindlessly typed while I worked out what to do next.

~

In all the commotion last week, I'd completely forgotten about handing in my timecard. I didn't even think about it until I rooted in my desk drawer for hidden candy mid-afternoon and saw the card flit across the cluttered drawer. After Maddox signed it, ignoring my billing for the afternoon I'd spent meeting his team, he looked it over once more, and erased my time out the night we discovered Dean's body. He carefully wrote in four p.m. and I blanched at my mistake, but didn't say anything.

One more sign off to go and the dollars would be hitting my account. With a glad heart, and the thought of fresh groceries and paying my rent, I paused by Vincent's desk and waited. After a moment or two of foot shuffling, I realized he had ear buds firmly wedged in his ears. Tapping him on the shoulder, I suppressed a giggle when he leapt half a foot into the air before swiveling around and yanking the ear buds out, his face red.

"Oh... hey, Lexi," he said, a smile breaking out as he ran a hand through his hair. His bald spot seemed to be expanding by the day. He tried really hard to be popular, but he had an issue with personal space, or more precisely, staying out of other people's. He didn't take hints well either. I decided to wrap this up quick.

"Hey, Vincent. I..."

"I'm rocking out to Nickleback," he interrupted, his head making a funny little thrusting movement, like a strutting rooster.

"Sounds like Bon Jovi to me."

Vincent's face fell.

"I like Bon Jovi."

"You do?" His face lit up as he seized the first thing in common between us.

"Sure. What's not to love? Big hair, big songs." I flapped the timecard between us hopefully.

"I think they all got haircuts," Vincent said, ignoring the card.

"Too bad."

"I have tickets to their comeback tour. Do you... want to go with me?"

"Oh, hey, well, I... gee," I spluttered, for once, at a

loss for words. Vincent and me out? Together? "Don't they have to go away to do a comeback tour?"

"I have no idea. We could grab some dinner, too, maybe." Vincent shrugged casually, but his eyes looked hopeful.

How hard could it be? Vincent might not be the guy of my dreams, but I could do a concert and a burger without talking commitment. "Sure," I said. "Sounds like fun."

"I'll give you my number and you can give me yours, and I'll let you know the deets." Vincent did a funny little hand move in his attempt at talking street. So, he had a haircut geeks wouldn't sport, but he was down with the kids, clearly. He scrabbled on his desk for a notepad, then a pen, his hands shaking slightly as he scribbled his number. He tore off the sheet, passed it to me, then extended the phone pad and I gave him my number, hoping I wasn't about to regret it. If Vincent wanted to be phone buddies, I would have to get a new number.

"Cool car," I said, nodding to the neatly clipped magazine pages Vincent had pinned on the felt walls of his cubicle. They all featured the same sleek Lamborghini Spyder in cherry red.

"She's a beauty," Vincent said reverently, his finger reaching to trace across the page. "I'll get her right before the concert."

"Wowsers." Wowsers indeed. The car easily cost six figures. I hadn't thought Vincent made that much, but clearly, company accountants did better than I assumed, unless he had a secret family fortune squirreled away. It was the same car that my car grew up wanting to be.

"Originally I wanted a DeLorean, but she is a

million times better."

"Sure is. Can you sign this, please?"

Vincent scribbled his signature next to Maddox's on my timecard. "And you'll be the first person I take for a spin in it," he said, looking up.

Well, I was a lucky girl indeed. "Looking forward to it. Later, Vincent."

"The seats recline," he called after me.

*Barf.* I pretended not to hear while hoping he was joking.

Maddox was waiting for me by my desk when I got back. "Hot date?" he asked as I dropped into my chair and foot walked to pull myself under the desk.

"Shut up," I scowled.

Maddox leaned over me, a pile of papers in his hand. That working together ruse was starting to wear thin for me, but as I spared a quick look from the corners of my eyes, I noticed everyone else focused on their monitors, fingers tapping away on keyboards. Maddox lowered his voice. "Seriously? He asked you out?"

"Yes! At least, I think he did. We're going to a concert." My voice edged into a higher octave.

"The man has balls."

"Why? You think I'm a bad date?"

"No. I think he has balls for asking a hot chick like you out."

"Yeah? I don't see you asking me on a date." That was two pretties, and one hot, not that I was counting. And Saturday, I'd decided while wallowing yesterday, didn't count as a date, unless someone said the "d" word.

Maddox's voice was low, but softer when he said, "You want to go on a date with me?"

"Nooo." *Oh, God, yes, please.* The impromptu dinner at my apartment had been pretty good. It would have been a whole lot better obviously without Solomon and Lily crashing it, not to mention ending with a dead body, along with pretty much everything else in between at Flames. Unless Maddox had seriously bad dating mojo, that was unlikely to happen twice. I hoped.

"I'll take you out when this is all over." Maddox smiled and my cynical insides melted a little. "I know where to get the best pizza in town."

"Monty's Slices. Everyone knows that." I picked up my stapler and attacked the pile of papers in front of me.

"Damn. How about Thai? I'll pick you up."

"I can live with that."

"Look at you. Five minutes, two dates." Maddox walked away before I could staple his tie to my desk. Inside, I felt pretty damn pleased with myself. I had a real date with a sexy cop.

# CHAPTER TEN

Maddox had already disappeared by five so I snuck out early and went home. My answering machine flashed with messages and I pressed "play" as I unbuckled my heels and lined them up by the door.

The first was from my mother, reminding me that Thursday night dinner had switched to Saturday because she had a crochet class; and did I remember her message about the belly-dancing outfit? Thankfully, I had forgotten all about that, its importance eclipsed by the corpses in my life. The second message was from Garrett, asking me to babysit Friday night. I deleted that one, then thought better of it and called him back. I left him a message saying I couldn't, but I would the Friday after and they could even stay out post midnight. I didn't feel comfortable looking after the kids while there was a murderer on the loose, one who might have an unhealthy interest in my reports, and thus, me. I felt confident I could look after myself, if threatened; but I wasn't sure about other people, and I'd never forgive myself if the kids got in the middle of it. Of course, there was a strong chance I'd change my mind if the kids pulled any tricks on me.

The third message was from Lily, saying hi. Finally, I pulled out my cell phone and there was a missed call from Maddox, but no message. I felt very popular all of a sudden. Instead of calling him back, I got my notes with Serena's demands and called the suppliers, double-checking everything was still on schedule for the baby shower. It had been surprisingly easy to organize, and I was half afraid something was about to go horribly wrong.

After I checked off my list, I called Lily back and asked her if she wanted to have a sandwich with me. Ten minutes later, she knew everything I knew from my day of snooping.

"I might call Scott. He was cute," she said after I remembered to tell her that he said hi.

"He's nice," I agreed. "I like him." And he was more available than my brother, but probably better not to mention that and send Lily mooning over Jord again.

"You know what I think?" she said.

"Tell me."

"I think we should stake out Anne."

"Why?"

"Did she look ill this morning?"

"No."

"Exactly. Maybe she's got the money? Maybe she's gone to hide it."

I couldn't imagine that somehow. Anne was mousey, past fifty and wouldn't say boo to a goose. But I hadn't gotten to speak to her and she was on my "unofficial suspects" list along with everyone else.

It was strange that Anne went home. "I don't think I've ever seen her sick," I told Lily.

"Exactly," she drawled.

"She lives on Burlington Avenue," I said. "I mailed some letters for her once and she had these cute little address stickers. Let's go check her out."

"You think she could have hired hit men and set them on Dean?"

I thought about it. Then I thought about Dean's secret hanky-spanky lifestyle. Really, who knew what other people were capable of? "Maybe," I said.

I drove, seeing as my car was slightly more inconspicuous than Lily's turquoise Mini, and pulled onto Burlington, around four houses away from Anne's, just as she was coming out of her house. She carried a large bag and seemed in a hurry as she climbed into a maroon sedan, gunning the engine and pulling out.

"I don't want to break in," I said. "It doesn't seem right while Anne is alive." Also, Maddox might not be as lenient. The lights were still on in the house and a shadow moved across the window. Someone was in.

"Yeah, plus I don't want to find any more bodies. Let's follow her. Maybe she's making a run for it. Maybe the bag is stuffed with money."

"It didn't look heavy," I said.

"How heavy are millions?" Lily tapped on the dashboard and pointed after Anne. "She's going to make a turn."

"I don't know. I've never carried more than two hundred bucks and that was a really good week." I pulled out and followed, keeping a few car lengths behind Anne. We trailed her out of her neighborhood, heading downtown, staying a firm two cars behind her the whole time until she pulled into a parking lot at the Elms Community Recreation Center. I pulled in after her, just as she climbed out the car and leaned into the back. We parked on the far side of the lot and stared.

Leaning forward, we both watched as Anne pulled the bag out, hurrying around the side of the building.

"Definitely not making a run to the airport," I said.

"Maybe it's the drop?" Lily gasped, opening the door. The overhead light pinged on. "Are you armed?"

I scrabbled in my tote for any kind of weapon and found nothing. "Only with my wit," I said, climbing out after Lily and beeping the car shut.

"Well, bring it." Lily shot off across the lot and I followed her in a half run, slowing to walk along the shadowed path to the front of the building. Lily pressed herself against the wall, to one side of the porch, and whispered, "She went inside."

"Guess we'll have to go in too."

The porch was dark, and one fluorescent light flickered in the lobby. The walls were littered with flyers and announcements for exercise classes and community events; and the only door that didn't lead to a kitchenette or bathrooms was straight ahead.

I pulled the door cautiously and peeped inside, jumping when a large woman coiffed in beehive hair with a silk flower stuck in it, appeared before us.

"Are you the new girls?" she asked, clapping her hands together.

"Uh... yes?" I said, my eyes riveted on her hair. It seemed to be hovering over her head like a spaceship.

"Fabulous! Wonderful!" She leaned closer. "Is this

your first time?"

"Yes?" I said, my voice sliding upwards in scale. First time for what? I wanted to ask. I couldn't remember the last time someone asked me that about anything.

"Great. Did you bring your costumes?"

"Pardon?"

"Your costumes, ladies."

"No, sorry. We didn't realize," said Lily, trying to edge her way past in order to get a better view.

"Oh, well. Maybe you just want to watch?"

"Yes!" I latched onto that gratefully. Watching I could do. Participating might prove a problem, given that I couldn't fathom what Anne was doing under the dim illumination. Across the room was a small stage, with a couple of women milling around on it.

"Well, alright. You can sit over there. Hello, ladies!" she called as the door opened behind us and we were swept forward.

"What the hell is going on?" asked Lily as we slunk along the back wall. "This doesn't look like a drop site. Do you think they're all in on it? Like one of those bad ass female gangs?"

I looked at the women. I couldn't see that somehow. They all looked like, well, normal, but then who could tell? Maybe they were gang moms. "You watch too much television." I picked out two chairs and pushed them into the corner.

"Do not."

"Do too."

We shut up then because the music started up, a big bass streaming through the speakers. A flutter of movement on the stage at the far end of the room drew my attention. Seven women stood in a vee formation; front and center; but dressed in a black corset, a skirt that wasn't much more than a ruffle of material, fishnets and Victorian-style lace-up boots was Anne! Her hair was swept back, her cheeks rouged, glasses gone, and she looked far from the dowdy Anne I knew. Like the other women, she held two large feather fans. Beehive woman stood on the floor below the stage and called time. Working as one, they danced, stomped, and high kicked around the stage, the fans working over time during the more risqué moments.

"Anne does burlesque?" I whispered incredulously.

"Well, she sure is shaking it!" Lily clapped.

We watched, captivated, as they went through the routine again, this time ending with Anne disappearing behind the fans and reappearing in only her lingerie. It was like a car crash moment. I wanted to look away, but I couldn't. I had to keep looking even as my jaw dropped open. Beside me, Lily whooped and all eyes shot in our direction. Anne took one look at me, panic registering in her eyes and she hurried off stage.

"Time to go," I said and we slunk towards the door.

"Lexi?" I halted at Anne's voice, Lily slid into me, and straightened up.

"Oh, *hiiii!*" I said, far too enthusiastically.

"What are you doing here?" Anne had wrapped a short robe around herself, her fishnets peeking out from underneath.

"We were...just...um..."

"Are you thinking about joining the troupe? We need a couple more." Anne looked from me to squint at Lily, sizing up our burlesque potential.

"It looks too energetic for me. Lily wanted moral support to check it out." Next to me, Lily nodded like a bobble-head. "I thought you were ill?" I said.

"Oh, please," Anne rolled her eyes, batting off my suspicion. "Like you've never snuck out when you're supposed to be working."

"Touché," I conceded, wondering if everyone on the team knew about my slacker habits. "Do you know where belly-dancing outfits are sold?" I asked, remembering my mother's message.

Anne frowned. "There's a dance shop near the train station. They have all kinds of stuff. I've seen those sarongs with the sequins. That could work."

"Thanks."

"We rehearse every Monday and Thursday at seven," said Anne. "Come and try it. We've all learned some great new moves for the bedroom." And with a wink, and a rustle of silk, she sashayed back to the stage. We slunk out. Lily thrilled. Me, horrified.

"You sure you don't want to learn some new moves to wow Maddox in the bedroom?" asked Lily, as we walked around the side of the building to my car.

"First off, I have moves. Secondly, Maddox isn't in my bedroom."

"Are they the same moves that you learned when you took your sex training wheels off?"

"Possibly. But if it ain't broke, don't fix it."

"Oh, sweetie," sighed Lily. "We have got to get you some new moves."

Later, I was sure I would have a great retort for that, but right then, I grabbed Lily's arm and we skidded to a halt a couple of feet from my car.

Something was stuck under my wipers against the windshield.

"What is that?" asked Lily.

"I don't know." We stepped forward together and I frowned. I pried the wiper open and pulled out the clump of foliage, careful not to catch my fingers on the thorns. "It looks like a bouquet of thorny rose stems. All the heads have been chopped off."

"Do you think it's a warning? Oh my God, Lexi, someone wants to chop your head off!" Lily grabbed my arm and I jumped.

I dropped the stems on the floor of the lot, and screaming in unison, we scrambled into the car and I hit the automatic locks. For a moment, we sat there, terrified, then Lily went rigid and whispered, "What if the murderer is in the car with us?"

I *never* exited a car so fast in my life.

"What do we do now?" I said as we inspected the car, from five feet away. It looked ominous under the patchy lighting, like it was going to come alive any moment and mow us down.

"We could call Maddox and get him to take us home."

"And tell him what? That we were scared of a bunch of rose stems?"

"No, that there's a murderer in the car. Can we call one of your brothers?"

"Are you kidding me? This would be their favorite story for months. I would never hear the end of it. Someone will probably put it out on the police channel and the whole MPD will know we're big wusses!"

Lily considered that as she played with the zipper on her jacket. "Good point. What are we going to do?"

"We'll check the back seat and the trunk for any sign of the murderer."

"Okay."

Neither of us moved.

"You first," said Lily.

I ran forward, pulled open the rear door and ran back.

"Well?"

I pulled a face. "I forgot to look." I crept forward but still gave the car wide berth. From three feet away, I could see the flat, and very empty, backseat of the car. When I felt a cold hand on my wrist, I jumped and screamed, then Lily screamed. Then we both screamed together. Finally, with my heart rate beating faster than a crackhead drummer at a rock concert, I grabbed the baseball bat I kept on the rear floor for emergency carjackings—well, you never know—and slammed the door shut.

"Why did you scream?" asked Lily.

"You scared me! I thought you were waiting over there." I flapped a hand towards where we were standing. "And your hands are really cold."

"Sorry. Have you thought about getting throw pillows for the back seat?"

I gave her The Look. "No, never."

"Let's check the trunk."

"Your turn." I pressed the button on the key fob and the trunk popped open. Lily crept forward, then around the car and leaned in. All of a sudden, she pitched forward and screamed, her legs disappearing from view. I gripped the baseball bat harder and ran forward, determined to beat the living crap out of whoever had pulled Lily in. My face twisted with anger, a bloodcurdling warrior's shriek on my lips, I raised my bat and… stopped.

Lily sat in my trunk, giggling. "Gotcha!" she said. "It's empty. You should at least keep a flashlight in here, you know, for emergencies."

"I have a mind to close the trunk with you in it."

"I'll bash out your taillights," she said. "And you'll get charged with kidnapping."

That decided it. "I need a drink."

Lily perked up and held out a hand. "You buying?"

Three double vodka and Cokes later, I wasn't confident about my ability to drive home without mowing down pedestrians and wiping out my car.

"I think we need to call for a ride home," I said, raising my hand to the bartender and ordering two more drinks.

"Tha shounds lik a gud idea," slurred Lily. "A big schlong man."

I was fairly certain she meant "strong," but I didn't like to correct her just in case she really meant what she said. The problem was, whom to call? I could call Maddox, but I fancied him and he was sort of my boss in my temping job, and sort of my boss in my super secret spy job. I did not want him to see me drunk again, right after putting me to bed Saturday night when I drank a couple too many medicinal beers.

Any one of my brothers would have picked us up, but like I said earlier, they would have made sure that I was the butt of every joke for months to come. Besides, I IOU'd Garrett too many babysitting vouchers already. Daniel would tell Alice, who would immediately telephone Traci, who would probably tell my mom. And Lily would probably drool all over Jord. "Is there anyone you can call?" I asked Lily.

She smiled and rested her head on the bar. "Officer Tasty," she said, smiling.

I figured as much. That left one person to call.

Solomon walked in a half hour, and two more drinks, later. He pulled the stool out next to mine and sat down, ordering a beer from the bartender. His jeans were worn, and his shirt untucked, with a couple of buttons open at the neck. I liked his casual attire just as much as I liked the way his sleek, black, work pants clung to his legs and hips. It was the first time I'd seen him clean-shaven and he looked even better than before.

"Are you really that drunk?" he asked, a small smile playing on his lips. I couldn't tell if he was amused or making some kind of comment about my drinking. He certainly didn't seem upset about playing my chivalrous knight.

"Yesh."

"We've hadda very shcary evenink. Alcohol was definitely necsheshary," said Lily as she hiccupped. She looked at him and sighed. "Prinshe of schecsky darknesh," she slurred, smiling goofily at him.

Solomon looked at me. "What did she say?"

"I have no idea."

Lily turned away and waved her fingers at the barman she had been eyeing during the past three drinks. She pointed to her glass, making a "one more" sign. "Exshcoozhe me. Bashroom," she said to us before knocking back her drink and walked shakily to the bathrooms at the rear, her skirt swinging cutely around her knees.

"She's going to have a terrific hangover," said

Solomon. "What was so scary about this evening that you needed to drain the bar?"

"Someone left roses on my car, except all the heads were cut off. Then Lily thought there was a murderer hiding in the car so we had to get out. And then—" I'm ashamed to say I did some kind of crazy arm waving move. "—And then she pretended to get pulled into the trunk, and I thought she was being murdered and needed rescuing. You can't tell anyone!" I slammed to a stop.

Solomon considered that as if I had told him something completely normal. "Why would your friend think there was a murderer in the car?"

I thought about Martin Dean with the bullet hole between his eyes, and his girlfriend with the one in her chest. "It seemed plausible at the time."

"Fair enough."

"You can't tell Maddox."

"We're not drinking buddies."

"Good job. Two smokin' hot guys sitting together would cause most of the female population of Montgomery to wilt."

"Smokin' hot, hmmm?" Solomon paid the bartender and took a long sip of his beer, his eyes closing momentarily. Smokin' sexy, I thought, watching him, but somehow kept my mouth shut. Alcohol had an embarrassing effect on me. It made me too talkative and too prepared to do things I would love to do, but regret later. It had no effect on Lily whatsoever, other than making her silly and moon-eyed.

"I won't remember I said it in the morning."

Solomon smiled.

"Why don't you like Maddox?" I asked, resting my

elbow on the bar, my chin in my hand. I tried, but failed, to stop myself from gazing at him.

"I didn't say I didn't like him."

"But you're not drinking buddies."

"That's right."

"Why are you leaving the you-know-whos?"

"The FBI?"

"Are you allowed to say that?"

He leaned in, his mouth close to my ear and I held my breath. "Yes," he said, his breath tickling the hair resting at the nape of my neck. "I like this top," he said. "Very feminine."

I gulped and ignored his comment, for fear of jumping him. He shouldn't make my heart race fast like that. He shouldn't look so good. Why did fate have to curse me with two of the sexiest men I had ever seen at the same time? "So, why are you leaving?" I asked, moving onto safer ground as the "Blondie" comment popped into my head.

"I feel like a change."

"I feel like a change too. I hate temping."

"Do you have plans to do something different?"

"No." That was always the fatal flaw in my plan. I had no idea what I wanted to do. Not in college, not in the years after.

"How come you're not a cop?" Solomon asked, surprising me. Then he added, "I read your file."

Of course he had.

"I didn't like the uniform."

Solomon laughed and I grinned, thinking how lovely his eyes were when he smiled. They crinkled slightly at the edges, enough that I thought he was older than I, but not so much that fancying him was icky. "So, I'm here to rescue you." He took another sip. "How do you know I'm not going to take advantage of you tonight?"

"How do you know I wouldn't let you?" Oops. That just slipped out. A squeak tried to emerge from my throat, but I stifled it and attempted to appear nonchalant. It would have been much easier four vodkas ago.

Solomon did that sexy half smile thing again, like he was having really dirty thoughts. I felt heat flush through me. My intoxication shut-off point was approximately two drinks ago, and I couldn't be sure if I were being sexy or just a lush as I met his eyes. I waited for Solomon to offer to undress me and do wicked things to my body, but instead, he sipped his drink, contemplating me. Finally, he said, "What's going on with you and Maddox?"

"John Solomon, gossip," I laughed. "Who knew?"

He waited silently and I shifted uncomfortably on the stool.

"Nothing's going on," I said. At least, as far as I knew, nothing was going on. So Maddox had stayed over a couple of times, politely taking the couch like a decent man. He brought me dinner and made me breakfast, but the "date" word had only just reared its pretty head and wasn't set in stone. So far as I knew, there was some kissing, and a lot of interest, but nothing that could possibly indicate any kind of girlfriend/boyfriend exclusivity or any promise that there would be some.

I did like Maddox a whole lot more now that I knew his secret side, but it wasn't just the undercover thing that excited me, and which I found very sexy. I felt like I knew Maddox a little bit. Not his favorite color, or his favorite baseball team, but I knew he was kind and caring and not afraid of bad guys with guns. I knew he had Garrett's respect, which counted for a lot because it meant he could probably survive my family.

I wasn't totally sure that he wasn't just being nice to me so that I would help him on the case.

"Do you want something to go on?" asked Solomon, appraising me with his dark eyes.

Now there was a question. Did I want that? Or was it lust? "I don't know. Maybe."

"Do you want something to go on between you and me?"

*Oh boy.* "I don't know. Maybe," I said, before considering it.

Solomon arched an eyebrow.

"Not tonight though. I'm too drunk and I'd rather remember." I don't know where that came from.

"You wouldn't forget."

Oh! Boy!

Lily took that moment to stumble back, hopping onto her stool and gripping the bar for stability. "I feel less drunk," she said, slowly and decisively, following it up with another hiccup. Somehow, between going to the bathroom and returning to our table, her top had opened a couple of buttons and her face was flushed. Plus, the barman seemed to be wearing her lipstick. I resolved to never use the bathroom here.

Solomon shook his head, his eyes twinkling with amusement. "C'mon. I'll take you two home."

"Yay us," said Lily, skipping out ahead.

"What about my car?" I asked as I slid into the passenger seat of Solomon's shiny, black Lexus. My car might not be chop shop desirable, but I didn't fancy its chances outside the bar overnight.

"Don't worry about it. I'll deal with it," said Solomon as he leaned around me to reach for the seatbelt. I held my breath as he buckled it after I fumbled it. He pulled away and fired up the engine.

By the time we got home, Lily was half asleep in the back seat so I woke her up and Solomon helped me walk her into her apartment. He waited in her living room while I rolled her into bed, taking a moment to pull off her shoes and pull up the blanket.

"You'rez the besht," slurred Lily. "Hunting murderersh is *sooo* much fun."

"Yeah. Loads," I sighed as I went to get her a glass of water. She was asleep by the time I got back. Using my key to her place, I locked her door behind us and walked up the stairs, conscious all the time of Solomon just inches behind me.

"Thanks for coming to get us," I said, unlocking my door and holding it open for Solomon. He slid inside and pushed the door shut behind him.

"No problem."

"Do you want a hot drink before you go? Or is this the part where you take advantage of me?" I said, half joking, as it suddenly occurred to me that we were very alone, sobriety was a vague memory, and I had no idea of how to play the situation.

Solomon moved closer and I took a step back, pressing my body against the wall that divided the small hall from my bedroom. His eyes bored into mine as he placed a hand either side of my shoulders. My heart beat a faster tempo as he stooped, his mouth irresistibly close to mine. He kissed my cheek first, then his lips brushed my jaw, moving closer with each butterfly kiss until his lips met mine, gentle at first, then teasing, then passionate. I responded like kissing Solomon was second nature and his hands wrapped around my waist, pulling me into him. His body was hard and unyielding, and when I ran my hands down his back to rest in the hollow just above his butt, he sighed. His hands edged lower, pulling at my top to run over my bare skin underneath, spanning my waist. Judging by his gentle rocking against me, and the extra hardness pressing into me, he was just as excited as I was about this new development.

Almost reluctantly, he pulled back, his hands still warmly gripping my waist. "I'm not going to take advantage," he said, and for a moment, my heart fell. "But that doesn't mean this is over."

"No?"

He kissed me again, slowly this time, taking his time to suck my lower lip, entangling his tongue with mine. "No," he said, and left, leaving me flushed and panting against the wall. In the morning, I would feel relieved, I decided. Solomon was not a man to get involved with lightly.

"Wow," I said to the empty hall.

## CHAPTER ELEVEN

It wasn't easy to concentrate on work with the pressure of Solomon's kiss burning my lips, while Maddox smoldered only a few desks away. Maddox struck me as a straight-talking type, so when he said nothing about Lily's and my drunken shenanigans the night before, I assumed Solomon simply hadn't told him. A large part of me was quite relieved. However, Maddox also didn't mention our future date. I spent a good few hours having an internal dialog about whether it was just a joke to him, after Vincent's invitation, or he simply didn't have the time to do anything about it.

Several times, I hovered the mouse pointer over the IM box, and several times I stopped, telling myself that not only was Maddox my boss here, and sort of my boss on the taskforce—though, come to think of it, I seemed to have unwittingly taken a volunteer position—I had kissed his colleague. I also didn't want to come off as needy. Kissing Solomon—what was I thinking? What was I doing enjoying it?

What was I doing analyzing it endlessly when what I clearly needed was a cold shower, not to mention some serious gossip time with Lily?

"You're looking very serious today."

I jumped at the sound of Maddox's voice. Tucking a stray strand of hair behind my ear, I looked up. "I'm very busy," I said, trying not to sound too surly as guilt prodded me. I had kissed him, and then kissed his colleague. Big oops.

"Do you have time for lunch?"

Duh. I always had time for lunch. "I guess," I said, looking forlornly at the stack of typing Dominic delegated to me. Seems like he was taking Dean's apparent absence as his opportunity to catch up. I just couldn't get motivated about it.

"It'll be here when you get back," said Maddox, apparently deciding I had some newfound work ethic. I did too, but not for this job.

"That's what I was afraid of."

I grabbed my purse and followed Maddox out, walking abreast across the park to the cafe. We got sandwiches and drinks, Maddox's treat, and we took a booth in the corner.

"This is going to start office rumors," I said.

"Eating sandwiches or... this?" Maddox's hand landed on my leg and slid a little further up, sending tingles through my spine.

A smile played on my lips. Perhaps the 'd' word was back on? "Definitely that."

"I was going to kiss you, but Anne just walked in and she would probably combust."

After what I'd seen last night, I doubted a kiss would even raise Anne's eyebrows.

"Raincheck," I said, just in case he thought I was

passing. Flirting away my lunch hour seemed like a lot of fun, but I had to get serious. I dropped my voice, "So what's happening with you-know-what?" I was going to say "case," but that sounded too ominous. I knew Maddox was concerned about public conversation, what with the walls having ears and not knowing whom to suspect. Somehow, I didn't believe that there were no suspects at all. I wondered just how much he held back from me.

"I'll tell you while we walk back." Maddox demolished his sandwich and unscrewed the cap of his mineral water. "In short, not a lot."

"Is that good or bad?"

"Neither, so far."

I ate my sandwich quickly and we gave our table up to a pair of hovering office workers; then walked slowly back to Green Hand.

"We got the coroner's report back on Tanya Henderson, aka Tallulah. We got her ID from a wallet in the jacket she checked. The shot killed her, obviously, and there weren't any defensive wounds. No epithelials or other trace evidence."

"She didn't see it coming until it was too late," I concluded and Maddox nodded. "Does that mean she knew her killer? Possibly trusted him?"

"It's a possibility that she felt certain nothing was going to happen to her. Or maybe she thought she was too valuable to off. We're checking into her history."

"Did you check her keys?" I asked. "It was odd that one wasn't on the key ring."

"Everything is being checked. Your lead on the call center was good."

"Thank you."

"We have a couple of people looking into what was set up there, but so far, it looks shady. I hope it's the key to blowing open the fraud case."

"I thought you had a bunch of information." I was fishing and he knew it.

"Some. Enough to show fraud, but not enough to find the perps, or how they are getting away with it. We always knew there was an inside man, and everything points to Dean. His mortgage, his expensive tastes and habits, the low pension pot all gave him motive to go for a big time payoff from the company he dedicated his life to. He had access to every part of the building and could feasibly have set up a fake office for claims. But without him, we don't have a lot to go on. If he were alive, we could have threatened prosecution and flipped him, like I tried to do the night he died. As it is, we need the rest of the team now. And the money," he finished.

"Do you have any ideas who they could be?"

"None. They might work for the company, or maybe not. It's a complicated thing. We're lucky to have the FBI involved. Their pockets are deeper than ours when it comes to surveillance for a case like this."

I'd heard plenty of times how badly the cutbacks had hit Montgomery. It wasn't just the PD that suffered, but every peripheral service connected to them. Victim support barely supported itself now. Only cut and dried cases were welcome at the precinct; every other resource was stretched beyond capacity. There were plenty of petty crimes that didn't get more than a cursory glance before being filed "unsolved." They simply didn't have the manpower to pursue everything.

"Hurrah for the spooks," I said.

"That's CIA," corrected Maddox. "I looked for you yesterday. You leave early?"

"Who me? No."

"Didn't think so." He laughed. I felt certain my timecard would be signed. "Do anything good?"

"Hung out with Lily. You?"

"Hung out with the team."

"Bet I had more fun." I wasn't sure last night counted as fun. One day, I hoped to look back on it and laugh, or preferably, wipe it from my memory. I wasn't sure about the bit with Solomon. I wasn't sure Maddox skirted the truth just as much as I had.

"I can't gamble on a bet I'll lose." We neared Green Hand and Maddox slowed his pace, forcing me to match him. "I want you to be careful, Lexi. Two people are dead. Two people that we *know* of," he emphasized. "The information you got already is good, but I don't want you asking the wrong person the wrong question. Saturday night could have been a lot worse." Maddox really didn't need to spell it out. A minute earlier and we might have been staring down the barrel of a gun.

"Are you saying I'm off the case?"

"I think it's for the best. I don't want you to get hurt."

"Keep my pretty little mind on typing and filing, huh?" I said, struggling to keep my cool. The only good leads he'd gotten so far had come from me, as far as I could see. "Got it." I heard a huff of annoyance from Maddox as I stalked off, but I didn't turn back or even think about apologizing. So I was good enough to kiss, but not good enough to work with?

It was petty, but I ignored Maddox for the rest of the afternoon. As soon as I finished Dominic's work overflow, I grabbed my purse, dumped the files on Dominic's desk and left.

I had to admit I was pretty cross at Maddox. I'd essentially provided him with a bunch of clues, ruined my good taste in fashion with hooker heels, stumbled on two corpses, and there was the small matter of the blood-stained dress, heels and purse that disappeared from my apartment the night Maddox drugged me. I really liked that dress and I was full on "say no to drugs." If he thought he could leave me out of the investigation, he was wrong. It had already become very personal.

By the time I got home, I had devised a plan. I went up to my apartment first and poured a glass of water, then pulled the phone book out, flipping through the pages until I found what I wanted. I drank the water, stuffed the phone book back under the couch, and clattered down the stairs to knock on Lily's door. Passing me yesterday's newspaper, she sat down. "Do you want to go to the movies Wednesday?" she asked. "That new comedy is out. I just checked."

"Sounds good." I needed a laugh without the danger of kissing a man. An annoying little voice in my head nagged as to whether I was maybe overreacting a little since I enjoyed kissing Solomon. Perhaps, just maybe, I was having a guilt attack. I told the little voice to shut up.

"Did you see the headline? There's been another hit-and-run. Mayor Mathis. Just got hit when he was taking an evening stroll and the driver sped off. That's the second one in a week! What's wrong with this town?"

It struck me that a lot was wrong with this town. My boss was dead, his girlfriend, Tallulah, aka Tanya Henderson, was dead and there was a huge stash of stolen money out there somewhere. Of course, I didn't say that. Instead, I just replied incredulously, "He was going for an evening stroll?"

"Yeah. Says here. He went out for a stroll after dinner and was struck. Some neighbors found him in the road."

"That's rough," I said, trying not to imagine Mayor Mathis squished all over the road.

"Tell me about it. You try and look after yourself, keeping fit, and what does someone do? Run you over, that's what! You want to go spin on Saturday again? Anton will be there."

"Yes, definitely. You think Mayor Mathis was trying to keep fit?" That struck me as funny. The last time I'd seen Mayor Mathis, he'd been cutting the ribbon of the new public library and his stomach hung pretty far over his pants. I doubt whether he'd ever seen a gym, but I'd bet he'd certainly seen more than his fair share of donuts.

Lily looked at me as I struggled to keep a straight face. "Maybe he turned over a new leaf. Like a mid-life crisis or something."

"I guess." It could happen to anyone. I'd already experienced my share of crises and none of them had been mid-life. I could only hope the universe wasn't waiting to whack me with a doozy. I'd take a mid-life sports car though. Not Vincent's Spyder, but maybe a cute little convertible. I shook the daydream from my head and got back on task. "I want to visit Tallulah's family," I told Lily.

"How come?" she asked.

"Maybe they know something."

"Awesome," said Lily. "We know nothing."

"Exactly."

"Where does she live?"

"I checked the phone book and there are three T. Hendersons in Montgomery."

"Did Hot and Hotter asker you to do this?" she asked.

"Which is which?"

"Does it matter?"

"Guess not, and no, they didn't. Maddox wants me off the case."

"Huh," said Lily. "Do we still like him?"

"I don't know. Maybe."

"There's nothing wrong in calling to pay condolences to Tallulah's family," decided Lily. "It *was* sad."

"It was," I agreed. "It was really sad."

"Let's call them first." Lily got her phone book and flipped through to the Hendersons, checking them off with a Sharpie. She dialed the first number and asked to speak to Miss Henderson, waited for the answer, said goodbye and put the phone down. "Miss is a Mr. Thomas Henderson," she explained.

The third call was the charm. "That was Tanya's sister. She told me her sister had just died and she was sorting through her things."

"Let's go over and talk to the sister. Maybe they were close?"

"Okay, and we have to go to *my* sister's baby shower afterwards." I looked down at my work clothes. I still passed as smart and neat. Clean, too. And, to my relief, I was hangover free.

Lily saw me looking at her sweater and jeans and took the hint. "I'll change."

Tanya Henderson lived in an apartment block on South Street in Frederickstown. The area, named after Montgomery's first mayor, was a melting pot of small, one-family homes, apartment buildings and independent businesses. It sprang up to house the overflow of a population boom in Montgomery more than forty years ago, but had quickly gone to the dogs. Its biggest problem was no one thought ahead far enough to connect the public transport system to the area. By the time they did, the commuters had moved out and the area had fallen to ghettoization.

It wasn't the nicest of neighborhoods, being mainly poor. The whole South Street block looked like it needed a coat of paint and landscaping around the communal gardens, but it wasn't the worst neighborhood either. My car—which had mysteriously appeared in my parking space sometime during the night—would most certainly be here when I got back, so I parked on the street and we walked over to Tanya Henderson's apartment.

"So, what are we looking for?" asked Lily. She pulled her sunglasses down her nose and looked at me expectantly, with the air of someone who trusted someone else to know what she was doing.

"I don't know yet."

"What are we going to say?"

"We'll say we're friends from the club and we heard what happened."

"Plausible," agreed Lily.

I located the button for 3B and pressed it. A moment later, a woman's voice called, "Hello?"

"Hi! This is... Jennifer and... Alison," I said, picking the first names to pop into my head. If the cops asked later, not that I could fathom why they would, she wouldn't have our real names. I was probably over thinking it, I decided. "We're friends of Tanya's."

"Come up," said the voice and the door buzzed open. The elevator was out of order so we climbed the two flights to the third floor. Someone had tried to jazz up the communal space outside Tanya's apartment with a little console table that held a plastic plant with a framed print above. A woman waited in the doorway for us. She was in her thirties and had waist-length, brown hair.

"I'm Tara, Tanya's sister. You heard what happened?" she said without preamble.

I nodded. "We're very sorry for your loss."

"Thank you. She was only twenty-eight, you know. Too young. What can I do for you?"

"I wanted to ask you a couple of questions. About Tanya. We were pretty concerned about her."

"Me too. Listen, come on in. We can talk while I sort through her things. The landlord wants everything out by the weekend. Harsh, right?"

"Totally."

Tanya Henderson had tried to make the best of her apartment. It was neat, although a little on the sparse side. She attempted to make it more cheerful by using bright throws and pillows. A modern art print had been tacked above a fake fireplace. I couldn't connect it with the red head in the tight leather dress. I couldn't picture Martin Dean in it either. It was a far cry from Bedford Hills and the grand piano.

"Did Tanya live here alone?" I asked.

"Yeah. Thought you knew that?"

"I did. I just thought she'd been seeing someone. Thought maybe he'd moved in."

"She didn't mention it to me. And she wasn't real sharey, you know, about the guys she was seeing."

"She was seeing more than one?"

"Well, you know about the clubs she went to." Tara moved around us to lift a carton off the small two-seat sofa and invited us to sit.

"You mean Flames?" said Lily. "We go there."

"Then you know monogamy isn't on top of the list. Tanya had a guy who took her there. I think he used to help her out with money and he was into all that weird shit. Sorry. I'm sure it's not weird to you at all, but the public spanking stuff? I just don't get it."

"No offense taken. Do you know this guy?"

"I think his name is Dean something? Like two first names, maybe. Tanya mentioned him a couple of times when he sent her presents. She seemed to really like him. I saw him once, dropping her off, but I never met him. Not the best looking guy, if you know what I mean. Plus, he was too old for her."

"Was she dating him for the money? He was loaded, right?" I watched her.

"Yeah," said Tara, with a shrug. "He was, but Tanya, she wasn't a gold-digger, ya know. She didn't ask him for stuff. She didn't have a lot either, but she always worked when she could and paid her own way. This Dean treated her nicely. She said he was respectful."

"Did she ever bring him home to meet your folks?"

"Hell, no. I don't think they had a relationship like

that, anyway. Tanya never said he was her boyfriend; and he had twenty years on her, at least. Maybe even thirty! She said he worked a lot and liked her companionship, that she was... What was it? Oh yeah—uncomplicated, whatever the hell that means." Tara shrugged and pulled a couple of paperbacks off a small side table, tossing them into a box marked "charity." "She used to go over to his place, too. Said it was really nice. Big. He had a thing for vintage cars and took her out in one once. She said it was amazing. She felt like a Hollywood screen siren in it."

"He's missing," I said.

"No shit? You think he was the bastard who did this to my sister?" Tara didn't question how we knew that, much to my relief.

"No, like you said, I think he really liked her."

"Then he got her mixed up in something?"

"Maybe."

"I told Tanya, seeing older guys was fine. Plenty of women do that, but these guys, they don't marry women who go to clubs like Flames. They get them in trouble and split. Again, no offense intended. But she said she wasn't after him for a ring."

"Had they known each other very long?" Lily asked.

Tara looked up at her. "A couple of years. I don't know where they met."

"Did Tanya seem worried about anything before she..." I paused. It seemed too soon to say the word "died."

"Before she was killed?" Tara asked bluntly. She was putting on a tough act, but nothing could disguise the red rims around her eyes. "Now I think about it, yeah, she did seem worried about something. She was real edgy."

"How do you mean?"

"Jumpy. Always looking over her shoulder. She mentioned taking a vacation too. Even bought a guidebook."

"That wasn't like her?"

"No, she always wanted to travel, we both did, but never have. This guy of hers, the one you say is missing, he bought her tickets to Paris. They were going to go there at the end of the month."

"Sounds romantic."

"Sure does. She said she might never come back." Tara stopped folding the throw she pulled off the floor and placed it in the carton. "Hey, do you want any of her stuff? Most of it is going to Goodwill."

"No, but thanks for the offer." I stood, and Lily followed. "Oh, there was one more thing. Tanya mentioned she'd been keeping something for Dean. Do you know what it was? It might have been a key or something?"

"No, she didn't say anything about a key, but she didn't tell me everything."

"No problem. Thanks for your time."

"Tanya's funeral is next week. It'll be in the newspaper. You're welcome to come by."

"Thanks."

Tara saw us to the door, and just as we were leaving, she said. "The tickets for Paris are here and they're in Tanya's name. What do you think I should do with them? Should I wait and give them to her guy?"

"No," I said. "Use them." Martin Dean would never need them.

"I can't imagine dating someone twenty years

older than me," I said to Lily as we walked down the stairs.

"I did. Once."

"Really?"

"Yeah. He was lovely. Very nice, mature, good in the sack."

"You never said. What went wrong?"

"I kept imagining ten, twenty years down the road, I would still be pretty young and he would just be getting fatter and asking me to get his slippers."

"It might not have been like that."

"I know, but the fear was there anyway. Plus, I didn't want to look like a gold-digger."

"I would never think you were a gold-digger."

"Everyone else would. If he was poor, but smart and handsome, people wouldn't care. Throw rich in and everyone's got an opinion."

I thought that was a good point, even though Lily's parents were loaded. "You think Tanya really liked Dean?"

"She was planning to go away with him. Plus, look at where she lived. She wasn't milking him for money or jewelry and stuff like that." The door banged shut behind us and we moved to the curb.

"Maybe it was the spanking."

"You are so fixated on the spanking. Did Maddox spank you in the club?"

"No!"

Lily smirked. "Maybe he should have."

"I'm going to spank you over the hood of my car."

"Take pictures and send them to Officer Tasty."

"Eugh!" I got in the car, trying not to think too much about that. "You know this wasn't a total waste of time," I said, sliding my key into the ignition and checking my mirrors.

"Why's that?"

"Because we found out Dean was planning on leaving the country. Maybe he was going to take his cut and go."

"And not come back," finished Lily. "Dude was going on the lam."

# CHAPTER TWELVE

We drove straight to Serena's house from Tanya's apartment, throwing theories into the air and hoping one of them would stick as the scenery turned from faded hope to expensive cars parked in driveways of upscale houses. It wasn't quite Bedford Hills, but it was still very nice.

"I just don't get the attraction," Lily said, still musing on Dean and Tanya Henderson, as we parked behind Serena's Mercedes and walked up the driveway.

I couldn't see the attraction with a number of guys Lily dated, so I figured who was I to understand what allured other people?

"Who knows?" I said. "Maybe it's one of life's mysteries. Did you bring a gift?"

"I had it delivered."

"Good thinking."

"You?"

"Gift vouchers."

"Smart."

We arrived a half hour early, in time to watch Serena direct the caterers. They brought a table with them, and set it up across one wall of the living room. They were now setting out platters under her scrutiny.

My mother had arrived earlier to put up decorations. Pleated paper bells were strung across the room, paper men in blue, pink and cream held hands, along with colorful paper cranes and vases stuffed with creamy roses.

"Great job, Mom," I said, kissing my mother on the cheek.

"The paper cranes were your father's idea. Apparently, they're supposed to be lucky."

"I like them."

"Did you find out about the belly-dancing outfit?"

"Anne at work says there is a dance shop near the train station that sells them. They have a website too." I still didn't ask her why. I just hoped to heaven my mother didn't find out about burlesque.

A therapist from a day spa that Lily and I liked had set up a small station by a leather armchair. Next to her sat a pile of towels and an open kit of nail polishes. She smiled at us and waved, her enthusiasm probably aided by the fat, short-notice fee we agreed upon that would have made me wince if Serena weren't paying.

The doorbell rang and Serena waved the caterers out, pointing them towards the kitchen, as she eagerly greeted her guests.

Two hours later, I was standing in the doorway, staring at the scene in front of me. I had to admit, I'd done a great job pulling off Serena's last minute demands for her baby shower. Her house looked great and the guests had made appropriate noises.

Serena even gave me the thumbs-up, which was rare for her. I guess she was looking forward to a baby shower almost as much as having her own baby.

I navigated past the cluster of chattering women to the long table, plucking a plate from the crisp white tablecloth and helping myself to pasta salad, smoked salmon blinis and my favorite dough balls. I poured a glass of something fruity from one of the pitchers of virgin cocktails; Serena had gotten her way with the mocktinis. Despite repeated pleas, Serena refused to allow any alcohol being served on the grounds. If she couldn't have any, neither would anyone else. Even though the table had been picked through, plates still groaned with finger foods and Alessandro's left extra platters in the kitchen.

The pocket doors to the dining room were opened and the dining table held a pile of onesies and craft materials. Around it, a gaggle of women sat, giggling and painting with non-toxic fabric paints while the remaining women got mini pedicures, manicures and facials. Serena sat in the middle of them all, like a fashionable Buddha; tranquil, resplendent and fully in her element as center of attention. I was happy for her.

Lily waved me over to the crafts table. While I picked at my plate, I looked over her shoulder at her creation. She had painted, in green letters, "What goes up must come down."

"She'll love it," I said, stifling a giggle.

Lily snorted. She knew there was no way on earth Serena was going to let her darling baby wear anything that these women painted.

"Why do all the women around Serena look so terrified?" I asked in a low voice.

"She's telling them her birth plan."

"Oh God. Not the breech story again?"

"I dunno. I left right after she said 'natural'. There's nothing natural about a human being coming out of your doodah."

"They all have kids, right?" I said, catching the word "episiotomy" floating towards me. I didn't want to know what that was. It sounded painful.

"Yeah, which is why they're looking at her like she's crazy."

"I'm gonna loiter at the gift table."

"Good luck," said Lily. "Just remember you're hosting this thing."

"Only because I heard God is giving out karma points on this one." The gift table held a pile of glossy, ribboned parcels. Lily had sent a basket of tiny, little sleepsuits, so miniature they made my ovaries twang when she pointed them out.

Serena broke away from the crowd, her exit offset by an audible gasp of relief. She linked her arm through mine in an uncharacteristic gesture of sisterhood. "This is fantastic," she said. "I've had a mineral facial and my toes are pink. At least, I think they are. I can't see them."

I peeked down. "They are," I confirmed.

"The girls love the spa theme."

"Told you so. Everyone loves pampering."

"And the food's great."

"And when it's all over, I'll send in the cleaning crew and your house will look perfect again." Well, until the baby is born, but I didn't add that. It was better to let Serena find out the babies just didn't fit into schedules and routines. Like renegades, they did their own thing, as my sisters-in-law were fond of saying. I was fairly sure Serena didn't believe them. I guessed she already had the baby's schedule plotted in six-minute increments.

"And Ted is happy with the boys," I reminded her. Daniel texted me a picture of them at the golf club bar. Ted was beet red, a baseball cap reading "Daddy" on backwards. I figured they would be there quite some time and Ted might have to pull a sick day tomorrow.

"I'm amazed you pulled this off so quickly." Serena beamed and moved on before I could ask her if that was a compliment. "Did you finish the puzzle you told me about at Alessandro's?"

"The puzzle?" I tried to remember our conversation.

"The number code you wanted to solve at work," she reminded me.

"Oh that. No, I'm still stumped." Really stumped. Despite pages of notes, nothing made sense. There was no discernible pattern or anything that could point to the numbers equating to letters.

"You tried matching the letters to numbers?"

"I went through the whole alphabet, moving everything one, two, three, four places up *and* down. It still came out as a jumble."

"Hmm, well, either you need to move up or down, higher and lower, or it's not an alphabet encryption."

"So, it could just be numbers?"

Serena nodded. "Only without some kind of reference point, you'll never know if you've hit the right sequence."

"How do I get a reference to work from?"

"Was there anything with the number set at all? A

name? A word?"

I thought about it. "I don't know."

"If you brought it over, I could go through it with you. Maybe I'll pick something up."

Serena probably would spot something, but I suspected I'd already put her in enough danger just telling her about the book, if it were even a clue. Generally a pain-in-the-butt, her pregnancy seemed to have mellowed her a little. Much as I knew her help would probably speed things up, my conscience told me not to put her in harm's way. It was bad enough someone had left decapitated roses on my car, I couldn't risk anything happening to Serena, too.

"No, it's okay. You're already so busy."

"I think it's time for a drink. You want one?"

"I would love one." A real one. One with a shot of vodka.

"Get me a fruit punch while you're there." Serena waddled off and plunked herself down in the middle of the gaggle, her bump narrowly missing the nail technician, who lurched to the side just in time.

I sighed. So much for mellowed sisterly bonding. I was back to my position of being Serena's gofer. I went to get my sister a fruit punch, seeing as I couldn't give her the fist variety with my mother watching.

~

"I hate to run," said Mom, as the first guests left, "but your father and I have a date at the community theater."

"Have a nice time," I said, trying to stomp the mental image of my parents out on a date night. On the other hand, dating in their late sixties was quite sweet. So long as they only dated each other. If they got into swinging, I was leaving town. I walked my mother to her car and she got in, rolling down the window to talk to me. "Be careful if you're out walking at night," she told me firmly.

"When do I ever go walking at night?"

"Well, be careful if you do. Someone ran over Mayor Mathis and left him to die in the road."

"I saw it in the newspaper."

"So sad, that poor family. They were really struggling and now to lose him like that."

"They weren't exactly poor." Mayor Mathis came from old money and everyone knew it. They owned a large house in Bedford Hills and their family was traced back to some of Montgomery's founders.

"Anita Mathis is in my crochet circle. They've lost a lot of money over the years. Things haven't been good. I blame it on the economic crisis. Anyway, just be careful. I don't want to get a call saying you're roadkill. Make sure you wear clean, matching underwear anyway."

"Thanks, Mom. Drive safe." I waved her off before joining Serena at the door to bid her guests goodbye and hand out the party favors—little truffles shaped into baby bootees with piped lacing—as we waved the last of them away.

"Fabulous shower," said Mindy Laws, the final guest to leave, as she air kissed first me, then Serena before sweeping out to her white Range Rover. Subtle, it was not.

"It's fun to do something different, isn't it?" Serena air kissed her back. "I hate her," she said, after the door was shut.

"She was your best friend all the way through school!"

"I think I hated her then too. She always did everything first."

"She never went to Harvard," I pointed out. "And she didn't marry Ted."

"I think she slept with him."

My mouth dropped open. I couldn't imagine Mindy as a harlot. Wait... yes, I could. She had been head cheerleader and a mean cow through my teen years, though she and Serena graduated before I started high school. "When?"

"In my second year at Harvard. She came to visit."

"But you don't know for certain?"

"No. But we were at a house party, and when we left, she had her panties in her pocket and she had just come out of Ted's room."

"Classy."

"But I married him," said Serena not as smugly as she normally would.

"And now you're having a baby," I reminded her.

"And I'm going to lose my job. And I'm fat!" Tears pooled in Serena's eyes.

I put my arm around Serena and gave her a little squeeze. "You're pregnant, not fat. And when you have the baby, you'll be skinny again and we'll all hate you too."

"Thanks." Serena dabbed her eyes with a cotton handkerchief, and yawned. "I need to sleep. I nap constantly."

"Go sleep. Lily and I will let the cleaning crew in, and you'll wake up to a pristine house."

"Thanks, Lexi. You're the best." That did it. There was definitely something wrong with Serena, but I chose to blame it on hormones. I shooed Serena off to her bedroom and Lily and I set about putting the house to rights. The leftover food was cling-wrapped and placed in the refrigerator, along with the jugs of juice. The stacks of onesies were left to dry in the living room and all the leftover craft materials were bagged for the trash. On second thought, I taped a note, suggesting Mom might want them for one of her classes or community projects. The cleanup crew finished the rest, and someone from Alessandro's came by to retrieve the plates and glassware along with the table, tablecloth and matching napkins.

"I hate to run out on you," said Lily, "but I have a date."

"You didn't say!"

"It's just a guy I met a couple of weeks ago. He's nice."

"I thought you were holding out for my brother." I didn't mention Scott from Green Hand. Or the barman.

"Oh, honey. I've given up on Officer Tasty." Lily said that approximately once a month. I never believed her.

"No! He likes you, I swear." I knew he did. Being several years older, Jord never looked Lily's way during school; but by the second year of college, that definitely changed. Not anything outlandish, although there were plenty of subtle looks when he thought no one saw him. He never lacked for a date, but never once asked Lily out even though we all gradually came to expect it. Even my father, usually oblivious to the dating lives of his children, asked Jord when he was going to pull his finger out and, "screw dating, just marry the girl." Jord said she was too young for him, and when she was older, he didn't want to ruin our friendship; then it was because he didn't want to settle down, not that Lily was asking. He looked at her like she was an ice cream on a hot day, so I didn't understand his reticence.

"Then he can do the chasing. I'm done," said Lily, spoiling her decisive tone when she added, "Maybe that'll put a spark under Jord's ass."

"I'll make sure I mention your date to him." I smiled conspiratorially. "Give me five minutes. We're almost done here anyway." Lily waited impatiently while I supervised the last of the cleanup, ushering the crew out a few minutes later and ensuring they all had their compensation.

After distributing the vases of roses through the house, and checking everything was perfect, I went to see Serena. She was snuggled under a blanket, her shoes kicked off, fast asleep. I bent over, kissed her on the cheek, raided her kitchen for leftovers, locked up and drove us home. I frowned when a car that had been following us the last couple of blocks pulled over a few houses away from our building. It was probably just a coincidence. Paranoia was clearly getting to me.

Lily said a quick goodbye and hurried to her apartment to change, so I went straight up to my place. I let myself in and grabbed a plate, taking it to the living room to unload my leftovers. After all my running around at the shower, making sure everyone had plenty to eat and drink, not to mention got in line for their spa treatments, I'd barely eaten anything. My lunchtime sandwich was ages ago and my stomach made ominous rumbling sounds. I changed into jeans and a sweatshirt, and switched on the TV, tuning in to watch the last half of a weepy Hallmark movie while I stuffed myself. During the end credits, I went over to the windows to close the drapes. Looking down, I noticed the car I'd seen earlier, parked a couple houses away, was still there. It stood out because it was pretty thrashed and the two occupants remained in it. I frowned again and went back to the movie.

Ten minutes later, curiosity gnawing at me, I crawled over to the window, kneeling up to peek out. They were still there. I lowered myself to the floor and sat against the wall for a moment, thinking. There was something off about the car's occupants. Why weren't they inside visiting or something?

On my hands and knees, I crawled to the hallway and rooted through the console for the binoculars my dad once randomly gave me for my birthday two years ago. I twisted off the lens caps and, feeling like an idiot, crawled back to the window, placing the binoculars on the sill. Kneeling up again, I placed my eyes to the sights and peered through, adjusting the lens and scanning until I had a clear view inside the car.

Something was definitely off alright.

I crept back to the hallway, closing the living room door behind me. Standing up, now blocked from view, I grabbed my keys and cell phone and tugged on my jacket, then went into the kitchen for a carving knife, which I slid into the waistband of my jeans. I pulled my sweatshirt over the top.

"Don't be scared, don't be scared," I chanted as I ran down the steps, wrenched the door open and strode across the road to the car. Hopping onto the sidewalk, I stooped down to look through the window. My stomach rolled over into a knot.

From my apartment and binoculars, I wasn't sure, but close up, I recognized the occupants. They were the men who killed Martin Dean.

Even worse, their glassy, dead eyes stared straight ahead. Each had a hole in the center of his forehead that wept congealing blood. Something was pinned to the driver's coat, but I couldn't make out the words; and there was no way in hell I was going to open the car door to get a closer look.

With shaking hands, I dialed 911, reported two dead males and gave my address and name.

"Lexi, honey, it's Traci," said the dispatcher when I finished.

"Traci?" I didn't recognize her voice as I shakily gave the details. "I didn't realize."

"Of course not, honey. You just got corpsed. You want me to call your mom and dad?"

"No, they'll just worry." And probably demand I move in with them. I could cope with the corpses two feet away better than the emotional blackmail.

"Sure. Sit tight, sweetie. Someone's on the way."

I heard a siren in the distance and Traci kept me on the line until a marked car turned onto the street. I didn't recognize the officer, but he seemed to know me, and he made me stand by his car while he checked on the bodies. First he took a cursory glance, then after opening the doors, he placed two fingers to their throats.

"Definitely dead," he said, shutting the door. "You just find them like this?"

I nodded. "They were dead when I came out."

"What did you come out for?"

"They hadn't moved since I got home."

"You see the note?"

"No."

"Did you touch anything?"

"No. I just looked through the window."

"Okay." The officer turned as another squad car drew up behind his and two more officers got out. Five minutes later, the street teemed with people and the medical examiner was called. I leaned against the squad car, shivering as my brother's SUV pulled up, double parking across my car and Lily's. Garrett got out, followed by Daniel. Jord climbed out of the back seat with a shaky looking Ted behind him.

"Traci called," said Garrett, crossing the road and giving me a hug. "Are you okay?"

"Yeah. Just cold."

"Where's Lily?" asked Jord, looking around.

"On a date. She wasn't here."

"A date?" Jord's lips set into a thin line.

"Yeah, with a guy who's not afraid to go out with her."

Daniel punched Jord on the shoulder.

"I'm not afraid," said Jord straight away. "I don't want to date Lily."

Garrett raised an eyebrow and Daniel laughed. Even Ted giggled, his face getting redder. "I'd do her if I wasn't married," said Ted, thrusting his hips.

Jord's fists clenched as he turned to Ted, and I stepped between them.

"I can't believe we're related to that asshole," said Daniel, in a low voice when I steered Jord away. "I swear, he was hitting on the waitress at O'Grady's."

"Eugh! I hope you left her a big tip."

"Huge. And we had to promise the manager not to ever bring Ted again."

Garrett went over to talk to the first officer on the

scene, and Daniel remained, his arm around me, as Maddox showed up. After what seemed like a short, tense chat, and a few glances in my direction, Garrett and Maddox walked over to us. Maddox shook hands with Daniel.

"Does the name Finklestein mean anything to you?" asked Garrett.

"Nothing."

"You ever seen these two before?" he persisted.

I looked over at Maddox, wondering what I should say. He gave a tight shake of his head.

"Don't know," I said, which was the closest thing to not lying outright to my brother's face. Fortunately, I was saved from anymore questioning by a kerfuffle next to the dead men's car. When I looked over, I saw Ted being muscled backwards, his face going from red to white. We all jumped back as he doubled over and vomited at the curb.

"Can you take him home and clean him up?" I pleaded with my brothers. "Serena will kill you if she thinks you didn't take Ted out for a nice, quiet drink and a game of golf."

"We did take him out for a nice, quiet drink," protested Daniel.

"It was when we took him to Tito's Topless Bar and Grill that things got out of hand," added Jord.

"Jeez." "Topless" and "grill" were two words that didn't need to be in the same sentence.

"Blame Ted. We could have stayed at O'Grady's," said Jord.

"The corpse show was a nice nightcap though," said Daniel, moving to slap Ted on the back. "Take a good look at the dead dudes, Ted?"

"Can we do this next week?" asked Ted,

straightening up, but swaying.

"No," my brothers all said in unison.

"Guys, go home. I'm going back to my apartment."

"One of us should stay with you," suggested Garrett.

"I'll stay with her," said Maddox. Kudos to him, he didn't flinch when my brothers turned to him; kudos to them for not smacking their fists into their palms. "I know Lexi," he said.

"How, exactly, do you know my sister?" asked Garrett, and, like a wall of a muscle, the three of them stepped closer. Ted slumped against the SUV and blinked. The big wimp.

"Mind your own," I said. "Maddox, meet Garrett—I think you know each other already—and these are Daniel and Jord, my other brothers. That's my brother-in-law, Ted. If you don't know each other already, this is Detective Adam Maddox."

"Yeah, we know each other," said Garrett, his eyes flicking from Maddox to me. "You sure you want him to stay with you? It's not a problem if you want family instead."

"Yes, already. Now can you please clean Ted up?" I pleaded.

"Call me if you want to stay at my place," said Garrett. "I can come by after dropping these idiots off."

"Appreciated, but no thanks. Good night."

My brothers made a proprietary show of giving me a hug, and kissing my cheek, but I drew the line at Ted, not just because he reeked, but because I didn't like him. I side-stepped him and headed towards my house, Maddox at my side.

"All your family are cops?" he asked.

"Nineteen cops and counting. Ted's a lawyer."

He waited until we were inside before leaning against my desk as I sat on the couch. "You recognized them?" was his first question.

"Yeah. The goons who shot Martin Dean. How come they were outside my house?"

"Good question and I don't know yet. We've had a BOLO on them, but it looks like they were lying low."

"I guess they'll be lying six feet under now. Who were they?"

"Twinkles and Knuckles Finklestein."

I raised my eyebrows. "Twinkles and Knuckles?"

"If you knew them, you'd never laugh. Twinkles was really Eddie Finklestein. He was light on his feet but you'd see stars after he punched you, hence the name. His brother, Rick, or Knuckles, was a bare-knuckle fighter. They both had rap sheets a mile long. Burglary, extortion, assault, witness intimidation, domestic abuse, and maybe a few killings besides Dean's too, not that the latter ever stuck. I've heard of them, but didn't put it together that night. This is the first time I actually got to match faces with names."

Maddox was intimating I was lucky to have found them dead.

"It's not a coincidence they were outside your apartment," he told me and didn't look happy about it.

I took a few moments to regulate my breathing instead of racing around the living room screaming. "They were waiting for me?" I said finally.

"I think it's likely, yes."

"Someone sicced them on me?"

"Probably."

I went for the obvious. "Then who shot them?"

"I don't know. But I do know I feel kind of grateful to them right now. Can you sit tight a moment? I have to go talk to the M.E."

"I'm not going anywhere."

"Lock the door behind me."

Ten minutes later, which I used to spy through the window, along with every other resident within peering distance, as the M.E. prodded the bodies, Maddox returned. Since I watched him enter the apartment, I opened the door before he had a chance to knock.

"Did you read the note on Knuckles?" he asked.

"You're not the first person to ask me that. The first officer on scene did too. And, no. Why?"

Maddox opened the notebook in his hand and read from his notes. "It said, 'Consider this a warning.' It was typed, so we can count that as an indication this was premeditated."

"You think someone planned to kill them outside my house?"

"I think someone planned to kill them, not necessarily outside your place. The warning could have been meant for you, or for whoever hired the Finklesteins."

"This sucks."

"On the bright side, they can't hurt you now."

"Yeah. There's just a lunatic out there who can outsmart, and is more dangerous than the Finklesteins, along with the person who hired them."

"It wouldn't take much to outsmart them. They're brawn, not brains. Besides, someone shot them in the back of the head, so it's not like they saw it coming. I'm a little worried about whoever hired them. We'll be checking their known associates."

"This still sucks."

"Once everything is cleaned up out there, I'm going to assign a car to your door all night. You don't have to worry."

"In the space of a week, I've found four bodies. Four!" I was worried. It seemed like an awful lot for one person to find in such a short length of time.

Maddox crossed over to me and pulled me into a hug. I wrapped my arms around him gratefully and sank my head against his chest. He felt warm and comforting. Despite everything, he made me feel safe. A little bit of me wanted to ask him to stay, but I imagined the cops on the door would know, and probably tell someone. That would get to my brothers, who would either decide to befriend Maddox (read: make his life hell) or, even worse, they'd tell my parents a man slept over. I was fairly certain my parents knew I had boyfriends, but it didn't mean I wanted a lecture about it or constant bugging about if it was "serious".

"What's this?" Maddox pulled the carving knife from the back of my waistband and held it up.

"I didn't want to go outside without some kind of protection."

"You could have called the police from inside."

"I wasn't sure they were definitely dead until I was outside." The flaw in my plan hit me but Maddox didn't comment on it.

"Next time, call me straight away," he said, his voice serious.

"There isn't going to be a next time. I'm not going

to find any more bodies." *And if wishes were fishes...*

"That's good to know. I was worried on the way over."

"About me?"

"That I'd find you hurt."

"I'm okay." Better than okay, now his arms were around me again. I looked up, into his lovely eyes, now ablaze with worry. "Thanks for coming."

"No problem." He kissed me and my evening didn't suck so bad after all.

## CHAPTER THIRTEEN

Lily got home to find a squad car parked at the door and immediately came up to find out what was wrong. After assuring her everything was okay and there was nothing to worry about, she went back to her apartment, and after a while, everything got quiet. Along the street, people returned to their homes, lights switched off, and dogs were brought inside. After one last look outside to make sure the cops were still at my door and awake, I went to bed with the carving knife under the pillow, and had a restless night.

Worry gnawed at me. Martin Dean was dead, so was his girlfriend, and the two goons who killed Dean were shot to death outside my apartment, with a note that may or may not have been intended for me. Someone had definitely left me a clump of dead thorns.

The thing was, I was pretty certain the Finklesteins hadn't killed Dean's girlfriend. For one thing, they were too large and cumbersome. The man in the alley could run pretty fast. Plus, even though I hadn't seen him clearly that night, I could tell he wasn't either Twinkles or Knuckles. He was shorter and had hair. Somewhere in Montgomery, a merciless killer was still at large.

I had a number of possibilities, and none of them reassuring. I made a mental list, working through the options. One, the man in the alley was behind Dean's killing, Tanya/Tallulah's, and the Finklesteins. Except, I couldn't see why the Finklesteins were shot outside my building unless it was to scare me. But in that case, how did that man know who I was and where I lived?

Second, the man in the alley only killed Tanya, and might have had a possible connection to everything else. Unless her murder was a massive coincidence.

Third, I knew the Finklesteins killed Dean, but could their employer have killed them?

Fourth, someone else killed the Finklesteins, except that seemed like too much of a coincidence as well. It was becoming unreasonable to think that the four murders weren't connected, since their common denominator was Dean. I just couldn't see how one person could be responsible for four deaths.

Maddox picked me up in the morning and drove me to work after dismissing the officers who were replaced sometime in the night. We hadn't arranged to carpool, but truth be told, I was relieved to have the company.

"How did you sleep?" he asked.

"Badly." It wasn't just the murders that caused my sleepless night. Maddox played a part too. The kiss had been heavenly, reinforcing how yummy I thought he was. The occasional thought about Solomon also crept into my mind. "How do you sleep at night after seeing so much bad stuff?" I asked. I was trying to extinguish my mental comparison about the way they kissed. *Me.* Not each other.

He smiled. "I'm overworked. I just keel over at night, then start all over again the next day."

Vincent was exiting his car when we parked and got out two bays away. He ran his eyes over both of us, his forehead puckering into a cross frown. Saying nothing, he strode on ahead, although he did hold the elevator.

"Carpooling?" he blurted, like he couldn't contain his curiosity anymore.

"Car trouble. I had to call Adam for a lift," I lied.

"Do you need a ride home?" Vincent asked hopefully.

"No, thanks, Vincent. Besides, I don't think I'm on your way. My friend, Lily, is picking me up." That was a lie, too, but I didn't want it to look like Maddox was picking me up *and* taking me home. As the temp, being careful to avoid becoming office gossip, as well as not sleeping with the boss, was part of my job description. So far I had succeeded at both; staying on the edge of the former, while seriously wanting to do the latter.

"Nothing's out of the way for you, Lexi," Vincent said, winking as we exited the lift. I thought he was flirting with me, but I didn't have the patience to play along today. I tried hard not to encourage him, but he was so hopeful, like a happy little optimist that truly believed there was someone special for everyone. There probably was for Vincent too, but I was not she. I would not ever be his honey.

"You're sweet," I said. Vincent flushed, but smiled happily at me and zoomed off to his cubicle. I hoped he hadn't taken my kindness as encouragement, or more than what it was, which was simply kindness.

"He's sweet on you," said Maddox, clearly not even remotely bothered. "Please don't marry him. It'll break my heart."

"No chance of that."

"Why?"

"I have my eye on someone else."

Maddox smiled down at me. "Anyone I know?"

"Maybe," I said, arching my eyebrows at him, as I peeled away to my own desk. I slid my purse underneath and powered up. Busying myself by arranging my notepad and pens while waiting for the password screen to pop up, I entered it and looked down again at my handwritten to-do list.

When I looked up, I shrieked and almost fell out of my chair seeing the screen. Instead of the generic background, big capital words spelled out "I'M WATCHING YOU."

Maddox's IM box immediately popped up.

Adam: *What?*

Me: *Someone changed my screensaver.*

Adam: *?*

Me: *Do that thing where you can see my screen.*

I waited a moment, then saw that Maddox was typing.

Adam: *Oh.*

Me: *Can you see it? Who did that?*

Adam: *I'll look into it.*

Me: *I'm getting rid of it.*

I closed the IM window, and changed the

screensaver back to the generic screen. It was bad enough that someone already deleted my files, but now they were in my computer leaving messages that they were watching me too. I hoped they weren't watching everything I was doing. That would be creepy as hell for me, and boring for them. Even worse, it made last night's note pinned on Knuckles even more frightening.

I snuck a glance at Maddox, wondering if he thought the same, but his brow was furrowed as he concentrated on his screen. There was no way I could work without caffeine, so I went to the kitchenette and switched the pot on, too shaken to function.

"Hey there. You need a caffeine boost too?" Vincent sidled past me, aiming for the coffee pot. He touched it with the back of his hand to check if it were ready, before pulling a mug from the open shelf above. "Pass the sugar, sugar! Hah!"

I rolled my eyes and pushed the sugar over to him. "It's a caffeine type of morning," I said, ignoring his attempt at flirting.

"You need a shoulder to lean on, I got two." Vincent patted one of them with a pasty hand.

"That's very nice of you," I said. "But I'm just going to dive into work."

"Maybe you want to get lunch later? A friend in need is a friend indeed."

"That's very true, but I have a half day today."

"Doing anything nice? Shopping? Spa?"

"Hanging out with my brother." After Garrett dropped my brothers and Ted off, he called and promised to take me to the shooting range so I could try out some different guns. Apparently, after the events of last night, he pulled some strings, got some time off work and booked the range for today.

Maddox had no problem giving me the afternoon off, especially after he heard I was going to be with Garrett. I hadn't told him exactly what we were doing though. I sensed he wouldn't be overly thrilled about me going to the range. After all, I was supposed to be avoiding danger, but I saw no harm in preparing for it, especially now that the threats were getting so much more personal. Plus, without requisite boyfriend status, he had no right to ask me not to do something, or expect me to answer to him.

"Any plans for the weekend?" Vincent persisted. He tapped the spoon against the countertop. He tried to flip and catch it, but missed and the spoon skittered across the floor.

"No. Not yet." So long as it didn't involve dead bodies, I was good. "You?"

He retrieved the spoon and leant against the counter casually. "This and that. Going to try out that new barbecue place. Want to come?"

"Oh, I..."

"Lexi, make me a coffee while you're getting yours and bring it to conference room one." Maddox's voice boomed behind us and Vincent jumped. "Fast as you can," he added.

"Sure. Coming right up," I said. I snagged the pot as soon as the light clicked off and made our coffees, scooting away before Vincent could ask me out again.

"Shut the door," Maddox said, barely looking up when I entered the conference room. I kicked it shut and placed the mugs on the table, sliding into a seat on the curve of the table, not quite next to Maddox, but not far away either.

"Thanks for saving me," I said gratefully. "Any

news on the Finklesteins?"

"Solomon is working on it. We're looking for the link between the brothers and whoever hired them. Let's hope someone got sloppy."

"Okay. Good. Great." So, not great. Someone out there was probably pissed off that their hired thugs were dead, and that meant more people pissed at me. The rational part of my mind insisted that I had nothing to do with the goons' deaths, it could have been just a coincidence that they parked on my street. It was simply unfortunate that someone chose to shoot them there, right outside my building. The irrational part of me wanted to run home to my parents and hide under their bed. "What do you want me to do?"

"Go back to work. Chat with the other employees."

"What do you want me to talk to them about? The night Dean died?" I didn't remind him that he thought I should be off the case. If he didn't bring it up, neither would I.

"No, don't mention that at all. We're going to announce it tomorrow morning. Just talk about whatever you normally talk about. See if anyone's body language is off. Has someone developed a nervous twitch, or a guilty expression about something? Someone having secret phone conversations or acting like they're doing something they shouldn't be."

"Can't you do this stuff?"

"I'm the boss. Everyone acts nervous in front of me."

"I don't. Do I?"

"You send me lingerie pictures."

"That was an accident." I got up and grabbed my coffee, flashing him an indignant look. My hand was on the door handle, when he asked, "So what did you get?"

"Hmm?"

"Did you buy that lingerie?"

"Like you don't already know. You forgot that you told me you can see everything I do on my computer."

Maddox grinned. He looked really happy. "The lemon set *is* sexy."

I rolled my eyes and walked out, trying not to imagine him looking at me while I wore it and nothing else. I spent the next five minutes Googling dating websites and dog houses, while hoping he got the message. Then it occurred to me that whoever else was monitoring my computer was probably getting very mixed messages about my personality. I shut the browser and pretended to work like normal.

Through the morning hours until lunch, I made excuses to talk to everyone from Dominic, Bob, and Anne, to a few of the suits that occupied the other half of our office. No one seemed abnormal at all, though Anne tried to persuade Lily and me to give her burlesque troupe a chance. I resigned myself to finishing the spreadsheet Dominic begged me to do, emailing it to him just as Garrett called to let me know he was parking in the lot. I waved goodbye to Maddox and went downstairs, pausing in the lobby to text Maddox. I let him know I saw nothing out of the ordinary, just in case he hadn't already used his detective instincts to work it out.

Garrett took one look at my neat shift dress and heels and drove me home to change.

~

The shooting range was a popular spot with the MPD. Garrett got a warm reception from the man behind the desk, who signed us in. Not long afterwards, we were ushered into a booth on the range.

"When was the last time you shot a gun?" he asked.

I wrinkled my face up in thought. "I was twenty-four," I said finally. It was a bleak period of my life that coincided with the army incident I tried to forget. "Rifles and handguns. I don't remember what type."

"So you're probably rusty?" he asked.

"I have no idea."

"Try this one." Garrett loaded a small revolver and handed it to me. Then he placed a pair of earmuffs over my head. "Aim and fire when you're ready. We've got the range to ourselves."

I readied myself, held the revolver forward, my arms straight and shoulders relaxed before squeezing off a shot. I hit the second ring out.

"Not bad," shouted Garrett. "Do a couple more."

I emptied the gun, scoring one inner ring, another second and the rest dotted around the outer rings. I made sure the gun was safe and laid it on the shelf in front of our booth.

"How's that?" I pulled my earmuffs off and Garrett grinned. He pressed the button to bring the paper towards us and we examined it.

"It's a Graves thing," he said proudly. "We can shoot anything."

"We can even shoot our mouths off."

"That, too. How about something bigger? A Glock? A SIG Sauer?"

We returned the revolver and booked out the SIG. "It's a good size, accurate too," explained Garrett as he showed me how to load the magazine and insert it. "It comes in compact too."

"Like a dangerous tampon," I said.

"Yeah, that'll make the bad guys run."

"They wouldn't need to run. They could rollerskate or windsurf with the SIG Tampon Compact."

"Fire the gun, sis'."

Garrett made approving noises about my aim, secured the gun and we went back to check out a different model. Garrett ran me through my paces on a variety of weapons until I settled on the SIG Compact. During our last twenty minutes, I fired round after round, my shots gradually becoming tighter together.

"This is the one I want," I told him, giving the weapon a friendly pat.

"Are you going to tell me why you need it?"

"Just to keep at home." I shrugged like it didn't matter.

"With you and Lily on your own, I guess it's a good idea to have some extra security."

"Right," I agreed.

We both thought about the Finklesteins. I hoped Garrett assumed that West Montgomery was just getting to be a bad neighborhood, and not that I was the target. He looked at me for a long time before he said, "We can set you up in a few days."

"I can't go get one now?"

"Baby steps. It's a gun, not a new sweater." I followed Garrett out of the range, waiting while he exchanged hellos with some buddies in the small lobby. I climbed in the car alongside him, but he didn't turn the engine on right away. Instead, he said, "You can tell me if something is wrong. I'm not going to blab to the rest of the family. Not even Traci, if you say not to."

"Nothing is wrong, honest."

"I gotta admit, Lexi, I'm kinda worried. The Finklesteins turn up dead outside your place, I get why you want a gun. But you wanted one before that and you were asking about Maddox. Then he turns up and you two seem to know each other. Something doesn't smell right."

"I may not be a cop, but we're a cop family. Of course, I know other cops."

"That doesn't really answer anything. So, I'm going to ask you again, Lexi, are you in any kind of trouble? Something you don't want to tell me about perhaps? 'Cause I gotta tell you, after fifteen years on the force, I've seen everything." I was quiet a long while, thinking what I could say. Evidently, Garrett got bored because he asked, "Is it Lily? Is Lily okay?"

"Yeah, she's fine."

"So it is you." This time it wasn't a question.

"Yeah, it's me. Garrett, you can't tell anyone about this." And despite orders to the contrary, I told him, because Garrett wasn't just on any team, he was on my team and he was a cop. And someone had left me the deadheaded roses and the creepy message, neither of which thrilled me to the core.

I told him about finding Dean and seeing the Finklesteins get rid of his body, then how Maddox and I got out of there, and how I found out he was a cop running an investigation with the FBI. I omitted plenty of stuff. There was no need to mention my breaking and entering moment, or the rediscovery of Martin Dean, or the stuff at the club, or when Lily and I visited Tara Henderson. I did tell him that I'd been snooping around the office.

"I can't believe Maddox got you mixed up in this." Garrett's face was impossible to read. I saw him look similar when his oldest kid got suspended after being caught spraying graffiti on the school gym's wall. It was his quiet, contemplative look while he decided whether to explode or not.

"He's just doing his job."

"He's putting you in danger because he wants a result."

"It's not like that."

Garrett inclined his head to look at me. "Please don't tell me he turned his puppy dog eyes on you and told you that you were part of the team."

"Actually his joint taskforce boss at the FBI approved it."

"Jesus!"

"No, his name is Matt Miller."

"This isn't a game, Lexi. You got mixed up with the Finklesteins, so someone means business. You did the right thing in applying for the permit. You should get a gun, but you can't carry it. You need a concealed weapon permit for that." Garrett leaned his head on the neck rest and closed his eyes. "I'll talk to Maddox's lieutenant tonight. We'll put you somewhere safe until whatever this is blows over."

"No. Garrett, I'm okay. Really, I am."

"Has he got someone watching you?"

"Not that I know of. But he had a car parked at my house after I found the Finklesteins."

"You shouldn't be wandering around."

"I'm not, I'm with you and Maddox picked me up this morning. You want me to come and stay at your house? Put Traci and the kids in danger? Or how about Mom and Dad? I don't think so, Gar'."

"You could stay with Jord?"

"Have you seen his apartment? Bachelor hell. It's covered in sports equipment and his roommate's girly magazines."

"You could take Lily. That would put her off Jord."

We laughed and took a moment to think about that. I wasn't sure what would put Lily off Jord, but after seeing her get-up for working the door at Flames, I didn't think a few editions of skin magazines would put her off in the least.

"The moment I disappear, or leave to stay with one of you guys, anyone who is watching me will smell a rat. Right now, all I can do is try to be normal. Go to work, go home, hang out," I explained. "Just be normal."

Garrett slammed the wheel and the horn honked, making us both jump, then laugh again. "I want you to get a tracker and keep it on you, along with an alarm. Then I'm going to talk to Maddox. Next time you see him, he might have two black eyes and be walking funny."

"I'll buy some ice." I didn't tell him that Maddox already bugged my cell phone.

"Let's get you home. I want to check the security on your place."

"It's shit," I told him. "But I have a carving knife."

"You ever carve anything with it?"

"No, but it's under my pillow, just in case I get the

urge to slice something in the dark."

"Jeez."

Garrett brought me home, staying for a long while to poke around my apartment and make a list of all the security improvements it needed. Everything, apparently, needed securing after seeing the way he rattled the windows and played with the door locks. After he left, muttering under his breath, Serena called in a panic and asked me to stop by her house, hanging up before I could ask why. Lily poked her head out of her door when I was on my way downstairs, so I figured that made it okay to strong-arm her into coming with me.

"Want to go out for dinner on the way back?" she asked.

I did. I really did. I wanted to go out and have a nice meal and a few glasses of wine and arrive home, feeling warm and safe. Unfortunately, after Garrett's lecture, I also had a healthy dose of paranoia and I wanted to lock my doors and hide in the closet, right after I made sure no one else was already in there.

"Let's pick something up," I suggested. "My treat. Chinese?"

"You're on."

Lily drove, seeing as she had to run a couple of errands on the way. "What does Serena want?" she asked.

"She didn't say. Just that it was important."

When we got there and knocked, I heard Serena weakly calling, "It's open!" so I pushed the door and went in, saying, "Hello?"

"Kitchen!"

"What's wrong?" I asked, clipping along the hallway, Lily at my heels. Serena stood hunched over in the kitchen, hands on thighs, breathing hard, a puddle of water by her feet.

"My water broke."

I looked down at the puddle around her toes. "Actually, I think you smashed a glass."

Serena looked up and frowned, then tried to look over her sizeable bump. "Are you sure? My belly is really tight."

"Maybe you're having those Braxton Hicks thingies?" suggested Lily. "It's too early to go into labor."

"Oh. Maybe." Serena levered herself into an upright position and blinked. "I guess if that was labor, it was a lot easier than I thought it would be."

"You'll know when you're in labor," said Lily, taking Serena by the arm and guiding her to the living room. Meanwhile, I plundered the cabinets for a dustpan to brush up the glass and a dishcloth to mop the floor.

"Is this why you called me over?" I asked. "Where's Ted? You should have called him if you thought you were in labor."

"Yes, and I don't know," Serena replied as Lily settled a pillow under her back. She also moved the footstool so Serena could put her feet up. "I called him and he said he had a business dinner and couldn't make it."

"You told him you thought you were in labor, right?"

"Yes. He told me the dinner was too important to miss and I'd have to cross my legs and wait it out."

Lily pulled a face. "He knows babies don't care about dinners, doesn't he? And if you were in labor this early, you would need to be in the hospital right away?"

"More importantly, does Ted know he's an asshole?" I asked.

"He really is an asshole, isn't he?" Serena groaned and stretched.

"Yeah. And anytime you think you're going to pop, call me first. I'll come straight over. You won't have to cross your legs for as long." My only hope was that Ted would arrive before it got gory.

"Thanks. I appreciate it."

"Aww. I'd hug you, but I don't think my arms can fit around you," I teased, but it was partially true. Serena was huge.

"Raincheck. I'll be skinny in a few months again. I've already booked post-pregnancy boot camp."

"What the hell is that?"

"Military-style weight loss and toning. I can even bring the baby."

"Sounds awesome." Sounded hellish, but that was Serena for you. "Can I get you anything before we take off?"

"No. I'm fine. Sorry for calling you out here for nothing."

"Not a problem."

We climbed back in Lily's Mini and buckled up. "So," she said. "Chinese?"

"Yes. I'm starved."

"Wing's?"

"You bet."

Lily backed out of Serena's driveway and pointed the car towards Wing's, both of us lost in our own thoughts momentarily. Mine were mostly on the menu, which I had half memorized.

"You ever wanted to be a mom?" asked Lily,

surprising me.

"I don't know. I guess." I pondered that some more. I had a crappy job, an okay car, a nice apartment, below market rate thanks to Lily's parents, and a distinct lack of commitment from a man. "Not any time soon though."

"Me either, but one day. I want to be a stay-at-home mom. It sounds nice."

"Nicer than working the clubs, eating out, drinking cocktails and sleeping in?"

"A different nice."

"Better than being skinny?"

"There's boot camp and I have great genes."

"I can see you being a mom."

"Me too. I bet Maddox would make beautiful babies."

"You want to have babies with Maddox?" My voice came out an octave higher than intended.

"No! Besides, he wants to make them with you."

"He might want to have sex with me. I don't think babies are on his agenda."

"What about Solomon?"

"I suspect he eats babies."

"Eugh!"

"Not really. I don't see Solomon as the type to change diapers and wear a Snugli. He's silent and dangerous."

"He's sexy and dangerous."

"You think too much about Maddox and Solomon."

"At least I'm thinking."

Wasn't I thinking about them too? I was probably thinking too much. So far, Maddox had starred in enough dreams that I'd lost count. Solomon had popped up in one, startling me enough to wake me up, panting. But back to real life, both had kissed me, and both held me when I needed them, their arms like steel girders around me.

I considered myself a powerful, in-control woman, since I hadn't gone in for a sneaky squeeze or given them the come-on. Well, I might have given them some indication that I liked them. But when I thought about that, I remembered Maddox kept inviting himself over, and the way he angled to get closer to me didn't strike me as strictly professional. Of course, that made me think about Solomon and his slow, sexy smiles. The way he looked at me with smoldering eyes and had no hesitation about crashing our not-a-date, or rescuing me when I needed him.

"What's the sigh for?" asked Lily.

"I just saw Wing's," I lied, firmly relegating Maddox and Solomon to the back of my mind while Lily parked in the lot. We ordered, loitering in the small, tiled, lobby area while it was being prepared. Then, with the hot paper sack filled with dinner in hand, Lily yawned, handed me the keys and we climbed back into her car.

For some reason, the main road into West Montgomery was all snarled up, so instead of twiddling our thumbs in traffic, I drove away from home and used side streets. We managed to bypass the majority of the traffic, backtracking and rejoining where it petered out and pointed towards home.

I pondered the Maddox slash Solomon thing as I drove and Lily snoozed, her head nodding towards the side window. Glancing in my rearview mirror as I switched lanes, I noticed a large, black car making the same maneuver. Perhaps they were just impatient, but like a good spy, I glanced in the mirror every few minutes. I signaled left but didn't turn, and slipped through the light traffic, while watching as the car matched our movements.

*Hmm. Suspicious!*

The SUV had tinted windows and I couldn't see who was driving, or the passengers. Now, however, I thought this was becoming less exciting and more scary, especially as Lily's Mini was just the right size to be their car's baby. I put my foot down and accelerated, trying to ignore the dial on the dashboard as it crept over the speed limit. The SUV never left us.

"Lily?" I whispered, "Lily?"

"Uhhhnn-err," snorted Lily.

"Lily!" I hissed, a little more loudly this time, finally shouting, "Lily!"

Her whole body shook as she jumped, her eyes flashing awake. "What? Was I talking in my sleep? I swear to God, none of it is true!"

"No, you weren't, but I think we're being followed."

"Whaaat?" Lily started to turn, but I shot my arm out, blocking her.

"Don't turn round. They'll know we're onto them."

"Why would anyone be following us? Are you speeding? You are so paying the ticket!"

"I'm not speeding." Actually, I was, but that wasn't the problem as I eased up on the gas. The problem was the car that stayed a regulation three vehicles behind us, kept weaving through the traffic whenever I did, and speeding up whenever I went faster.

"What's going on, Lexi?"

"I don't know what you mean."

"Don't play dumb with me, missy. I've known you too long. There were two dead dudes in the street last night, and now someone is following us." Her suspicious face, combined with the dark sky, infiltrated by the flashes of streetlamps ahead, made me shrink lower into my seat. Her mouth dropped open. "Oh my God! They really *are* following us!"

"They might not be following us," I squeaked.

"Tell me the truth!"

I broke. "They probably are following us."

Lily spoke slowly, in the no-nonsense voice she usually reserved for people trying to creep past the bouncers to get into one of her clubs. "What really happened last night?"

"The dead guys are the men I saw getting rid of my boss' body and now someone has offed them and Maddox said they might want to kill me." I sucked in a breath. Wow. Getting that off my chest felt so much better. "And I promised not to tell anyone!"

"Maddox wants to kill you? Cute Maddox who isn't your boyfriend?"

"No, he doesn't want to kill me, and yes, that Maddox. Is there any other?"

"Huh. What else haven't you told me?" To Lily's credit, she didn't say a word until I finished filling her in on the extra details from the ominous note to the creepy screensaver at work. "Holy crap," Lily said at last. "Someone is after you."

"So, you believe me?" Hell, I wouldn't have.

"And now you think this car is following us?"

I glanced in the mirror. Yep, the car was still behind us, and thanks to the traffic snarling up again, we were still far from home. "I'm sure," I replied. "It's been on our tail for a while."

"What are we going to do? What are they going to do?"

"It depends who they are."

"Maybe they're from Maddox. Maybe he's got someone watching over you to make sure you're okay?"

"I guess." But they were being kind of obvious about it and I thought Maddox was more subtle than that.

"We need to call him." Lily reached round, careful not to look up and grabbed my jacket, pulling my cell from the pocket. She tapped in my pin number, ignoring me when I scowled, open-mouthed, at her. "You're not exactly discreet with the pin. It's also the same as both your credit cards."

"I'll change them on Monday."

"Do not change them to the same code as your laptop."

Drat. That was the first sequence I thought of.

"It's ringing." She listened, for a moment, then, "Hey, Adam Maddox? It's Lily, Lexi's friend. Yes, she's fine, but we were just wondering... *Arrrgh!*" Lily didn't finish because right then, the Mini suddenly hurtled forward, the wheel sliding through my hands as the SUV rammed us from behind. Instantly, we were both screaming and Maddox was shouting, his voice sounding tinny through the phone's earpiece. My future flashed before my eyes: Serena screaming at me for ruining her baby's birth by dying; my parents' sad faces at my imminent funeral; and Lily in the hospital, injured, because I couldn't ever think of her as dead.

Then the SUV came at us again, ramming for a second time.

# CHAPTER FOURTEEN

"Breathe," screamed Lily. "In! One, two, three. Out! One, two, three. Are you with me? Breathe, Lexi. Breathe!"

"I'm breathing," I screamed back, the wheel securely under my hands. I gripped it so hard, my knuckles went white. Slapping my foot down and pressing the pedal to the metal, we shot forward as fast as Lily's little Mini could manage. Unfortunately, that was no match for the SUV bearing down on us. Somehow, I became vaguely aware of Maddox still shouting my name, his voice sounding from somewhere near our feet.

"Maddox!" I yelled, then to Lily, "Ask Maddox what to do!"

Lily grappled for the phone, pressing it against her ear then turning it the right way up. "We're okay," she screeched, "But the car rammed us. Uh, a big, black one. No, I can't see, it's got tinted windows. It's not yours? No shit! Yes, we're going faster!" In a calmer voice, she said, "Lex, he wants to speak to you."

My first thought was, "I'm driving," but considering we were now fifteen miles over the speed limit, and I'd just pulled through lanes without signaling, speaking on a phone while driving probably didn't even count as an offense anymore. I inclined my head and Lily pressed the phone against my ear.

Maddox's worried voice exclaimed, "Lexi? Thank God you're okay."

"For now! Adam, are they trying to kill us?"

"Ohmygodthey'retryingtokilluuuuus!" Lily screamed.

"Breathe!" I snapped, then concentrated on Maddox. "What do I do? There isn't a turnoff for miles and we're in a Mini being rammed by the equivalent of a tank."

"Keep going forward."

"Good thinking, Adam! Keep 'em coming." I could barely avoid the sarcasm in of my voice.

"You're going to have to anticipate their every move and outsmart them until I can get someone out to you."

"How am I supposed to do that?"

"You've got to put as much distance between you and them as possible. As soon as you see them start to turn, you've got to use that to your advantage..."

"Lexi... Lex... Uh..." Lily gestured frantically behind us as the SUV sped up, dodged past a car that had slid in front of them, into the inside lane, and jumped in right behind us. I swerved into the right lane, causing the car behind to honk at us, and put my foot down, jetting us forward as the SUV got stuck behind a slow moving truck. Lily put the phone back to my ear.

"What happened?"

"I lost them behind a truck. What now?" I asked Maddox.

"Put your foot down, Lexi. I'll have someone meet you at the next junction."

"Who..." Then Lily and I were both screaming again as something blasted through the rear window and lodged into the dashboard. The phone tumbled to the floor. We looked at each other in horror as it registered that whoever was following us wasn't content just to take us off the road. They were now shooting at us. Simultaneously, we both slunk lower in our seats until I could barely see over the steering wheel.

"A few minutes, Lily. That's how long we've got to the junction. Just a few minutes." I could only hope we would last that long.

"Lexi, I just want you to know that you're the best friend I ever had and I'm really sorry for ruining your purple dress."

"You're my best friend too. And I'm sorry for taking your yellow bag and never giving it back."

"It suits you better anyway." Lily sounded so horribly resigned that I risked taking my hand off the wheel to reach over and give her a little squeeze. "Get us out of here and you can keep it," she said.

"You got it." I would have sounded so much more confident if my words hadn't turned into a scream as I slammed on the brake with scant seconds to spare before the SUV tried to sideswipe us into the guardrail. Instead, sparks flew off their side. I pulled hard on the steering wheel, taking us into the next lane and sped past while Lily flipped them the finger.

"The turn's coming up." Lily pointed to the sign indicating how far before the road would split away.

I crossed my fingers on the wheel, hoping with every last bit of my body that Maddox had come through for us as we sailed past, the SUV increasingly gaining on us. My mirror glances were every ten seconds now as I tried to anticipate what they would do next. That was how I spied the motorcycle hurtling forth from nowhere. It came veering out from behind the SUV. The rider drew a gun, pointed, aimed and my heart stopped.

Then the SUV slowed, and wobbled slightly as it sped onto the side, clipped the guardrail, bouncing a bit before entering into a spin. We pulled away, the distance finally growing between us. The motorcycle, however, was gaining, but I saw the rider putting the gun away into some kind of sling over his shoulder and he... he signaled to us. Lily leaned forward, frowning.

"Hello, Nighthawk," she said; then to me, "I think we're supposed to follow."

"You sure?" I asked, blood rushing in my ears.

She shrugged. "He didn't shoot us. He shot them."

Good enough for me. The rider waved again before pulling in front of us, slowing down to the speed limit and forcing us to as well. We followed him as he pulled off into a gas station and drew to a stop in the parking bays off to one side. I pointed the Mini at the furthest bay, leaving the engine running, just in case we were duped and about to get an unwanted hole in our heads. We watched silently as the rider swung one leather-clad leg over the bike and strode purposefully towards us, sliding the zipper of his jacket down. By gosh, that was sexy. He reached for his helmet, pulled it off, and I realized I hadn't even taken a breath.

Solomon stopped, bent down and smiled, making a little winding motion with his hand. I hit the button and waited while the electric window unwound the full length. I returned my hand to the wheel, gripping it hard.

"Thank you so much," gushed Lily, leaning across me while Solomon's eyes ran over me, assessing me for damage and finding none. "They tried to kill us!" She jabbed a finger at the hole, still smoking in the dashboard.

"Open the hood," he said and Lily leaned down a bit further, giving Solomon a marvelous view of her cleavage while she found the lever. I switched the engine off and leaned back against the seat, closing my eyes and taking a few deep breaths. We were safe. After rooting around under the hood for a moment, he slammed it shut, moving back to crouch next to my door. "You're in luck. The bullet didn't hit anything crucial so you're good to drive home. You okay to drive?" he asked me.

"I... I think so." My hands were still gripping the wheel so tightly that I had no idea if they were shaking or not. I wiggled my toes. My legs felt okay. I could probably hit the gas and brakes. "Yes."

"I'll follow you back." He stood up and turned to move away.

"Solomon?" He turned, placing one hand on the roof as he stooped to look right at me, with darkened eyes. "Thanks," I said feebly, "for helping us."

He just nodded and strode off, the helmet sliding over his closely cropped hair as he swung astride the bike.

"Yummy yum yum," Lily breathed.

"Solomon is not yummy," I said. "Solomon transcends yum."

"He's eye candy-on-a-stick."

Privately, I agreed. Everything tasted better on a stick.

"I'm glad you told me," Lily continued. "I had no idea your life had turned into Scary Shitsville. Plus, that would have been scary even without all the other facts."

"I'm glad I told you everything too. Shitsville was getting lonely."

"If you disappear, or turn up dead, I promise I won't rest until your murderer is caught and convicted."

"Um, thanks."

"No problem."

Maddox was waiting for us on the doorstep by the time I drove the beat-up Mini into Lily's parking space. Solomon pulled his motorcycle in behind us, kicking out the stand as he dismounted.

Lily paused with her hand on the door handle. "I gotta say, Lexi, this was not my favorite way to end the day."

"Sorry," I muttered, getting out. I slammed the door and the bumper fell off. "We still have Chinese though."

"Is it possible to panic eat egg rolls?" Lily asked, opening the bag.

"Glad you're okay," said Adam, his face filled with concern as he approached us, ushering us inside. Lily dropped her bag inside the door of her apartment and followed us upstairs with the sack of food.

"Did you get the guys? The people who rammed us, shot at us and tried to bump us off the road?"

Well, I tried not to let my slightly resentful tone make its way through, but failed miserably. It was there, loaded and angry. Four murders were bad enough, but I didn't want someone to find Lily's and my bodies, boosting the corpse count to six. I imagined my parents' heartbroken faces again, my coffin covered in white lilies—my vision becoming more solid the longer I thought about it—and the anger mounting a bit more. I breathed in and out through my nose, trying to calm down.

"No. They were gone by the time our team got to them," Maddox told us.

"Were they really going to kill us?" I asked.

"Yes, I think so." He spoke gently, despite the harsh reality of his words.

"You warned me."

"I did."

"They're going to keep trying, aren't they?" I huffed an annoyed sound.

"Probably."

"We'd better find out what the connection is between the fraud, Tanya Henderson and the Finklesteins then," I said.

Lily added, "She's your best hope of cracking this case."

"Dear Lord," said Solomon, behind her. I hadn't realized he followed us in, but Maddox just smiled in his gentle way and escorted all of us into my apartment.

Lily, who seemed to have recovered from our ordeal remarkably fast—though it could have had something to do with two handsome men in close proximity—fussed around us. She made drinks and raided my cookie jar while I sat down. Then I keeled forwards, my head in my hands, until I stopped feeling sick. My only other option was to curl up in fetal position and start bawling. Knowing how unproductive that would be, and the likelihood of Maddox drugging me again, I decided I might as well get to know my potential enemies better. I would freak out, privately, later.

Then I'd get a gun.

~

For the second night in a row, I had a car parked outside my door, and again, Maddox picked me up in the morning. To avoid gossip, I decided to walk in ahead of Maddox, saying my hellos to my colleagues as I made my way towards my desk.

When Maddox arrived five minutes later, he gathered us all together.

"You may have noticed that Martin hasn't been at his desk this week," he began, his eyes scanning the small assembly. "I'm sure this will come as a shock to all of you, as it did to me, and there's no easy way to say this. Martin was found dead at his home over the weekend. I'm afraid I don't have anymore details, but I will keep you informed. For now, let's just keep working."

"Probably a heart attack," said Anne, next to me. "He wasn't exactly a healthy eater."

"Mmm," I said, noncommittally.

"Mind you, my first husband was as fit as you like and he had a heart attack too."

"It could happen to any of us," I replied. Last night, for example, I could have died in a car crash, but I decided not to mention that. On the way in, Maddox told me the SUV was reported stolen and found clean of prints. As the driver left the scene, he was alive, although possibly injured, and definitely pissed off.

Anne nodded. "Certainly could. I wonder what happens to Green Hand now? Maybe we'll get a new boss, and you know how new bosses are, they always want to shake things up. I'm three years away from retirement. No one will hire me now," she finished, gloomily.

"Sure they will," I said, trying not to think how many years away from retirement I was and whether that whole time would be filled temping. Perhaps it was time to get my résumé in order.

"Maybe. I don't think the company was doing that well." Anne turned to walk away and I followed her to her desk. She didn't seem to mind.

"Why do you think that?" I asked.

"I think Green Hand were paying out on more policies than they anticipated. I heard Dominic mention to Martin and Vincent that it was unusual." Anne had worked here almost as long as Dean, so they had been on first name terms. I still didn't know what Anne did, and it seemed impolite to ask, especially when she made an effort to look busy, and I'd been here a while and really should have known by now.

"What was so unusual about that?"

"Just a lot of the policies that hadn't been open long and were already paying out, especially when it came to damage. The ratio between theft and damage usually stays the same, but over the last quarter, the ratio was skewed."

"Odd," I said.

"I know. It's probably just one of those things."

"Probably," I agreed, returning to my desk. I

opened a file, ruffled some papers over my desk and went internet surfing.

At lunch, Lily stopped by and we walked over to the café where I'd had lunch with Maddox. We bought sandwiches and grabbed a couple of tall stools by the window.

"Insurance will cover the Mini's damage," she told me. "It got picked up at nine. And I filed a police report this morning. They want your statement too."

It struck me that I was spending far too much time at or with the Montgomery Police Department lately. "Sure. When do they want me in?"

"Anytime in the next couple of days," she said. "Are you sure it's okay to use your car? I wouldn't ask, but I have so much stuff to do today, and I'm on the door at eight."

"Yeah. Just replace whatever gas you use. Maddox is giving me a ride home."

"Is he staying for dinner?" Lily winked.

"I don't know. Maybe." I shrugged, taking a bite of my chicken sandwich. "He told everyone Dean was dead."

"No way. Anyone wig out?"

"No, but Anne mentioned something odd. She said the ratio between theft and damage was skewed."

"I don't follow."

"I don't so much either, but Dominic, Dean's assistant, apparently thought it was odd that there were more claims for damage than usual and the policies hadn't been open long."

"What kind of damage?"

"I don't know. This office handles the policies for all kinds of stuff. Not cars though, that's the Boston office."

Lily sipped her coffee and looked thoughtful. "I guess theft has to have a police report, and damage doesn't."

I nodded. "It would be easier to file a fake damage claim." Something niggled at me, something was missing, but I couldn't squeeze the thought into fruition.

"You have any idea which claims were fake and which weren't?"

"No. And if Maddox does, he hasn't told me." As far as I knew, they were no closer to breaking the case.

"Maybe you could have a look in the files? See if anything raises a red flag?"

"I guess. Did I mention Anne said a lot of the newer policies had paid out too? Some policies can run for years without a payout."

"Sounds like a place to start."

No one was in the office when I got back, except Vincent, who gave me a cheery wave and offered me a donut. His lips were covered in confectioner's sugar. I declined and he shrugged as he went back to work. I switched my monitor on and clicked through to the shared server, calling up some of the recent payouts files.

Using a pen, I scribbled the names, dates, addresses, account numbers and length of policy on the payouts. I wasn't sure what I was looking for, but I was interested to see if a pattern emerged. I continued until my hand cramped and made a possibilities list of one hundred policies, all of which had paid out in less than six months of their opening date. I exited the files and called up an internet browser, typing a few of the local addresses into

Google Maps, just out of curiosity. Most of the addresses were average family homes or apartment buildings, nothing out of the ordinary.

I went down the list, ticking off the ones on my way home, and came up with twelve and the crazy idea that I was onto something.

# CHAPTER FIFTEEN

Picking up my cell phone, I checked to see if anyone was nearby, but the desks were empty, my colleagues still out to lunch. Only Vincent was there, wearing his headphones. I called Lily. She was in my car when she answered. "Hey, I got the weirdest idea. Are you doing anything right now?"

"I was going to go to the gym. I want to punch the crap out of something," she replied.

I knew what she meant. "Can you check on something for me instead? You'll need a pen." I heard shuffling noises, then Lily said, "Shoot."

I reeled off the twelve addresses while she jotted them down. "Can you just drive by these places and tell me if anything stands out?" I said.

"Sure. What am I looking for?"

"I really don't know. It was just a hunch."

"I feel like a private detective. Should I go home and get a disguise?" Hopefulness was hanging in her voice.

"No. Just drive by. Call me if you see anything

odd."

I hung up and slipped my notepad and cell phone into my purse, before closing the browser. I jumped when I felt a presence suddenly behind me.

"Only guilty people jump," said Vincent, hitching one cheek onto my desk with utter disregard for any of the papers I had strewn about. The papers didn't mean anything; I just wanted to look busy, but that wasn't the point.

"I didn't hear you sneak up on me."

"I wasn't sneaking. I have light feet. How would you feel about dinner tonight? You. Me. A little wine."

"That sounds like a date to me."

"Call it how you see it, babe." Vincent winked at me and my stomach churned. The niceness would have to stop, clearly.

"I don't think we're allowed to date colleagues," I said as gently as I could.

"The boss is dead. Who cares? Let's live a little."

Wow. Cold. I backtracked, scrambling for an excuse that Vincent could actually take without wanting to screw up my timecards. "I mean temps. We're not allowed to date people we work with. It gives us a bad reputation."

"I don't think you can get a bad reputation dating an accountant."

He was probably right and it would also make my mother very happy. Unfortunately, the Vincent-shaped package didn't strike a chord with me. "Vincent, you're a great guy..."

"I feel a 'but' coming on."

I nodded. "But we can't date while we're colleagues."

"So you would date me if we weren't colleagues?"

"Absolutely," I lied.

"Maybe I should have you fired."

My mouth dropped open as my gentle let-down backfired. "No! Don't do that! I need this job," I replied, flashing indignant eyes at him.

"If we were dating, you wouldn't need to work. I would support you. You could be a lady who lunches, goes shopping, gets her nails done."

My mother would be planning the wedding at this point, but still, Vincent was just not appealing. He was a lowly cheeseburger, and twice this past week, I'd been tempted by filet mignon. "I like working. Besides, I'm very expensive." And there it was; I sounded like a prostitute.

"We're all going to be out of a job soon anyway, so maybe you should think about my offer," Vincent said solemnly.

"Seriously?" My squeaked question seemed to cover both his points nicely.

"Yes. Be my girlfriend and I'll make sure you have anything you want."

I clicked my tongue against the roof of my mouth and pulled an apologetic face. "Thanks, but no."

"I have a lot of money."

"How come?"

"What?"

"How come you have a lot of money?" I knew the concert tickets cost a lot, because the only ones left were the ones Lily and I couldn't afford. (I was seriously reconsidering accepting the ticket.) The car Vincent had set his heart on was easily a six-figure model. You didn't grow up with three motor-minded brothers and not know that. And the offer of being a kept woman? Priceless.

Vincent shifted so he was fully perched on my desk, his feet not quite making contact with the carpeted floor. "I made some good investments this year and they're about to pay off," he said, his nostrils flaring slightly.

"Oh, well, good for you. Hey, there's our current boss. I don't want to get in trouble chatting when I'm supposed to be working."

I could see the words, "it's never stopped you before" forming in Vincent's mind, but he seemed to think better of it. Instead, he said, very matter-of-a-factly, "Adam will look a lot less appealing when he's unemployed." And with that, he stalked off, leaving me frozen at his menacing tone. I saw Maddox glance at me, then at Vincent as he stomped away with his shoulders set backwards. I swear Vincent had developed a swagger.

Maddox looked back at me and raised his eyebrows. I rolled my eyes and shrugged, returning to the pile of filing that was dumped on my desk while I was at lunch. I locked my purse in the desk drawer, remembering to take my cell phone with me, in case Lily called, and lugged the foot-high pile to the filing room. Forty sheets of paper later, and my phone rang.

"Hey, Jord."

"Hi, sis. I heard you and Lily had some car trouble last night." Clearly, he knew. At least, he knew enough to know that we hadn't blown a tire.

"Some asshole tried to run us off the road. I'm fine, thanks for calling."

"When we get him, I'll break his knees anyway."

"You're the perfect big brother. Tell me you're not using a phone at the station."

"No, I'm at home. No witnesses. How's Lily? She okay?"

"She's fine."

"Not injured?"

His casual tone didn't fool me one bit. "You could have called her, you know."

"Oh, I don't know about..."

"Chicken," I interrupted and made clucking noises.

"Maybe I'll call her just to see if she's okay."

"She might need help with the insurance forms. You'd be doing her a favor. And then she wouldn't have to call the desk sergeant who gave her his number this morning."

"Who the fu..." Jord spluttered and I held back a giggle. Teasing him was fun. "What's his name?" he asked calmly.

"I don't know, but I'd call her soon."

"Maybe I'll call her up, take her to dinner, take her home and make very loud love to her all night," threatened Jord. He knew my bedroom was right over hers; but I also knew what jealous sounded like.

"Do it," I said. "Lily will probably pay me to stay at a hotel. I'll get room service."

"I gotta go."

"Need to take a cold shower?"

"Need to glue a desk sergeant to his chair. Not that I care," Jord added quickly. "Lily can date whomever she likes."

"Sure. Whatever. Thanks for checking that I'm alive." Just as I slid my phone back into my pocket, it rang again, Lily's picture flashing onto the screen. "Hey," I said. "Jord just called."

"Did he ask about me?" was the first thing she

wanted to know.

"Yeah. I told him you got the desk sergeant's phone number and he got all pissy."

"I didn't get his number!"

"Jord doesn't know that. He said he'll call you later. Ask him to help you on your insurance forms. He likes being needed."

"Awesome. So, I drove past those addresses and I did see something odd."

"What?"

"Seven of the addresses are just average houses, but they were all in foreclosure. On the others, three were rentals and two were empty."

"I knew it!"

"You want me to check anything else out?"

"No, that's it. Thanks."

I clicked off and rested against the filing cabinet for a moment, wondering if it was a very good idea to let Lily use my car. On the other hand, there was no way she could be mistaken for me. I mused over our conversation as I began filing.

Every policy needed an address and it stood to reason that the fake ones were empty. Even so, I didn't think it could be that simple. A fraudulent damage claim wouldn't pay out much money. The bigger payouts would be in burglaries or fire damage, but that would mean having paperwork falsified at the police and fire departments. Maybe realtors were being paid off so the properties could be used. I had a horrible feeling the insurance fraud ring was more widespread, and there were a lot more people involved, than I guessed. I wondered if Maddox already knew. I wondered what Solomon investigated when he wasn't rescuing me and if he had any leads.

Despite feeling like I was barely part of the investigation, I was looking forward to going home because I thought I might have something to work on with the notebook. I felt certain it was connected to the fraud somehow, and the particular addresses Lily noted had given me another idea. I might have found a reference point to work from.

Halfway through my filing pile, Bob stuck his head around the door. "Adam is letting us all go early," he said, adding, "on account of Martin's death."

"It was *very* sad."

"Yeah, I'm devastated. I'm going to O'Grady's to drown my sorrows. Want to come?"

"I think I'll just head home."

"As you like. See you tomorrow." Bob nodded and ducked out.

"Bright and early," I called after him cheerfully. I slid the filing on top of the cabinet, ready to pick up tomorrow. My work ethic might have bucked up lately, but I wasn't prepared to stay if I'd been given a free pass. Plus, I could almost certainly still claim the time on my timecard. After I got back to my desk, everyone else had already cleared out. I craned my head around to check Vincent's desk, worried that he might be hovering, ready to ambush me.

"Don't worry. He's gone."

I jumped at the sound of Maddox's voice. "I hate it when people sneak up on me."

"Sorry. I'll give you a ride home, then I have some stuff to do."

"Thanks."

I decided not to tell Maddox about Lily's and my snooping. So far, it was just bits and pieces, not enough to go on. And okay, I was a little worried he was going to laugh at me.

"Your brother got in touch with me," he said.

"Garrett?"

"Yep."

"He said he would." I gave him a surreptitious once over for injuries and saw none. That was positive.

"He's pretty mad."

"I know."

"He thinks I've put you in danger."

"Have you?" It wasn't an accusation and I didn't think he was putting his career before my safety because I thought there was more to Maddox than just a career detective. I remembered what Garrett said about Maddox's "puppy dog eyes." Maddox struck me as a stand-up guy, but having it confirmed was fine by me.

"Maybe. For my career? No." He looked sincere. He was breathing deeply like he wasn't sure if I believed him, but he wanted me to.

I nodded my acceptance. "Good to know," I said, feeling relieved.

He waited while I gathered my stuff and turned off the computer. We left the building and headed towards the parking lot. When we climbed in the car, Maddox reached into a compartment under the seat and pulled out his gun, strapping it to his waist. I thought about my own order for the SIG and said nothing. We easily slipped through the afternoon traffic, Maddox steering his car into the empty space in front of my building, now that Lily's Mini was in the shop. He shut the engine off. "You going to invite me up?" he asked. His eyes were smoky. Even if he asked for tea right now, it would probably sound filthy in my mind.

"Sure. Come up."

I let myself into my apartment and within a few steps, I knew something was wrong. I froze, causing Maddox to bump into me as I held up a hand. I looked around. My jackets on the coat rack by the door seemed rumpled, and my shoes, that I hadn't put away, were out of their neat rows.

"Someone's been here," I said.

Behind me, I heard a rustle as Maddox drew his gun and stepped past me. "Wait here," he said. He pushed the bathroom door open and scanned inside. Then he stepped into my bedroom, searching. From the doorway, I saw him drop to his knees and check under the bed. I cringed inwardly and hoped I hadn't kicked any used underwear there. I heard him open and close my closet doors, and held my breath, waiting for an assailant to jump out. Instead, Maddox closed the doors and stepped out, taking a cursory look into the kitchen before moving onto the living room. He walked around checking the windows, then opened the apartment door and peered at the lock.

"It's all clear. But you're right. Someone's been here. See these scratches around the lock?" Maddox pointed to light scratches before shutting the door.

I followed him into the living room and looked around. Someone had ransacked the room, but were careful about it. If I weren't such a neat freak, I might not have noticed the way the couch cushions were pulled out, or that the pillow zippers weren't quite zipped all the way up. I might not have noticed the drawer of the desk slightly out of its slot, or that my laptop wasn't square with the corners of the desk. But that wasn't what captured Maddox's attention. He was looking at the bunch of flowers on the table.

"They left me flowers?" I squeaked. "Someone broke into my place and left *flowers*?"

Maddox just stared at the yellow blooms. "You didn't have them before? Maybe Lily brought them up?"

"She didn't say anything when I saw her earlier, but I guess it's possible."

"Call her and ask."

I did, keeping my fingers crossed while I asked her. Lily was in the gym and hadn't seen any flowers. Moreover, she left the house as soon as her car was towed and hadn't been home since.

"That narrows the timeline a lot."

"This is creepy," I said, entering my bedroom. I felt sick when I saw my underwear moved around in the drawer and the lid not quite back on my favorite perfume. I imagined the burglar poking through my things, a lascivious expression on his face, and I made a mental note to go lingerie shopping. "This is creepier than the dead flowers."

"Say what?"

I explained and Maddox ran a hand through his hair, his face growing angrier. I skipped the before and after parts of that evening, along with the bits about Lily and I scaring ourselves stupid, obviously, and he didn't ask.

"I hate to say this, Lexi, but you can't stay here anymore," said Maddox, looking up from the flowers and fixing his attention on me as I returned to the living room, trying not to shake.

"It could just be a random burglary," I protested.

"You see anything missing?"

I looked around. My television was still there, along with the DVD player. On my desk stood an iPod dock, with my iPod still in place. There was my laptop along with some loose change in a dish and my car keys; Lily had the spare set. They were the most valuable things in the apartment. My wallet with all my cards and cell phone were in my purse.

"No," I conceded, "I don't."

"You nearly got ran off the road last night, and someone's been inside your house. This isn't the freakiest warning I've ever seen, but it's creepy. If I were a betting man, I'd say someone had you under surveillance."

"The killer?" I asked, gulping.

Maddox nodded. "We knew it was a risk letting you carry on your life as normal, but obviously someone suspects you know something. Even if we keep you under a twenty-four hour watch, things can still go wrong."

Double gulp. "What are you saying?"

His voice dropped to a whisper. "We need to discuss putting you in a safe house."

"Like witness protection?" I asked, just as quietly. My knees felt weak and I sat heavily onto the sofa. Witness protection was the one thing I wanted to avoid. Call me crazy, but I liked my life. Sure, maybe it wasn't an exciting, glamorous one, but I had an apartment I liked, a big family who loved me, and a job that I... could tolerate. I wasn't about to give all that fabulousness up for a life on the run.

Maddox knelt beside me, his hands resting on my legs. "It won't be for long. Just a couple of weeks," he said softly. "We'll catch them. Then everything goes back to normal. We do this all the time."

"*If* you catch whoever is responsible for this," I said, because that was the stipulation Maddox should have included.

"We're going to catch them," Maddox assured me. "But I'm not prepared to leave you as bait. I don't want to find you..."

"Dead," I finished. Me neither.

~

"The building is definitely being watched," said Maddox. He stood to one side of the window, looking out onto the street below. I had waited quietly for the past hour while he made phone calls, talking cryptically. "Don't worry," he said to me.

"Why would I worry, Adam? You're here." I didn't ask, *Can you stay over?* But I wanted to. I really wanted to. I didn't want to leave my home, but I didn't want to be alone in it either.

Maddox shook his head. "I can't guarantee your safety here."

A knock at the door interrupted us. I flopped backwards, my shoulders hunched, while Maddox went to answer it. After a moment, he returned with Solomon. Solomon held a small plastic bag, which he handed to Maddox. Maddox looked inside it, then at me, and I had a feeling I wasn't going to like what he had to say. But first, he put a finger to his lips as Solomon took out a black device and moved around the apartment.

"It's clean," he said after a while.

"Thought so, but can't be too sure," said Maddox.

At least my thoughts about a bug hadn't been totally wrong. Given that I'd forgotten about it pretty quick, I was glad my apartment was confirmed bug free. "What's in the bag?" I asked.

"You need a disguise."

"Like a costume?" That wasn't so bad. I could do costumes.

"Think of it as a makeover." Maddox held out the bag and I took it reluctantly, peeking inside. After a moment, I looked up and frowned, not quite believing what I was looking at. Maddox continued, "If we take out a pretty blonde, all they have to do is follow us, and we don't know what kind of manpower they have. If one of us walks out with a different woman, maybe we can throw them off. Your upstairs neighbor is a brunette."

I didn't know how Maddox knew that. I didn't even know that.

"You want me to dye my hair," I said flatly. I looked back in the bag and a tear pricked at my eye. Okay, call me vain, but I really loved my hair. It had been a boring, dark brown all through high school and college, and only a couple of years ago, I'd taken the plunge and bleached it a gorgeous, glossy blonde. I'd grown it out so it swung to mid-back, and, if I didn't say so myself, it was my crowning glory. And now it would all be gone.

"You can fix it later," said Maddox. "After this is over."

"I guess." But I knew I couldn't. It had taken too much work, too long and too many dollars to get my hair to look like this. Now my job was in jeopardy, I probably wouldn't be able to afford the disaster relief session with my hairdresser to get it this good again, or the upkeep either. Still, blonde or dead? The decision should be easy, but it was compounded by all the other horrible things over the past week. Combined with the murders, the creepy gifts, and the home invasion, it was all becoming a bit too much.

I blinked back the tears as Maddox continued, "You'll need to pack a few clothes. A week's worth maybe. I'll take them out so it doesn't look suspicious."

"Then you'll come back for me?"

Maddox shook his head. "No, they probably already associate me with you. Solomon will take you out in an hour."

I glanced over at Solomon. He leaned against the doorjamb, hands in pockets. He nodded, just a slight incline of his head. They had probably already discussed what would happen if it came to this. It should have reassured me that they had contingency plans. But it didn't.

"Okay," I said, the box of hair-coloring clutched in my hand. "I guess I'll pack and dye."

Maddox flinched.

I slid past Solomon and walked down the hallway to the bedroom. The lights were on, and someone, Maddox I suppose, had drawn the curtains. I opened my closet doors and stood in front of them, wondering what someone on the run would pack. That immediately discounted all my dresses and pretty shoes. I shoved jeans and tops and a couple of sweaters on the bed, adding underwear—with a grimace—socks and a pair of pajamas. Moving to the bathroom, I packed my travel bag with a few items of makeup, deodorant and my hairbrush, tucking them in the middle of the clothing. I left them all on my bed.

Back in the bathroom, I pushed both doors closed and pulled the box of hair dye out of the bag, placing it on the sink. After a few deep, calming breaths I snapped the carton open and pulled out the instructions and the plastic gloves. It was now or never. I took one final look in the mirror, swung my blonde hair for the last time and got on with the job.

First, I pulled my hair into a ponytail, and took out my scissors. Snip, snip, snip. Three inches of hair fell to the floor. I gathered it with my hands, brushing them off over the little plastic wastebasket under the sink. Standing in front of the mirror, I pulled out the band and let my hair swing free. I pulled on the plastic gloves.

Forty minutes later, and a new me reflected from the mirror. In place of the blonde was a glossy, dark brown, cut shorter and fuller. It framed my face and still swung past my shoulders. It seemed to enhance my coloring. My face looked paler, my eyes bluer, my lips more red. It lifted my spirits a little; actually, I didn't look too bad at all. Not blonde and pretty anymore, but still pretty. I felt slightly better.

I scrubbed the last little blotches of dye from the tops of my ears and pulled out some nail polish remover. After a couple of minutes rubbing, my nails were plain and I cut them shorter, too. Next went my clothes. I switched the dress for black skinny jeans, a pale blue top and a zip-up, black sweatshirt, pulling on sneakers last.

When I went back to the living room, both men turned to me and I stood there hesitantly, awaiting their verdict.

"You look different," said Maddox. "I like it."

"Better than the blonde?"

"Yes, most definitely. You look sensational."

I smiled, a little color rushing to my cheeks. "Thanks, Adam," I said. "I laid out everything I'll need on my bed. I wasn't sure if you wanted them in a bag or something else."

"I'll take them now." He nodded to Solomon. "Wait close to an hour, then take Lexi to the safe house. I'll meet you there."

Maddox moved over to me. Placing both hands on my shoulders, he looked down at me. "You'll be okay," he said. "Keep calm."

"And carry on?" I asked, aping the slogan.

"You bet."

I wasn't sure what to do when Maddox left, so I got a soda from the refrigerator and offered Solomon one, but he declined. We watched television for a while, but I only stared at the box without really seeing any of it. All I could think about was what was going to happen next. It struck me that the most dangerous few minutes would be leaving the apartment and making our way to wherever Solomon's car was parked. There was every chance that my disguise was for nothing. I gulped.

A hand landed on my thigh, making me realize my leg had been nervously jiggling up and down. I followed the hand, up the arm, to Solomon's face.

"Don't worry," he said, his hand unmoving.

"Easy for you to say."

He shrugged. "We wouldn't move you like this if we didn't think it would be the easiest and safest way."

"You really think it'll throw them?"

"I think they're looking for a pretty blonde all alone, not a brunette going on a date," Solomon replied. "I don't think they're experienced; if they were, they would know we had already spotted them by now. So, yes, I think you'll be fine. This is just a precaution. Maybe they just want to see what you're going to do, *if* you're going to do something."

I tried not to gulp when he said "date," choosing to keep my face passive.

"Why don't you just arrest them?" I asked.

"Because we still need the other gang members to lead us to the money. We don't want to spook them." Solomon checked his watch. "Time to go," he said. "You need anything else?"

"Uh. My cell phone and wallet."

"Leave the phone. It's traceable. And you won't need the wallet."

"I guess I don't need anything then." I stood up, moving toward the light switch. But just as I reached for it, Solomon's hand closed over mine. I spun, stumbled, and planted my back against the wall for support as he stepped closer. For a moment, all I could feel was my heart hammering in my chest.

"Leave the light on. We want it to look like you're staying home," said Solomon, his hand still on mine. With his free hand, he reached up and pushed a lock of hair behind my ear, resting his hand for a moment as my heart raced a little faster. His lips were inches from mine, and his eyes dark. At first, I thought he was going to kiss me. I felt my eyelids flutter and I licked my lips. "I like this." He twirled the lock around his fingers and leaned in. "Sexy," he whispered, his breath warm against my cheek. "I guess I can't call you 'Blondie' anymore."

Thank God for small mercies, I thought as he pulled back and moved towards the door.

I took a moment to compose myself, then grabbed my purse and followed him.

Solomon took my keys and locked the door

behind him as we stepped out of my apartment. The lights were on in the living room and kitchen, the curtains drawn, so it looked like I was in for the night. As we went downstairs, Solomon took my hand in his and I was surprised at how warm he felt. It was strangely comforting too. At the door, he pulled a cap out of his back pocket and mounted it on my head, tweaking the peak so it covered my forehead, but not my eyes. Outside, instead of taking my hand, he slung his arm around my shoulder and tucked me into his side, turning off to the right and walking a little way down the street. I nearly jumped when his car lights flashed ahead.

"Relax," he said, leaning into me as he guided me towards the SUV, and not the Lexus I expected. "This is my car."

When he deposited me into the passenger seat, I realized my teeth were chattering, not so much from cold, but fear. I hadn't seen anyone observing my apartment, even though I'd stolen glances here and there.

"Where were they?" I asked Solomon when he slid in and started the engine.

"Don't look back," he said and I had to fight the natural urge to look over my shoulder. "They were parked in a blue sedan three houses down from yours."

"You think they were onto us?"

"Let's find out." We slid out into the quiet street and moved off. I saw Solomon glancing in the rearview mirror, and after a few minutes, and a couple of turns, he seemed to relax slightly. "No problem," he said, eyeing me as the corners of his lips turned upwards into a barely noticeable smile.

The safe house wasn't what I expected. I was thinking perhaps it would be an underground bunker, surrounded with high security fences and guard dogs; but instead, it was an average suburban house with a neat lawn, surrounded by a street full of family homes. Solomon pulled onto the driveway and used a key fob to open the automatic garage doors, parking the car inside and closing the doors after us. We entered the house through a side door into the kitchen where Maddox was waiting for us.

"I got Chinese," he said, indicating the cartons on the eat-in counter. "Figured we'd be hungry. Any problems?"

"None. They didn't notice us leaving," answered Solomon.

Maddox nodded to me. "How're you holding up?"

"Okay," I said. "Hungry."

Dinner was quiet. Maddox poked through the cabinets and pulled out plates and forks. We shared the food, forking chunks of egg fried rice, mu shu pork and chicken black bean onto our plates. Maddox took an egg roll, and deposited one on my plate. Digging into the bag, I pulled out fortune cookies and napkins.

"What does yours say?" asked Maddox as I snapped the cookie open.

I unpeeled the strip of paper. "It says, 'The one you love is closer than you think'." I screwed it into a ball and tossed it onto the counter. *Stupid fortune cookie.*

Maddox raised his eyebrows.

"Let's hear yours."

He snapped it open. "Patience."

"Come on," I prompted.

"No, that's it. It says, 'Patience'."

"Oh."

Maddox nodded at Solomon. "How about yours?" he asked as he slid off the stool and moved to the refrigerator.

"A thrilling time is in your immediate future." Solomon met my eyes and smiled. I think my heart skipped a beat.

"Well, how about that," said Maddox, but he didn't sound particularly peeved as he uncapped three beers, sliding them down the counter. I swallowed my bite of egg roll and took a sip. Cool, refreshing libation washed down my throat, and for a moment, I just closed my eyes and enjoyed it. I tried to pretend I was just having dinner with friends and not hiding like a big wussy-pants.

When I opened them again, Solomon had finished eating and was washing his plate over the sink. I hadn't even heard him move. Afterward, he walked back over and tossed his keys to Maddox, who caught them in one hand, before offering his own.

"I'm parked a block down the street," said Maddox. "The Ford Focus."

"Where are you going?" I asked Solomon.

"Only one of us needs to stay," said Solomon. "I have work to do." He shrugged his jacket on and walked out of the kitchen without a backward glance.

"Adam? What now?" I asked. I picked up my plate and followed him to the sink, drying after he rinsed.

"Now we wait it out. This safe house is only known to Solomon and me, so we're not expecting any activity. The perimeter is wired for movement and sound and the house is alarmed. The house is only partially furnished, so there's not a lot to see. We can watch a DVD on my laptop if you like?"

"Sure."

I followed Maddox along a narrow corridor and he pointed out a bedroom. I ducked my head inside and saw a bed with a pillow and quilt folded on top. A bag was on the floor at the foot of the bed. He beckoned me and I followed him into the living room. Sparse wasn't the word. There were two sofas and a coffee table, with a lamp in one corner. A desk on one wall held boxes of electronic equipment and the other walls still had the faded outlines of picture frames.

Maddox's laptop sat on the coffee table and was open, showing a four corner split screen, each with a different image of the outside of the house. One quarter showed the garage door; another the front door and a patch of lawn; the third showed the rear door; while a fourth monitored the street.

"Our team is also watching these images," he told me.

"Any cameras inside the house?" I asked.

Maddox shook his head. "No, not necessary."

A thought occurred to me. "Where are you going to sleep?"

He pointed to the sofa and I noticed a second quilt and pillow folded and placed to one side. "There."

"Sorry." I didn't like the look of the bed much, and the sofa looked like it had seen better days.

"No worries. I've done it before."

I dropped onto the sofa and looked around at the blank walls and the stripped room, my heart sinking. My apartment wasn't overly cozy, but it was home and I missed it already. I missed my things and the familiarity. I missed my normal life. I missed my family. I wanted to go out with Lily and have fun, or work up a sweat at the gym. I even wanted to go to the concert with Vincent and wave my new hair around like a rocker. Suddenly, everything seemed uncertain—I didn't know when, or if, I could go home. My job was almost certainly over, which meant I would be back at the temping agency soon. Potentially anyway.

"It'll be okay, Lexi. It's not for long."

"How do you do this?" I asked as he settled next to me. "How do you wait it out? Knowing that the bad guys are looking for me? That anything could happen?"

"I just do," he said. "And this is better than leaving you alone as a target. I don't want yours to be the next dead body I see."

Well, if that didn't drive it home, I don't know what would.

"What about work tomorrow?" I asked.

"You sprained your ankle," Maddox said. "And I'm at a conference."

Maddox had thought to bring a small selection of DVDs with him, so I thumbed through them and handed him a comedy. He slid it into the laptop's disk drive and we sat there, neither of us really watching. With beers in hand, it could have been any night, but I couldn't shake the frightened, no, *terrified*, bit of me that knew I was hiding. In the space of a week, I'd seen more bodies than during my entire lifetime. I didn't know which was more upsetting: being chased by the SUV, having my home invaded, or losing the blonde. Before I could stop myself, my shoulders shook, and a big, gaspy sob escaped me.

"Hey," said Adam. "Hey, it'll be okay."

"No, it won't!" I wailed, pushing the heels of my hands against my eyes. Not that it stopped the tears sliding over my cheeks. "This has been the worst week *ever*. I loved being a blonde and you took my favorite dress because it had Dean's blood on it!"

Maddox chuckled. "I thought you were going to say the corpses creeped you out."

"That too!" I sobbed.

Maddox wrapped his arms around me and pulled me into him, stroking my hair while I soaked his shirt. He was big and warm and comforting and I relaxed against him as I sobbed the frustration and fear away. I didn't have to worry as long as Maddox stayed with me. I knew he would protect me. I just wasn't keen on the idea of what he had to protect me from.

Most of all, I wanted it to be over.

# CHAPTER SIXTEEN

I jolted awake, completely disorientated. Looking around the beige, sparse room, I couldn't work out where I was. Then it all came flooding back to me. I was in a safe house, on the sofa in the living room and there was a warm, heavy arm draped over me.

For a moment, I froze, then relaxed, because, actually, being stretched out on the sofa with Adam behind me was quite nice. Better than nice. For the first time in a few days, I'd gotten a full night's sleep. I was warm and not panicking about what was going to happen because I already knew I wasn't going anywhere; and Maddox had assured me several times that no one could get to me here.

Although Maddox told me to pack for a few days, we both knew this could stretch on a lot longer than that. That depressed me slightly. It wasn't just that I missed the opportunity to have this week's timecard signed so I would get paid, but I could be missing many more days, even weeks. I closed my eyes for a minute and tried not to think about that. I tried to think about my mother saying "What will be will be," but it wasn't all that soothing, given that there were quite a few scenarios that I didn't want to be in.

I wriggled, working the cricks out of my neck and stretched. Adam's arm tightened over me and I stopped. I could feel something pressing into my back as he pulled me against him, our bodies in full contact. Shame we were wearing yesterday's clothes.

"Morning," Maddox mumbled sleepily as he looped his leg through mine.

"Hey," I replied, pausing before adding, "I didn't mean to fall asleep here." I didn't remember much after crying my eyes out and wailing about my hair. I had a vague recollection of curling up next to him, but I didn't remember stretching out with him.

"No problem."

"Adam?"

"Hmm?"

I couldn't help it. I'd slept awkwardly and I needed to wriggle. Behind me, Maddox tensed and his arm held me still, his palm flat against my stomach. He groaned softly. "Could you move your gun?" I asked, my head still fuzzy with sleep.

"My gun's on the table."

"Then, what's..." *Oh!* My eyes widened.

He moved, and a moment later, a CD container landed on the coffee table. *Ahh.* Not quite what I expected. I giggled and rolled my shoulders, working out the kinks. Something still prodded me.

"If the next thing you remove is a bunny rabbit, I'm outta here," I told him.

Maddox's breath was soft against my neck, and, if I weren't mistaken, his lips brushed my skin. "It's morning," he said, by way of explanation for the continued prodding. "I'm warm. I don't want to move, but you need to stop wriggling or it's not going to go away."

*Oh.*

Did I want it to go away? I wasn't sure. Truth was, it was nice being snuggled up to Maddox. There was a heat spiraling through me that suggested less clothing might make it even nicer. A bed would make the moment fantastic, but I couldn't work miracles. Also, he smelled really nice. Warm, masculine, and a little citrusy. Being this close to him made my breath quicken and other parts of me dance a jig.

Like he could read my mind, I felt a tug at my t-shirt, before Maddox's hand slid underneath, caressing my stomach, while his lips settled on my neck. I was pretty certain now that Maddox's morning condition had as much to do with me as it did with waking up, but it struck me as rude to point that out. Without thinking, I pressed against him, rubbing slightly. His lips slid from my neck to nibble my shoulders, while his hand slid further upwards, over my stomach, then softly over my bra. I knew he felt my breath quicken.

"Lexi," he murmured.

I twisted next to him, finding his mouth and kissing him hard, my hands running over his morning stubble to his muscular shoulders. Then we were moving, shuffling, and somehow I ended up under Maddox. I had one knee drawn up against the back of the couch, while the other foot dropped to the floor as he lay between my legs and returned the kiss eagerly. He fumbled the zipper on my sweatshirt, tugging it down and pushing it apart while my shirt rode up at his hands.

I moaned when he pushed himself against me, sending a spark of fire through me that shot south, his kisses becoming more urgent. I wrapped my arms around him, a moan escaping me when his lips left mine. He slid down my body, his lips returning to the soft swell of my breasts as he kissed them through my bra. Then on the skin, then back to my mouth as my hands fumbled with his fly.

I'd only just tugged it open, my hand sliding inside his jeans, when I heard the front door open. Maddox looked up, his body suddenly tense. I caught the brief register of annoyance as it flashed across his face.

"Breakfast," called a man's voice. *Solomon's.* The door banged shut and his footsteps sounded in the hall.

"Shit," said Maddox, scrambling off me and falling to his knees on the floor. I rolled onto my side, pulled down my shirt and leaned over.

When Solomon came through the door, I pretended to be tying my laces. When I looked up, running fingers through my hair to smooth it, Maddox was on the other side of the room, his shirt untucked and his jeans zippered. At least, I thought they were.

"I brought bagels," said Solomon, looking from me to Maddox, his face blank. "Anything happen?"

"Not a thing," said Maddox, glancing at me, and I thought I heard a hint of regret. I knew how he felt, though I couldn't help feeling a little relieved that our first time hadn't taken place on a crusty couch in a stark, safe house, rather than in, say, my lovely bed.

On the plus side, I was really hungry and Solomon had fresh bagels, so I couldn't be too miffed.

I finished my bagel in record time and reached for another, washing it down with a glass of orange juice, already curious what we were having for lunch. It may have been a good thing for my waistline that I couldn't invade the kitchen for a snack, seeing as we had, literally, nothing in the cupboards, but I was starting to think like a prisoner... or a puppy. I wanted to know where my next meal was coming from, something I never had to think about before. Being in the same room with Maddox and Solomon was uncomfortable enough, body heat-wise, but being solely reliant on them was intolerable.

"What's wrong?" asked Maddox.

"Nothing," I said thinking about my mother's roast chicken. "What's happening today?"

"Nothing." Maddox and Solomon exchanged glances.

"I know that look. What's going on?"

"Someone left a gift at your house last night," said Solomon.

"What kind of gift?"

"Chocolate."

"I like chocolate."

"These had tire marks across the box."

"Someone ran over chocolates and left them for me?" I frowned. "That's nutso."

"Dead flowers, creepy screensaver, flowers in your living room... the chocolates look like another warning to me. I'm glad we got you out of there," said Maddox.

"I don't suppose..."

"What?"

"Did you bring any chocolate with you?" I asked Solomon and his chest did a fast rise and fall like he was trying not to laugh.

Maddox's face clouded. "Someone threatens you, but you're more concerned about the chocolate?"

"It's part of my five-a-day diet."

"That's fruit and vegetables."

"Chocolate comes from the cocoa bean and a bean is a vegetable," I justified. Maddox and Solomon just stared at me. "Ask any woman," I told them. "It's true."

Maddox just shook his head and turned to Solomon. "Did the ballistics report on the Finklesteins come in?"

"No traces in the system. The gun was probably a throwaway. The bullets in the Finklesteins didn't match the bullets in Martin Dean."

"The Finklesteins shot Dean. They couldn't shoot themselves," I pointed out, just in case no one spotted the obvious.

"She's smart," said Solomon. He winked at me.

I suspected he was being sarcastic, but I thanked him sweetly anyway. Two could play at that game.

"She's got a point," said Maddox and I smiled at him. "Our perp hasn't left any prints, his gun isn't in the system, and we have no idea who he is."

"And no one saw him leave the chocolates?" I asked.

Maddox shook his head. "The car watching your apartment left an hour after us. We had someone do a tail, but they lost it. No one was watching." Now he sounded annoyed.

"What about Tanya Henderson?" I asked.

"What about her?"

"Did anyone cross reference the bullet in her during the autopsy?"

Maddox looked over at Solomon. "Did they?" he asked.

"I'll check," said Solomon. "No one mentioned anything."

"So what now? We wait for another body to show up?" I didn't need an answer. I just sighed. This majorly sucked.

"We have some leads to work on," said Maddox, right before he and Solomon sloped off to the kitchen. Alone, the only thing I could do was turn on the television. I flicked through the channels, finally selecting car racing. Not my cup of tea, but there was something soothing about watching the cars whiz around the track, one after another, time and time again, knowing exactly where they were going.

There was something else about the cars that niggled at me all morning. At last, I was sure that I knew something else, something creeping on the periphery of my mind, but the thought stayed half-baked, just like the idea I was formulating about the policies I felt sure were fraudulent.

Finally, like a little light bulb going off in my head, I knew the answer. "I've got it!" I exclaimed, racing through to the kitchen where Maddox and Solomon looked up at me in surprise as I burst in. "I've got it," I repeated.

Maddox looked at me expectantly. "Got what?"

As soon as I realized, all the pieces clicked into place. I knew who was involved in the Green Hand Insurance scam and how the whole scheme had come about. I knew who was after me and I knew why. And it was all down to one casual little photograph in the files I'd innocently given to Martin Dean, the same files that had been stolen, the same files that I imagined the task force perused repeatedly, but came up with nothing. I knew the perpetrator had put it together too.

"Everything," I said. "Adam, do you have copies of the files I worked on for Dean?"

"Yes. I have them on my laptop in the living room."

"Pull them up," I told him. We huddled around the laptop while the files whirred into view, with me wedged between the men on the couch. I tried not to savor it.

"Which one?" he asked, the pointer hovering over the window.

I pointed to the file in the top right. "This one here." Maddox double-clicked and we waited for it to open. "Scroll to the second page," I told him. The page moved down and then the photograph appeared. Below that was the photograph that explained everything.

"It wasn't anything to do with legislature, or research or all those surveys Green Hand does. It was this silly puff piece for the feature-style, ad Green Hand wanted to place in the Montgomery Gazette. The one where Martin Dean wanted to look like every householder's best friend."

"Keep going," urged Maddox.

"Green Hand wanted Dean to look like your average Joe," I explained. "He was supposed to be the guy next door, your friend, your brother, the man you trusted to look after you. The guy you wanted to buy insurance from. The idea was to show a montage of pictures that portrayed that, alongside the slogan of how Green Hand insurance would make you feel secure. Here's one where he's playing basketball with underprivileged kids. Scroll down. And here's one where he's planting a new tree in the park at the corner of the kids' playground Green Hand helped fund. But it's this picture that tells us everything."

I took over the mouse and glided the page up until the not-so-innocent photo embedded in my report filled the screen. "This is Martin Dean at his car club. He was a member for years. They restore vintage cars and drive them, put on races, stuff like that. Look who he's with." Tara Henderson had even mentioned how cool her sister thought Dean's car was. I pointed to the man next to Dean. "That's Ron Harris. He's an award winning insurance broker. Green Hand underwrites his insurance deals. I think he wrote the fake insurance certificates, set up fake addresses, and got the fake policies into the system. All they had to do was wait it out, then make their claims and get paid. He was killed recently, a hit-and-run. But look who else is in the picture."

Simultaneously, Maddox and Solomon leaned forward. "That's the mayor, Chris Mathis," said Maddox and I nodded.

"Right. Old money, you think? Town gossip says the family money was running out. They can barely keep the estate afloat." Town gossip was actually my mom, but I didn't think that lent a lot of credibility to my claim.

"How was Mathis part of it?" asked Maddox.

"He was the money man. Well, what little he had left of it. He helped create the fake policies too and funded them until it was time to claim. He was killed in a hit-and-run too. Kind of a coincidence, right? Three men in this picture are dead." I pointed to the fourth man. "Ten points if you guess who he is."

"Tell me," said Maddox.

I smiled. "He's Hector Ramos, president of Montgomery First Bank."

"Another money man," said Solomon.

"That's right, but Ramos doesn't just fund the policies. I checked a bunch of accounts that paid out recently, all paid through his bank, all fake accounts, I'll bet. I've been thinking. He could manage the expenses to fund the policies and then re-gather it when it got paid back, maybe transferring it to another account or offshore. This is how they remained unconnected, how no one could put the gang together. You were looking for people who knew each other, but on paper, they didn't. They didn't go to school with each other, or college. They didn't particularly socialize with one another either. All they had in common was their car club and it's not member-based. There's no register. It's just a loose, informal, thing for a bunch of guys who love old cars. This picture is only around because someone snapped it randomly and it made its way into an old edition of the Gazette, which is where I found it."

"We know what happened to Harris and Mathis. You're right, that it's too much of a coincidence they were killed. My money is on Ramos getting rid of the other three," said Maddox.

I had come to the same conclusion, but now I wasn't so sure. "You think Ramos planned to take the money and run, cutting the other three out of the deal?" I asked.

"No, I think Dean got cold feet when he saw your report and realized they were connected. I bet he called his buddies and said he wanted out. He probably knew we were onto him, but not how or when we would strike. I suspect he wanted to take his money and split, pulling the plug on the whole operation."

"But they didn't want to." I sighed. Money made people do such stupid things.

Maddox shook his head. "No. Maybe the other three got greedy. We'll run their financials. Maybe it was Mathis' mounting debts. Maybe they just wanted a little more. Or maybe they knew the scam couldn't last much longer. They were cashing in more and more policies. They would want as much as they could get. With Dean out of the picture, maybe they thought they could keep going and split it three ways instead of four."

"There's just one thing I don't get," I said. "With Dean dead, they could keep going for a while, maybe even get someone else in Green Hand to funnel the fake claims through. But someone killed Harris and Mathis. I can understand wanting to eliminate Dean, but the other two? And Tanya? And who is after me?"

"That still points to Ramos," pointed out Maddox. He placed a call, giving instructions to have Hector Ramos picked up.

"If you thought Ramos had it in him, you would have said that straight off, right?" pressed Solomon. He had a little knowing smile on his face, one that told me he had reached the same conclusion.

"Yep. I think there's someone else."

"Who?" asked Maddox.

I threw my hands in the air, the flat photograph of the four men smiling proudly back at me. "That's the problem, I don't know."

We went through the details over and over and

nothing emerged. If anything, I just felt more frustrated. When Maddox's cell phone rang, he answered on the second ring, listening briefly then hanging up. "Ramos' wife reported him missing two days ago," he told us, sliding the phone back into his pocket.

"That's not good," I said.

"Ramos *could* be the killer. Maybe he ran?" persisted Maddox. "He could be out of the country by now."

I shook my head. "Mathis, Harris and Dean are all dead. Unless Ramos really hated his wife, I think he's dead too," I said. "Plus, he wouldn't go missing without the money and I don't think they've got it yet. He's worked too hard for it. That's why someone came after me. Whatever Tanya Henderson had, they think I now have." It hit me. "They can't get the money."

We all stared hard at the photograph, but I shook my head. There were a couple of faces visible in the background where a cluster of people stood. "I don't know anyone else in this picture," I said.

"I'll send it to the team. They can run facial recognition." Maddox took over the keyboard, his hands flying across it. "Done. Let's see if they get any hits."

"What now?"

"Now, we wait," said Maddox. "I need to stretch my legs."

I hated waiting.

When Solomon and Maddox went out of the house to talk together about secret stuff, or their weekend plans—who knew?—I went into the living room and pulled out my notepad and the sheet of notes I'd made in the office. Keeping my finger on the first address Lily had checked, I flipped through the notebook. On the third page, I struck gold. The first set of numbers before the slash matched an account number on my list. After that first slash, the numbers were still a mystery. I suspected that the digits were made up of a partial encryption, with the first part simply an account number. But what could the second, third and fourth parts mean?

I ran my finger down the list and found a policy opening date near to the first one that I matched. The account number matched another one on the list. The month read March. I penciled "March" on a sticky and added it to the notebook page as I flicked back to the beginning. Every few pages, there was a blank, and the same pattern continued until I counted twelve sections. I wrote the months on sticky notes and added a note to each section. Now that I had a way of differentiating the numbers, I quickly found seventy-six of the accounts on my list written in the notebook, each with a corresponding six-digit policy opening date. All I had to do was work out what the last two parts of Dean's notes meant; but I folded it away when Maddox and Solomon came back. I would share when I had the whole thing worked out.

There was one thing I was sure of. This innocent looking notebook was the master list for every fraud the gang had committed. The question was, did whoever was after me want this piece of the puzzle too? Was this what they needed? Not the key Tanya Henderson held?

Solomon took off after an hour to who knew where—I'm not even sure Maddox knew all the time where he went—leaving us alone again, a shared pizza between us. Both of us were on edge, knowing how close we were to breaking the case. I paced the floor, munching a slice, waiting while Maddox filed his report. Every so often, he would look up and ask me a question, his forehead furrowed with lines, then duck back down, typing quickly as I gave him my answers.

Try as I might, however many questions he asked, I couldn't imagine who the fifth person could be.

"I don't think the fifth person is connected to the group at all," I said finally, coming to a standstill in front of him, my hands on my hips. "Five even sounds too many for a group. It's another person they trust to keep quiet, another person to split the proceeds with. Maybe we shouldn't look for a connection to the gang. Just like they weren't really close, this fifth person isn't close to them either."

"What does your gut tell you?"

"Blackmail. I think someone found out and wanted a piece of the pie."

"But they didn't get it?" Maddox leaned back and stretched.

"No, because Dean was killed. But it would make sense how the others started dying, or disappearing. The fifth person was chasing the money. Not just a little bit of it, all of it, and I don't think he can get it. Maybe each of them had part of the puzzle to recover the money," I mused. I was thinking about the object Martin Dean's girlfriend had died to retrieve, the keys I'd pried from her hands. It had to have been something small and something the water wouldn't damage. "It was probably the fifth person who killed Tanya." Another thought occurred to me. "None of them seemed extra wealthy at their time of death, right?"

"We combed Dean's records and there was nothing, which was why we were spying. When Dean's name kept coming up in the investigation that was when I got put into his department. I was trying to find out who exactly in Green Hand was part of it, as well as how it was going down. My team is pulling Mathis', Harris' and Ramos' financials now. We can comb them, but I think we'll find the same thing. Nothing." Maddox sounded exasperated. "They probably have it stashed somewhere?"

"In a bank account? Ramos would be able to move and collect the money. If he turned it into cash, it could be in storage or in the vault. Somewhere safe where they could collect it when the time came, when and if, any suspicion was gone."

"So, if none of them trusted each other to keep the money, and they all had something that enabled them to collect it together, all the fifth person had to do was find all four pieces of the puzzle and wait it out." Maddox folded his arms behind his head.

"Except the heat is on," I noted. "If that person connected the dots, they must know we can too. They need to get the money and fast."

"This mystery person is going to go for the money and disappear," said Maddox with a sigh. "Then he's gone."

"Unless we get there first." If we cracked the case, I could go home, back to my own bed, and, more importantly, my own life. I took a deep breath and put a dent in my plan. "The only thing is, Adam, the fifth person knows who I am, but I don't know who he is."

"The Finklesteins?"

"If they weren't dead," I replied. I paced the floor while Maddox watched me. "But some of those creepy messages came after they were shot. It has to be the person who shot Tanya. They knew we were following her that night. Maybe they think I'm after the money too, that I know all the fraudsters are dead except Ramos. They just think I know who they are," I surmised.

"It's not enough to keep you safe. You figured out the rest of it. Until we stop that person, you're still in danger."

Shit.

"I believe Dean's girlfriend's key is one of the items he needs," I said. "It's still the only thing I can think of that could have been hidden in the toilet tank. It wouldn't have gotten damaged like a map or a code, and was easy to move. No one else knew Dean went there, so it would be a safe place to hide it. We need to look at lockers. The bus station? Ramos' vault for sure."

"None of her effects have been released so we have the key at the precinct. Maybe she was after the money too?"

"I don't know, maybe. Maybe Dean told her to hide it, and she never knew what it was for. She might have been threatened and told to get it, or maybe she thought she was getting a share once she handed over the key."

"But she was killed anyway."

"Yeah."

"The key wasn't a high priority item." Maddox took out his cell phone and placed a call, instructing someone to pull the keys and find out what they fitted. And fast.

I yanked my notes and the book out of my purse, settling in the corner of the sofa adjacent to Maddox. I started with the first number I'd identified and checked my notes on the corresponding page. I sighed and ticked off a four-digit number. It was so obvious, it hadn't even occurred to me to check. The first set was the policy number, the second the policy date. The third set of numbers, which varied between three and six figures, was the claim amount; in this case eight thousand, two hundred and fifty dollars.

"What's the sigh for?"

I held up my hand, my eyes focused on the sheet. "Do you have an account at Montgomery Bank?" I asked.

"No. Why?"

"Do you know if the account numbers have any pattern?"

"I can find out, if you tell me why."

"I'm not sure yet, but I think I found something. Hang on." I moved to the next number on my list. The claim amount fitted there too. Just to be sure, I checked the next three. All matched up. I moved over to Maddox, snuggling on the sofa next to him.

"Don't get mad," I said, "but I found something that belonged to Dean. I wasn't sure what it was at first. It just seemed like a random list of numbers." I flipped to the first page and pointed to the numbers. "They're all like this. A series of numbers then a slash, a shorter series, another slash, then another series of numbers." I explained the significance of the numbers. "I don't know what the final set of numbers mean, but I think it's probably the fake bank account." I moved my list to the front. "And see here? Most of these claims say Boston Test Group or

BTG. The test group Scott in the call center told me about is really a front for the fraud op. It was a way for Dean and the others to bypass the claims inspectors and make sure they got their money. It's no wonder it looked like it was all streamlined. It was all fake."

"Where did you find this?"

"Um... at Dean's," I said vaguely.

"His office?"

"Not exactly."

"His house?" Maddox pressed.

"Well..."

"Please tell me you didn't tamper with a crime scene."

"I didn't tamper with a crime scene," I said solemnly, and with the exception of removing two important clues, I hadn't. Besides, the police had already been through Dean's house before me, so really, I was in the clear. "Anyway... Dean is hardly going to come back from the dead and say, 'Hey, that was in my house'."

"I didn't hear that." Maddox studied the list, cross-referencing it against my notes. "You know what you've got here, right?"

"Yes," I said, a smile spreading over my face. "The master list of the whole scam."

"I can't believe we missed it. I have to take this to my boss. It's key evidence."

"But, there isn't going to be a trial unless Ramos turns up."

"And when he does, we have enough to put him behind bars for years."

"Awesome." Since no one else was going to say it, I would. I was good at this. Really good.

Maddox placed a call to Solomon, but evidently, he didn't answer. Maddox said, "I have to take this in right away. You'll be okay here by yourself. I'll lock up. Just stay away from the windows and don't answer the door."

Panic gripped me. "Are you sure?"

"Yes."

"Isn't it safer if I go with you?"

"No. I don't want you seen. Plus, your family is ready to lynch me."

"Seriously?"

"I told Garrett you were in my custody until this was all over, and he threatened to do scary things to my nuts."

I warmed with pride. My brothers always took it upon themselves to gang up on my boyfriends when I was younger. I found solace in that the older two ended up with no-nonsense women, and if Jord got his head around it, he'd complete the set with Lily, who wouldn't put up with any macho shit either. None of us had any choice about Ted, so I was pretty sure my brothers wanted to make sure that I got someone better. Their concern ran side-by-side with interference and self-preservation. My future husband would have to be a pretty awesome guy to pass their roadblocks. Clearly, Maddox hadn't been warmed to yet.

I wondered what they would think of Solomon. Solomon could probably take all three of them without breaking a sweat.

"Fine. But hurry please, because if anything happens to me, they'll never find your body." I was pretty sure this was true.

"Point taken."

Maddox walked the house, inside and out, before showing me how to operate the controls for the cameras on his laptop, and finally locking up. He left me with a key, but gave firm instructions not to go anywhere, which he repeated four times, just in case I didn't get it. He was gone a total of forty-three minutes, not that I was clock-watching, and returned just as my mind started to taunt me with every strange creak and groan in the house.

I pounced on him as soon as I opened the door. "What did your boss say?" I asked.

"Matt's happy that we have the list. He's passed it onto our tech guys to crunch the numbers. We should know exactly how much the scam is worth inside a day, plus, we'll be able to build a paper trail of every account, who opened it at the bank, what addresses were used. Maybe find a digital trail too. The techies are thrilled. They had too much information to wade through before, hundreds of thousands of policies. You blew the case wide open." Maddox hugged me, the clinch lasting a little too long to be friendly, but just as I thought about standing on tiptoes and kissing him, his pants started to vibrate, which, I have to say, wasn't an altogether bad feeling, but there was the possibility I'd been indoors too long.

"Solomon," said Maddox, suddenly attentive. When he hung up, the news wasn't good. "Hector Ramos' body was found in a dumpster this morning, and only just identified. To make matters worse, his thumb was cut off."

"He was tortured?"

Maddox nodded. "The coroner thinks it was pre-mortem."

"That's all four of the gang dead," I said, my heart

sinking. "Five if we add Dean's girlfriend." Seven, if I added Twinkles and Knuckles to the list.

Maddox hugged me tighter. He didn't need to say it. We were both thinking the same thing. There was definitely someone else out there.

And I really didn't want to make eight.

# CHAPTER SEVENTEEN

I had been counting on puzzling through the notebook as my entertainment in the absence of anything, oh, like fun. Instead, Maddox laid his own sanity on the line and played game after game of Twenty-One with me with a pack of cards he produced from his laptop bag.

"What do you normally do with witnesses?" I asked as I added another game to my winning streak. "Is there a section in the PD handbook with a list of entertainment suggestions?"

"Nope. I just have to hope that they stay more scared of living outside than in, and that usually keeps them put."

"Even bored rigid?"

"Sorry that you're bored."

I produced the lamest line in the handbook. "It's not you, it's me."

"I get it. It's okay. It's no fun being a witness."

"Too right. Have you heard from Lily? Is she okay?"

"She's fine."

"What about my family?"

Maddox shuffled, cut the deck, shuffled again and dealt. "Garrett is making sure your parents don't know anything."

"Good." I was anxiously concerned about my parents being worried. My dad had been a cop for more than thirty years when he retired, and he and my mom were finally enjoying a more quiet life. Well, for my dad, anyway. Life remained busy for my mom. I wondered if my dad still kept a gun in the house. "Will the... whoever it is, go after my family?"

"Unlikely."

"How so?"

"Too many of them. Where would they start? Stop worrying, okay? We'll catch him."

"You have new leads?"

Maddox studied his cards, placing them flat on the counter. "Yes," he said, but I think he was lying.

"Excellent," I lied, tossing my cards down, winning another game.

I poked around the house while Maddox checked in with his team. I found a paperback lodged and perhaps forgotten, at the back of a cupboard. It was a sappy romance, but given the circumstances, beggars couldn't be choosers. I took it to the living room and curled up, reading about heaving bosoms and rakes in frock coats, while Maddox watched reruns of a game on the television.

"What happens if he isn't found?" I asked, folding the corner of the page and placing it on the couch next to me. Paranoia was creeping in the longer I waited. "How long do I stay in the safe house?"

"We'll do a risk assessment. If nothing happens

and it appears danger-free, we'll let you go back to your normal routine. Maybe we'll keep an eye on you, just in case, maybe not."

"On the off chance that he shoots me in the head?" I gulped. It seemed pretty risky to let me go back to my life with a murderer out there, even if *they* thought it seemed safe. If the mystery man truly thought I was after the money, or knew how to access it, I could be picked off any time. He might just be waiting for me to surface. The alternative neither of us wanted to broach was the possibility of never seeing my family again. Never seeing Lily again... never meeting my new baby niece or nephew. Starting new, alone, in some distant town where nobody knew my real name. And if I were really unlucky, filing in crappy offices for the rest of my life.

I wondered if Maddox would miss me, or even think about me.

"It's not gonna happen," said Maddox, passing the cards to me. I shuffled and dealt as he said, "If Ramos was alive, we'd have picked him up, and you would have been home free by now. We just have to wait it out a little longer. This person is desperate, assuming there really is someone other than Ramos. He's close to the cash, but he can't get it. He's going to make a wrong move."

"And you'll be there to catch him?"

"You bet."

"Will I see you again after this is all over?"

"If it goes to trial, we'll both have to testify." That wasn't what I meant, and Maddox knew it, but if he weren't going to say he hoped to see me again, I wouldn't be the one to press the point. I had some pride. Instead, I won the game and Maddox declared himself out.

I picked up my book and read a while longer until Solomon turned up with some take-out cartons, a box of breakfast cereal, and a bag with orange juice and milk. They conferred for a while and didn't seem to mind that I eavesdropped, seeing as I learned that little had happened. The techies had located all the accounts in the notebook, crunched the numbers and estimated that the fraud now stood at a cool three point nine million.

"That's not a lot to split between four people," I pointed out, calculating each share. "Not even a million each."

"Sounds like plenty to me," said Maddox as Solomon shrugged, apparently not willing to commit to a price. "It's a lot for one person."

I got plates and forks from the drainboard, feeling oddly domestic. "Are you staying?" I asked Solomon.

"Not tonight. I'll swap shifts with Maddox tomorrow."

"You're going to stay with me?" I said, taken aback. Somehow, being alone with Solomon hadn't fit into my freaking out schedule yet.

Solomon smiled. *Oh boy.* I tried not to imagine being alone with him, in an isolated house, with nothing to entertain us, but each other. Instead, I tried to focus on feeling safe with Maddox and reminding myself that another night in the safe house meant another night closer to home.

I knew Solomon would protect me, but given the way he kissed, I wasn't too sure of my personal safety with him. There was a good chance he could charm me into anything, and, come to think of it, it wouldn't take much charming.

I figured a night with Solomon would be wildly entertaining; but come the morning, he would just be an indentation in the pillow and mattress. He intrigued me. I knew he could make the perfect shot and drive a motorcycle. I knew he was smart and I knew his name. I suspected it would be fleeting and brilliant, but exciting and untamed didn't stick around. I wasn't sure that was what I wanted.

Maddox, however, seemed like a man who would happily wake up with a woman, snuggle, make breakfast and do the whole nine yards. I knew plenty of cops like him. I understood his life. I understood that type of man. *That's* what I wanted. I had thoroughly enjoyed waking up with him this morning, even though it had only gone two yards. I would have enjoyed it a lot more if Solomon hadn't arrived. My resolve weakened a little more. I wondered what Lily would say about my predicament. She would have loved it.

"We need to rotate shifts," explained Maddox. "We don't get a lot of sleep doing this."

I nodded, collecting plates from the drainer, passing them around, though I suddenly didn't feel hungry at all. Solomon didn't eat with us this time, but he stayed a while, then left, saying something about needing to sleep before getting an early start on the mounting evidence. I was still picking at dinner when he left, wondering how much punishing exercise I would need just to work off all the fast food.

"You're quiet," remarked Maddox. "Should I be worried?"

"No."

"Will I have to handcuff you to the bed tonight?"

I looked up. "Kinky."

"To stop you from running, but now you mention it..."

"I don't think there's a headboard."

"Too bad."

"Should I be worried about you?"

"No, my intentions towards you are very, very good."

"What a shame," I said, leaving the room to go splash some cold water on my face.

Maddox cleared the kitchen while I was in the bathroom and when I came out, I found he had set up the DVD player on his laptop. "This doesn't seem like you," I said as the credits rolled. "Shouldn't you be watching hardboiled detective shows or Die Hard Twenty-Nine?"

"I don't watch a lot of TV. Work doesn't leave much room for a life."

Not what a potential girlfriend wants to hear. "So what do you do in your spare time?" I asked.

"Go to the gym. Catch a movie once in a while."

"You're such a man."

"I like cooking, too."

"The surprises never cease. What do you cook?"

"Meat."

"Ahh. Man cooking."

"I'll cook for you some time, then you can eat your words."

"I like them sautéed."

"Do you now?"

"You know I'm going to hold you to that?" I answered.

"Do that," said Maddox, leaning in and I was suddenly aware how close I was sitting to him. I could feel his body heat radiating against me. The evening was certainly looking up now, and I thought he was about to kiss me. Then he leaned back, frowning. "Do you hear that?"

It was a tinny beep from his laptop. He pressed a few keys and the film disappeared, leaving the four-screen display of the outside cameras. One quarter fizzled with static. "The feed on camera three is down. I've got to check it out."

"Is that safe?" I asked. "Won't someone from your team come?"

"Sure," he said. "It happens sometimes. These are only temporary units. I can fix it before anyone from the team gets here." All the same, he took a small gun out of his ankle holster and laid it on the coffee table. "I'm going out the kitchen door. Watch the feed and shout when it's back on." He pulled a screwdriver out of his bag, slipped it into his pocket and walked out. I stayed in the hallway until I saw him exit the back door, then returned to the living room to wait for him. As I watched the screen, the upper right camera blinked out, replaced by static.

It struck me as very unlikely that both feeds would have loose wires at the same time. Instantly, I was on alert. Angling the laptop so I could see the screen from the doorway, I crept to the door and peeped out. As I did so, a loud crack sounded outside, then the thud of something heavy dropping. I fell to the floor, my breathing fast and shallow, crab-walking until I was next to the sofa.

Instinctively, I knew what I heard was a gunshot. I wasn't sure about the heavy thud.

The back door opened and closed and I held my breath, waiting to hear Maddox's voice, but there was nothing.

I looked around for some place to hide, but there were barely any hiding places, just the couches and the coffee table. Behind the couch would be the first place they looked in this room.

Soft footsteps came through from the kitchen into the hallway and stopped. I heard them move into another room. Grabbing Maddox's cell phone from the coffee table, I huddled into the far corner, vanishing into the shadows. It took me a couple of attempts, but I managed to scroll through until I found Solomon's number, my heart pounding as it connected.

"Solomon."

"It's me." I whispered. "I need help."

"Why are you whispering?"

"Someone's in the house."

"Where's Maddox?"

"I don't know. He went outside."

"Can you get to a gun?"

"Yes." I shot forward, grabbing the gun Maddox placed on the coffee table and checked the small barrel. It was fully loaded.

"I'm on the way."

Solomon didn't disconnect, so neither did I. Instead, I placed the phone in my back pocket, scuttling backwards until my back hit the wall, and prayed that Solomon had no problem with breaking the speed limit. I knew I didn't have any way out. My only exits were the front and rear doors, which involved moving through the hallway, where someone now stood, the floorboards creaking with every step.

I looked around. The windows were locked, the

room sparse. All I could do now was wait and hope Maddox overcame whatever was stopping him. Unless, the bullet… No, I couldn't think about it.

The footsteps grew closer and the door creaked as it suddenly pushed wide open. A man stepped into the room. Shorter than Maddox and bulkier, he wore all black. Black camo pants, a hooded top and a knit cap pulled down low over his brow. Despite being in the shadow of the door, ominously, in his gloved hands, I could see he held a gun, the shape of it quite clear in his hand. I saw the whites of his eyes flicker as they swept the room and settled on me. With my hands behind my back, I stuffed Maddox's small gun up my sleeve and tried not to quake with fear.

"Stand up," said the man, his face hidden in the shadows. "Stand up slowly and keep your hands where I can see them."

I raised my hands above my head, as the gun jolted down my sleeve, and stood up slowly, my knees protesting after being cramped. There was something awfully familiar about his voice.

"Palms flat," he said, stepping forward into the light.

I uncurled my fingers and my mouth dropped open. "Vincent?"

Green Hand's accountant took another step closer, his gun pointed at me. His eyes darted around, scanning the room, registering that we were alone. He stepped to one side, and, with the gun still aimed at me, checked behind the couch just in case anyone else was concealed, repeating the strategy with the other couch.

"Where's Adam?" I asked, trying not to panic. My best bet was to stall for time. If Solomon got here before Vincent shot me, I would be okay. If he got here moments after I was shot, I stood a better chance of surviving; and that's what it all boiled down to now: Solomon's speed and my oral skills. I was so glad I hadn't said that out loud. Lily would say it was totally Freudian.

"Shepherd? Shot him in the yard," said Vincent bluntly.

My breath caught. "Dead?"

Vincent ignored my question. "You're my last loose end," he said. "If it wasn't for your meddling, I'd have my money by now and I'd be outta here. Where is it?"

The final puzzle piece clicked into place. Vincent was the fifth man. The unnamed suspect responsible for blackmailing, then killing the rest of the fraudsters. I saw it so clearly now. He was the man Maddox chased down the alley, the man who forced Tanya Henderson to Flames. He was also the one person who knew how to access all the cash, and as an accountant, he knew how to hide it. It was more than enough to buy his precious Spyder and then some.

"I'm not alone," I stalled.

"Yes, you are. I've been watching the house. I knew Adam Shepherd, or whoever he really is, was mixed up in this somehow. I saw him earlier, when he was supposed to be out of town, and all I had to do was follow him. Imagine my surprise when I saw him talking to a couple of detectives, thinking no one spotted him. Actually, I wasn't surprised at all. I'm smart, see? I'd already figured out he was a cop and when I saw you at Flames, I figured out you were part of it too. Everyone thinks I'm just Vincent the dull accountant, but they're wrong. They're all wrong!"

"I never thought that."

"I asked you out a bunch of times and you turned me down."

"I... was seeing someone else."

"No, you weren't. You just didn't want to go out with me, even after I left you all the gifts to show you how much you meant to me."

"What gifts?" I asked, confused.

"The flowers, the screensaver I put on your computer. The chocolates. Is nothing good enough for you?"

"You left the dead flowers on my car?"

"They weren't dead!"

"They didn't have heads!"

Vincent sucked in a breath, and his mouth pinched in frustration. "Those punks! They must have ripped the heads off when I left. The good for nothing little assholes! I left you twelve red roses!"

"I just got thorny stems!"

"What about the screensaver? That was great!"

"It was creepy! It said, 'I'm watching you.'"

"You didn't like the animated hearts that came up after it?"

"What hearts?" I screeched, my voice slightly hysterical.

"When the note screen faded out, it erupted into hearts. I programmed it myself. I learned how to at night school."

"I went to get coffee right after I got creeped out!"

"So you didn't get coffee just to bump into me?" Vincent's face crumpled.

"No."

"I left flowers in your place." He watched me closely. "I arranged them in one of your vases."

"You burgled my apartment!"

"I didn't," he sniffed. "I didn't *take* anything I just wanted to know what you knew. And I thought I'd leave your flowers for you. I was being nice!"

"Well, gee, thanks, Vincent."

"Did you at least get the chocolate?" he asked. "I stopped by later to see if you were okay. Maybe you needed a guy to lean on. It's been a rough week."

I didn't like to point out that it had been a rough couple of weeks entirely because of Vincent, but I couldn't help saying, "The ones with a great big car tire print across the box?"

"I only ran over them once and it was an accident, I swear. They were still okay to eat. I checked."

"OhmiGod! Vincent!"

Vincent was quiet for a while, his gun wavering slightly. "So, you'll still go out with me?" he asked hopefully. "The concert will be great."

"You just killed Maddox," I said in a small voice.

"For fuck's sake!" Vincent steadied the gun. "I give up. Wooing you is hopeless. I've tried everything. You're impossible! Give me the key. I know you have it. I saw you take it from Tallulah. I'm going to be rich. I have millions. I can get anyone I want now. Have anything I want."

"I don't have it with me," I said, stalling for more time. "But I can get it."

"Tell me something. Does the money make me appealing now?" asked Vincent after sighing. Clearly, his plan was dissolving fast, but I didn't have the heart to laugh. Not with Maddox outside, alone. Dead.

I had to be honest. No. Billions wouldn't have made Vincent any more appealing, never mind millions. But I couldn't say that with a gun pointed at my head. Not when I knew how many murders he was responsible for.

"Figures," said Vincent when I hesitated. "But no matter. All I have to do is shoot you and all the witnesses will be gone."

"Where will you go?" I blurted. I could feel my forehead breaking into a sweat as my eyes crossed to the barrel pointed at me.

"Hawaii for a nice vacation. I've always wanted to go. I won't be coming back to Montgomery, that's for sure. I've lived in this town all my life. I've worked at Green Hand ten years and what recognition do I get? Nothing. Even the bimbo temp won't go out with me. Maybe I'll go to LA or London or Paris, after that. Finally, see the world."

"Sounds nice," I said.

"Shame you won't be coming. What's with the hair, by the way? And where's the key?"

"It's at my place," I lied. "What's wrong with my hair?"

"Nothing. It's okay. I liked the blonde more is all. You had the whole fabulous thing goin' on."

"I felt like a change." *And it's all your fault*, I added mentally. I could feel tears pricking at my eyes again and had to fight to keep my chin from quivering.

"The key?" prompted Vincent.

"I said it was at my apartment. I can take you there."

"No, it isn't. I searched and it wasn't there. It's here, isn't it? I told you I'm smart! I told you! You can't fool me! I'll get it when you're dead. I'm armed and dangerous, you bitch!" Vincent shrugged and pointed, his finger scraping the trigger guard.

At the same moment, I dropped my arm, tipped the gun into my hand and fired, yelling, "And I'm armed and fabulous!"

Vincent screamed as his shooting arm dropped. I saw a blur behind him, just a shadow against the wall. Like slow motion, I watched Vincent steady himself, position his finger, extend his arm slightly forward and then... there was nothing.

When I came to, it was to look into beautiful blue eyes. I raised a hand to my head, brushing my fingertips across my forehead then down to my chest, feeling for a bullet hole and finding none. Next, I pinched myself hard. Yep. That hurt all right. And was probably a very good sign that I was still alive. Just to make sure, I pinched the man holding me.

"Ow," he said and Maddox's face swam into view. "I've been bashed over the head and shot. What was the pinch for?"

"Just checking."

Maddox helped me sit up. I looked over, following the sounds of grunting and swearing. Vincent was flat on the floor, face down. His glasses had fallen off and lay, the frame twisted, a little to his left. His hands were cuffed behind his back along with his ankles. He drew his legs up so his heels bounced off his butt as he struggled against the bindings. Solomon knelt next to him and delivered a punch to Vincent's side, which stopped him struggling for a moment. Solomon looked up briefly and I think he smiled.

"What happened?" I asked. I was dizzy and sick and really, really angry. And in pain. Oh boy, the pain that hit me suddenly was enough to knock me off my feet.

"When I went out to check the camera, Vincent came up behind me and knocked me over the head. I went down and the bastard shot me."

"That is so rude," I said, commiserating with him, overjoyed that he wasn't singing with the angels. "What else happened?"

"When I came around, Vincent was inside the house already, and I could hear him talking to you. I snuck up behind him. You fired. I went for him as he fired. Great shot, by the way. You got him in the hand."

It turned out that when I crumpled to the floor, Maddox thought I'd been killed. As it was, Vincent had squeezed off a shot, the bullet slicing past my arm, causing a very bloody, but not life-threatening wound and I'd simply passed out from shock. A few stitches, some rest, and I would be right as rain.

Maddox helped me to a sofa and filled me in on what happened in the minutes I was out. There had been a brief struggle, during which Vincent had turned on him and stuck his finger into the wound in his shoulder, causing Maddox to nearly pass out from the pain.

Maddox managed to grab the gun from him, throwing it into the dark hallway just as Solomon came to the front.

Ranting and raving about how I'd spoiled everything, Vincent didn't know whether to go for his glasses or the gun, so it had been easy for Solomon to subdue him. I don't know where Solomon was when I called, and he didn't volunteer the information, but it was close enough that he'd beaten the rest of the team who were on their way.

"You're just a temp," spluttered Vincent, lifting his face off the floor enough to stare at me. His face was bright red and he puffed angrily, pulling against the restraints from where Solomon had him hogtied. "How could you have figured any of this out?"

Maddox had one hand clapped to his shoulder. I could see blood seeping through the rag, blooming between his fingers. I could only imagine I must have mirrored his bloody image. We were lucky Vincent was such a crap shot. "She may be a temp, but she's also a highly trained government operative," said Maddox, his voice quietly menacing.

Bless him. He was such a good liar. And he had my back too. He was really growing on me. Well, the kissing helped define my opinion, but the whole saving my life thing helped too. Obviously. Maddox looked at me with mutual admiration.

"Really?" said Vincent, his voice belying surprise.

"No," I said, with a painful shrug. "I'm just a temp."

"Christ," said Vincent as he stopped struggling, his cheek resting on the floor. I think I heard a sob escape from him.

"I didn't figure it out," I told Vincent, just to add to his misery. "Not all of it anyway. I didn't know it was you. I only knew for certain when I saw you here. If you'd gotten the money and disappeared, I may never have put it together. You could have been in Hawaii, home free in weeks. Instead, you'll be sending me a postcard from the big house."

That sounded so cool, the way I said it. Unfortunately, the first part was true. I had no doubt that the taskforce would have pieced everything together, and that Vincent's name would have come up in the investigation, but it would have been too late by then. He and the money would have vanished. We were lucky that in his desperation, he made the wrong move as Maddox anticipated.

Solomon hauled Vincent to his feet. For a serial killer, he looked so pathetic with his shirt untucked, his hair mussed up, and a bloody rag wrapped around his hand from where I shot him. "Will you visit me?" Vincent asked.

"Are you kidding?"

He looked so perplexed, I nearly laughed. "No," he said, his forehead marred with frown lines. "I'll write you!"

Solomon hauled Vincent away before he could embarrass himself any further.

I heard sirens approaching, paramedics I hoped for Maddox and me, and a ride to the can for Vincent. Once word got around that he'd attacked a Graves, his stay at the precinct wouldn't be pretty. I struggled to care, but couldn't.

"Let's go to the hospital and get patched up," said Maddox, his arm sliding around my waist.

"It's a date."

## CHAPTER EIGHTEEN

Garrett picked me up from the hospital after my arm was stitched closed. He drove me home, very quietly, eyes forward, fingers gripping the wheel until his knuckles turned white. He hadn't said a word about Maddox, or Solomon, and I figured he might explode soon. He just hadn't decided on whom to explode yet. I was glad I wasn't playing baseball with him and the guys at their regular weekend game. With Garrett's temper simmering just below the surface, it had the potential to get brutal. At least Vincent Marciano's arrest had assuaged some of his anger.

"You could have been killed," he said quietly, after settling me on the couch.

The weight of his comment lay heavily on my chest. "I know," I said simply because there was nothing else to say. "But I'm here."

"You're not indestructible," Garrett pointed out. He took my overnight bag to my bedroom and came back, looking down at me. I leaned against the back of the couch and took a deep breath, waiting for the lecture about safety, why you should never trust an accountant, and how to avoid getting shot at. Instead, he surprised me. "As soon as your arm is healed, we're going to the range," he told me.

~

Vincent was arrested for six murders, two attempted murders, assault with a deadly weapon, extortion and fraud, which wasn't too bad for a guy who had never even gotten a parking ticket.

Two weeks later, Lily and I were sitting in my living room. She had run out first thing after the verdict came in, and bought double-pump mochas with extra whip and sprinkles along with the biggest chocolate croissants she could find. I was in heaven. Plus, now the court case was over, and quickly solved given my rock-solid evidence, I could tell her everything.

"How did that little creep Vincent get involved?" she asked.

Vincent squealed with barely any prompting. Some I even overheard as we exited the safe house to the waiting paramedics—Maddox's boss, Matt Miller nodding to me as we limped out—some Maddox filled me in on more in the days after; while I got the rest from the court case.

With Vincent behind bars, we wouldn't see him again.

"As company accountant, he had access to all Green Hand's financial records. After Dominic mentioned an irregularity, Vincent noticed other irregularities in the payouts," I explained. "On investigating, he realized the extent of the fraud, piecing together who was part of it from weeks of patient watching and waiting. But instead of turning his evidence over to the police, for their forensic accountants to comb, Vincent got fat dollar signs in his eyes and decided he wanted his slice of the multi-million fraud pie."

"Whoa," said Lily. "I did not think Vincent had it in him."

"It's always the quiet ones," I agreed.

"No, that's not it. It's that people are never what you expect them to be."

"Can't argue with that."

"So... he didn't just kill Dean straight off?"

"Vincent didn't kill Dean at all. Dean was killed by the Finklesteins." I licked the cream from the top of my mocha and snuggled against the couch as I told Lily everything.

Vincent's first step was to blackmail Martin Dean, but Dean didn't have access to the money. When Vincent threatened to turn Dean in, Dean 'fessed up his connections and bought the tickets to Paris where he intended to flee with Tanya, with or without the cash. He simply couldn't get the money without alerting Harris, Mathis and Ramos, his car-crazed conspirators, and he wasn't going to jail for the fraud without a payoff awaiting him.

The four never trusted each other much from the start. They decided it was in all of their best interests that none of them could access the cash without the other members present. With more than three million of it already converted to cash, it was the smart thing to do. Not as smart as not committing a crime in the first place, but I didn't like to be picky.

The cash was stored in a special bank deposit vault in the city. Each conspirator had something that was needed to access it, and none of them could open the box without the others. Dean and Ron Harris each had a key; Chris Mathis had the code for the electronic keypad; and Hector Ramos was the signatory. His thumb print provided the extra security, which was why Vincent hacked it off. It was found in his freezer, between the ice cream and peas.

"And Dean gave his key to Tanya?"

I nodded. "Dean knew he was in big trouble. On one side, he had Vincent blackmailing him, on the other side were Harris, Mathis and Ramos who wanted to get more money, and then there was always the potential that the authorities would discover the crime."

This much was guesswork, given that none of the gang could corroborate the truth. We surmised that faced with the evidence and the threat of the police, Dean stalled for time with Vincent, telling him he could get the money, but to be patient. Vincent knew who was in the gang and since the money couldn't be moved, he was okay to wait it out.

Then Dean saw my research for the Gazette and knew that I had put together his connection to the other three members of the gang. He panicked, putting in a call to Ramos. "He gave his key to Tanya to hide as collateral," I explained as Lily hung on my every word. "If anything happened to him, the others wouldn't be able to access the collated money. He couldn't pay off Vincent without any ready cash, and he knew there was a discoverable connection between the four of them. All he wanted was out. He confided in Ramos all about the problems he had."

Lily frowned. "So why did the Finklesteins kill Dean?"

"In his panic, Dean became the weak link so

Ramos put out a hit on him. Ramos' wife is Knuckles Finklestein's wife's cousin, so Ramos hired the brothers to take out Dean, get the key and the report, thus reducing the pot. It would have finished off the fraudulent claims, but they could take a cool million each. Importantly, Ramos wanted the evidence between him and the rest of the gang obliterated before pay day."

"Who knew this kind of stuff went on in Montgomery? Makes you wonder what else is going on under our noses."

I didn't want to think about it. I'd had enough "fun" for a while.

"When did the police get involved?" asked Lily. "They knew, right?"

"They knew there was fraud, but had no clue who was involved. Green Hand is huge, they have hundreds of thousands of active policies and pay out thousands every day. It took them months to narrow it down to Dean's department." Apparently, Dean didn't know that Maddox was already in the department spying and collecting evidence to implicate the whole gang, until the night he died. "Without his notebook, they didn't have any place to start looking for the fraudulent policies."

"Do you think Dean knew he was going to die?"

"When the Finklesteins came by that night? Yeah, I think so."

"Sucky," said Lily.

To Dean's credit, once he realized he was going to be killed, he didn't give up my name or Tanya's to the Finklesteins. I don't know whether he thought that would keep us safe or just make things difficult for Ramos, but since he also didn't give up Vincent, it was hard to tell. Perhaps that was his revenge. He knew even if he were dead, Vincent would go after the other three to get the money. In a weird sort of way, Vincent was his insurance policy just as much as Maddox was and he'd seen the whole thing.

However, what Dean hadn't banked on was Vincent knowing about Tanya, or that he would be desperate enough to kill her, too. I think Tanya was the one person Dean trusted, and probably the one person he really tried to protect. He probably hoped she would take the Paris tickets and flee.

"And the Finklesteins and Ramos thought you and Vincent were the same person?" prompted Lily.

I nodded. This much I knew from Vincent's testimony. "Once Dean was dead, Vincent knew he didn't have long to shake down the rest of the gang for the money. The gang knew already from Dean that someone was on their tail, and had discovered a connection. They also knew Dean was being blackmailed. The only problem they had was that they didn't know who the blackmailer was and who had the evidence connecting them. Vincent said Ramos told him they figured it was the same person."

"People should never jump to conclusions."

"But they did. Harris, Mathis and Ramos weren't career criminals. They were opportunists." Once Ramos saw my name watermarked on the research, he knew I could connect them.

Unfortunately for Ramos, Vincent was one step faster and had come up with another plan. He planned to stall any investigation into the fraud as he bumped one gang member off at a time, until he was the only one left with the knowledge of the crimes and access to the money. Earlier on the day Dean died, he overheard Dean telling Ramos about the file on his desk. He couldn't get to it before the Finklesteins, so he counted on deleting my files as a guarantee to ensure that neither I, nor anyone else, would be able to put the pieces together. He just didn't count on my amazing ability to accidentally delete everything, thus ensuring I always, *always*, backed up my documents. And he also didn't count on the authorities putting together the task force that put Maddox in the building to spy.

"I knew there were too many hit-and-run accidents," said Lily. "It was too much of a coincidence."

"I agree. Vincent got the first key from Ron Harris and, so he claimed, killed him by accident when he was desperate to get away. After that, everything came easy. Chris Mathis gave up the box number and the bank where the money was stashed in a deposit box, along with the key code, and paid for the information with his life. Vincent couldn't risk leaving anyone alive. After all, he would never be safe while they were after him, determined to get 'their' money back. And that left Ramos, the most dangerous one. He was the signatory and Vincent needed his thumbprint. He chopped it off before he killed Ramos."

"Why didn't Ramos cut a deal with Vincent?"

"Too greedy. Ramos wasn't too bothered about the deaths of his co-conspirators. He just wanted the money, and like hell would he give it up to a pipsqueak like Vincent, not after they'd put all the effort and money in to pull it off."

This came out during the investigation too. Ramos had been playing fast and loose with the bank's money and was in debt up to his neck. It was only a matter of time before he was investigated for banking fraud. Even with Vincent threatening him, Ramos couldn't afford to get out, not while his bank was on the verge of collapsing. He would have lost everything, not to mention facing a hefty jail sentence.

With Dean, Harris and Mathis dead, Ramos could get enough money to wipe his slate clean and start over with millions. Vincent got to Tanya before Ramos could. Vincent forced her into retrieving the key from the safest hiding place she knew, Flames, and he shot her to cover his tracks. Except I picked up the key and it was safely stored in the evidence locker at Montgomery PD ever since.

"Ramos figured I must have taken it and sicced the Finklesteins on me. Ramos assumed getting rid of me was the last step before claiming their cash." I don't know what they were supposed to do to me to keep my mouth shut about the file, but given their rap sheets, I was sure it wouldn't have been pretty. "This is where Vincent actually saved the day. He recognized the Finklesteins outside my apartment and shot them both, effectively saving my life."

"Hurrah for Vincent?" Lily looked hopeful.

"Not really. When the Finklesteins showed up dead, Ramos thought I killed them. He was the one who tried to ram us off the road the night we visited Serena. Ramos didn't know Vincent was also following us. When Ramos' car wiped out, Vincent picked him up, jumping him while he was injured. Faking a signature wasn't a problem, but he had to cut off Ramos' thumb to get the print."

"Gross. Also, did Ramos think you were Ramboette or what?"

"I know, right? Ridiculous."

"Far out, Brussels sprout."

"What?" I shook my head. "Anyway, Vincent figured I had the key and followed Maddox to the safe house." The money was nearly his. That one little key has caused a lot of problems for everyone.

The Green Hand Gang, as the Montgomery Gazette dubbed them, were dead, most of the witnesses were gone and the money was recovered, rendering the fraud aspect of the case cut and dried.

Vincent's trial, however, generated a lot more interest. The whole thing lasted three solid days. In the end, the only way he was getting out of prison was in a body bag. I figured between Ramos' wife and Finklestein's, it might be sooner rather than later.

"I'm glad this is all over," said Lily, thoughtfully chewing her last bite of croissant.

"Me too."

"How's your arm?"

"Better."

As for me, well, no serious damage done. Green Hand Insurance's future is currently uncertain, given the scale of the fraud. I didn't even know if I still had a job. I just decided not to go back. So, I was out of a job, plus, I had a small scar on my upper right arm from the bullet. It was a small price to pay for getting to live. As a bonus, I swiped Vincent's concert tickets when I went in to clean out my desk, and Lily and I had an excellent time.

Solomon disappeared right after Vincent was arrested and I saw him once, briefly, at the trial, but we didn't talk. Although he did stay around long enough to hear my statement. I was told he did his best not to laugh when I burst into tears after telling the court how I had to dye my hair brown. Lily told me she saw him at the hospital, but she was a tad hysterical at the time, after discovering I had been shot. I figured he was checking up on Maddox.

Maddox, on the other hand, I've seen plenty of. We're dating, and I'm looking forward to finding out where that goes. After undergoing surgery to remove the bullet from his shoulder and some recuperation time, he went back to Montgomery PD to face the wrath of my family. I think he's hoping he won't have to go undercover again for a while. Unless it's my covers. That sounded fine to both of us.

"I have to go," said Lily, "But I'm glad you got to tell me what really happened."

"Me too." She was careful not to squeeze my arm when she hugged me, and I was careful to give her the biggest hug I could.

~

So here I was a month later, no work and nothing to do. I had a coffee, a magazine, a strong resistance to daytime television and a new alarm system for my apartment, courtesy of Lily's parents who were shocked when they heard everything that happened.

When someone knocked at the door, I took my time answering.

Solomon was waiting in the hallway, his hands in his pockets, casually lounging like he had nothing better to do than loiter in my hall. He was clean-shaven, and his eyes were soft like liquid chocolate. He wore black pants and a shirt with tonal black stripes, two buttons open at the neck. He looked elegant, strong, smokin' sexy. After I got over my initial surprise at seeing him, my stomach doing the usual little flip whenever he appeared, I smiled warmly and so did he.

"Come in," I said, opening the door and stepping aside. Solomon pushed himself off the wall and stepped through, entering the living room. I watched him walk, wrenching my eyes, with a mental sigh, from the way the pants molded to his butt. He was a fine, fine man. Funnily, it hadn't occurred to me that I would never see him again. I just assumed he'd turn up one day and here he was. With the case wrapped up, I wondered what he could possibly want.

The apartment was neat and tidy, though I had to replace a few things Vincent ruined when he rummaged through it. Solomon, as usual, saw everything and said nothing, finally turning to me in the doorway. I held still, the sound of my heartbeat echoing in my ears, as he ran his eyes over me.

"You're still a brunette," Solomon said at last, surprising me as he gave an approving nod.

I self-consciously smoothed a hand over my hair. I missed the blonde and it had taken some getting used to, but I liked what I saw in the mirror. "I kinda like it."

"And you're not working?" Solomon asked, glancing at the half-drunk coffee on the table and the open magazine.

I shrugged. "My temping agency can't find anything for me right now." Actually, I hadn't asked. I wasn't in dire need of the cash. Maddox ensured that my last couple of paychecks came through, and the taskforce had, surprisingly, made a contribution, given the work I'd done for the case. I earned a commendation too, plus, they covered my excess medical expenses. The only thing they couldn't do for me was advise me where to go from here out. That was something I hadn't decided yet either.

"How about you come work for me?" he said.

I tried to keep my face passive, but I think a little surprise leaked out as my eyes widened. "Work for you?" I asked, the words slipping from my throat easily.

"It's part time at first, flexible hours."

"Doing what? I'm over filing." So, *so* over filing. Though I wasn't totally sure what I wanted to do with my life, the last couple of months had made it clear what I didn't want to be doing. I didn't want to be the admin monkey anymore. I wanted more. I owed it to myself.

"There will be some filing, but only your own stuff," Solomon clarified before my spirits dropped. "I'm opening a small agency here. Private investigations for individuals and corporations. The usual stuff. Surveillance, tracing, background checks for starters. I could do with another private investigator to work with the team I've put together."

"I'm not exactly qualified," I pointed out.

"You don't have to be an ex-detective or have been in the field. You just have to be smart. People talk to you. They like you. And you think like an investigator, only..."

"Only?"

"Only different," Solomon concluded and there was the ghost of a smile again. One that told me he believed in me. "I have an ex-detective, two agency men, and a cybercriminal on my team already," he told me, intriguing me further.

"So why do you want me?" I waited, breath stilled.

"Because you're *nothing* like them at all."

I pondered his offer. My own hours were appealing. A wage was definitely appealing. Not being Serena's sounding board for every aspect of her pregnancy while she waited to pop was appealing too. Working with Solomon? Not so sure about having him as my boss, working beside him every day, but I figured I would never be bored. I might even get a work ethic. Maybe this was exactly what I was waiting for.

"How about you try it on for size? Give it a few months. See if you like it. If you don't, no harm done." Solomon shrugged nonchalantly. "I'll train you."

The words were out of my mouth before I really thought about it properly. "When do I start?"

"Monday. Ten a.m." Solomon pulled a business card from his pocket and passed it to me. I took it, flipping it over to read. Stretched in large black letters across the thick white card was "Solomon Agency." Underneath: "Investigations." Then there was a phone number and an address downtown in what I vaguely recalled to be a nice building that had been vacant for a while. I tucked the card into my shirt pocket. "Don't be late," he warned, starting towards the door.

I followed him. "Solomon?"

With his hand on the door handle, he turned to me, one eyebrow raised, waiting.

"What do I wear?" I asked.

"Whatever you like."

"What do PIs wear?" I pressed. I had suits, dresses, jeans, but I had no idea what would be suitable and I hated getting it wrong.

"That's the whole point, Lexi. I don't want you to

look like a PI. I want you to be the person it doesn't occur to people to suspect."

"Hah." Clear as mud.

He pulled the door open.

"So you do like me, huh?" I said, following him out. I don't know why I said it. It just slipped out; maybe because I still wasn't sure. And I guess I missed him popping up when I least expected it, his cool eyes assessing everything.

Solomon turned to me, just on the threshold, and stepped closer, back inside my apartment. I held my space, unmoving as he leaned in. His lips brushed my cheek, moving a little closer, then landing on my lips for the briefest of moments. "Oh, I *like* you," he said. Then he was gone. For a long time, I stood in the hallway, my heart beating fast. I shut the door and went back to my magazine. Gossip counted as keeping up with current affairs, right?

A couple of minutes later, another knock sounded at my door. Maddox smiled broadly when he saw me and I stood on tiptoes to kiss him. "Hi, Adam."

"I think I saw Solomon," he said, taking hold of my hand, lacing his fingers through mine and kissing me again. He carried a grocery bag in one hand for the dinner he had promised to make me once, a promise I decided to collect tonight.

"He was here. You just missed him."

"You know, he was never really with the FBI." Maddox shut the door behind him as I tugged him inside. He shrugged his jacket off, no sign of stiffness in his shoulder, and hung it next to mine on the rack. "He was on some kind of loan due to his financial crime expertise and field experience. I don't know who the hell he worked for. I'm not even sure Miller knew. I don't even know if Solomon is his first or last name!"

I thought about it for a moment but felt no surprise at the revelation. Solomon was quiet, strong, and probably deadly. I didn't know about romantically, but I did know I would always want him on my team. I also knew his first name. "Strikes me that he was working the right side, whomever he worked for."

"I guess. He's left, anyway. I haven't seen him in a couple of weeks." Maddox stepped closer, his hand running over my hair as he smiled down at me. His eyes sparkled.

"I figured."

"He never struck me as an agency man," said Maddox, but he didn't expand on that, instead asking, "Did he say what he's doing now?"

I relieved Maddox of the bag and walked through to the kitchen, Maddox close on my heels. "You really haven't seen him?" I asked, glancing over my shoulder.

"No. Not since we wrapped the case up. I'm back at MPD now the task force is disbanded. I caught a homicide case. The guy gambled with dudes way out of his league. I'm working with your brother Garrett on this one."

"Hope you catch them." I flashed a smile at his pleased face. Catching criminals suited him far better than watching television while he healed. I wondered how working with Garrett would suit either of them. "Well, I guess he won't mind me saying. I don't think it's a secret. He's staying in Montgomery. He opened a business."

"Doing?"

I repeated what Solomon told me, "Private investigations." Dang, if that didn't sound mysterious.

"He came to tell you that?" Maddox frowned, but he didn't seem overly surprised at the news.

"Yeah. Offered me a job, too. Private investigator."

Maddox's face darkened as he looked at me sharply. *That* surprised him. "Seriously? You told him no, of course." Maddox stated it simply, like there wasn't even the possibility that I would say anything else.

I narrowed my eyes and shook my head, feeling strangely possessive of my new job. And, I thought, with sudden amusement, the whole Vincent thing had been the world's worst interview. "Actually, I said yes." I grinned. A big, excited smile to reflect my inner excitement. Me? A PI? Stranger things have happened. And as for Solomon being on my team; I bet being on his team would be pretty cool too.

Maddox sidled closer. "Can I persuade you to say no?"

"Why would I say no?"

Maddox's jaw stiffened and he ran a hand over it thoughtfully, before placing it on my shoulder, caressing me right where he knew it didn't hurt. "Because Solomon is scary. No one really knows him. I couldn't tell you a damn thing about him and I just spent the last four months with him every day."

"You worked with him. You must have some idea about his character," I pointed out, turning back to the grocery bag and unloading the contents onto the counter. "And you're a detective. Didn't you find out *anything*?"

"Only that he was working this job for fun. Miller

told me the FBI wanted to give him something to keep him out of trouble until his loaner contract expired. His words, not mine."

It hadn't been a lot of fun for me, but whatever floated his space cruiser. "What did he usually do when on loan to the FBI... or whomever?" I asked, curiosity biting.

"Beats me." Maddox waited. "So...?"

"I'm going to take the job," I said decisively. Like before, when Solomon offered, I didn't even have to think about my answer. I was intrigued and more interested in seeing what Solomon's world had to offer than ending up as a temp in another office, doing the same thing day in, day out. Frankly, filing could bite me. "I'm not exactly rolling in offers here," I added. "And lounging around was fun for oh, a day and a half, tops. I need to work."

Plus, Maddox's warning made it sound even more appealing. Working with Solomon would *never* be dull. I might even learn a bunch of cool stuff. So long as I didn't get shot again, I was fine with that.

Maddox inched up to me, his hands snaking around my waist and drawing me to him. Through the open neck of his button-down shirt, I could see the pinkish scar of his wound, now healed, but still fresh and shiny looking. "I could make you a nice offer," he murmured, his voice smoky.

"It's not a job offer is it?"

"No, but it'll keep you out of trouble for the next few hours."

"Mmm," I purred, my arms going around his neck. "I think you better tell me more."

Lexi Graves returns in *Who Glares Wins*, out now in paperback and ebook!

Only a few weeks into her new job as a private investigator, Lexi Graves thinks she may have bitten off more than she can chew with her first solo cases.

In between going undercover as a plush pony at a "Bronies" conference and following her cheating brother-in-law, she's got a saboteur-turned-killer to catch and a missing woman to find. Two of her cases may be connected, but how? There's no short list of suspects to investigate, but the closer Lexi gets to the killer, the more her life is put in jeopardy. Trying to avoid being framed for a murder she didn't commit, Lexi knows her luck is running out.

To make matters worse, her boyfriend, sexy detective, Adam Maddox, thinks she's out of the PI game faster than she got into it. Her boss, the mysterious Solomon, meanwhile, hopes to get her between the sheets by night, as well as solving cases by day, and Lexi's "just say no" resolve might not be as fortified as she believes.

All she wants is to be taken seriously and there's only one way she can do that—solve the cases, no matter what.

If you enjoyed *Armed and Fabulous*, you'll love *Deadlines*, a spin-off from the bestselling *Lexi Graves Mysteries,* out now in paperback and ebook!

Shayne Winter thinks she has everything she ever wanted: a job as chief reporter at *The LA Chronicle*, a swish, new apartment in a fabulous neighborhood, and a California-cool lifestyle. But on the very first day, it all goes horribly wrong. The apartment is less "young professional" and more "young offender," as the only furnishing is a handsome squatter with roving eyes. Even worse, Ben Kosina, her predecessor at *The Chronicle*, has returned to claim his former job, leaving Shayne nothing but the obituary column and a simple choice: take it or leave it.

Her first assignment should be easy: eulogizing the accidental death of washed-up former child-star, Chucky Barnard, and filing her column. Yet when Shayne interviews the people closest to Chucky, his sister claims Chucky had everything to live for, suggesting his untimely death could only be murder.

Convinced this could be the perfect headline to put her life back on track, Shayne vows to find the truth, persuade a reticent homicide detective to investigate, and bring a killer to justice, all before Ben grabs her story and the killer makes Shayne his or her *personal* deadline.

Made in the USA
Middletown, DE
04 July 2024